MW01128525

The Madness
of Grief

Panayotis Cacoyannis

Acknowledgments

With thanks to Oliver James of bluepencilagency for being so incisive and inspiring as an editor, to Keith Voles for the cover design, to Javier Lopes and Keith Voles for the website design, and to Michael Duerden for his technical wizardry.

For Yannoulla

I

1969

1

Karl

'I *hate* him!' I said.

'No you don't,' said Karl.

'Yes I do.'

'Jane, he's your father.'

'So?'

'You're not allowed to hate him.'

'Says who?'

'Says the Bible.'

'I don't believe in the Bible,' I said matter-of-factly.

'You'll go to hell if you're not careful.'

Karl was sweet. He was always looking out for me. I was glad we were friends.

'Nonsense,' I said.

'Shh! God can hear you.'

He ran his fingers dextrously over the keyboard, as if to smother my profanity with something irrefutably divine – the heart-stopping opening of Beethoven's 5th. That was something else I liked about him: no one ever knew if Karl was being ironic. Even when I tickled him to try and make him laugh, Karl wore his straight face like an iron-faced mask. But when he played the piano for me seriously, then he wouldn't so much lose as *surrender* control, giving himself over to the music completely. Or perhaps it was the other way around. In fact it was both. Becoming as one with it, he had a way of interpreting the music that added to it something mysterious, an inscrutable extra dimension. I didn't know all this because I knew a lot about music, I knew it because someone important had written it and Karl had read it out to me, and although I'd be the first to admit that I *didn't* know a lot about music, every time I heard him play I could *feel* what it meant. Karl gave an edge to the music that made his performances "visionary", a word that made me proud to be his friend. And it made me even prouder that Karl said he was proud to be *my* friend.

'Of course he can't hear me,' I yelled over Karl's playful thumping. What I liked best was the lack of complication in our friendship. The other boys I knew were all after only one thing, or at least made a show of being after one thing – which they wouldn't have known what to do with. My interest had always been in *much* older boys. They too were after only one thing, which they would know what to do with, after they had bullied the younger boys out of the way. But though I relished their attention, I had only ever let them go so far – about as far as holding hands and a dry kiss on the lips, which wasn't very far and fell short by a very great distance of the one thing they were after, and which really I only imagined they would know what to do with. Probably they were just better at pretending.

'Yes he can, or he wouldn't be God,' Karl yelled back as he marked his finale by pounding the keys with all his fingers at once. When the music had reverberated into silence, he turned his stool to face me squarely as I stood beside the rickety grand. 'You've filled your head with too many books. Have you been reading Nietzsche again? You do know he went mad in the end.'

I never lost my patience with Karl. I was fond of his confident manner, even though I never knew precisely what he was being confident about. Swooping down on his gaze, I held on to it fixedly. I wondered why I wasn't attracted to him physically. It wasn't because he was young (he was seventeen, one year older than me, but looked almost twenty), or because he wasn't good looking – he was *very* good looking. Perhaps it was because he was so dauntingly unique, a virtuoso pianist destined for greatness. I was clever; I didn't just parrot what I read, I was able to digest it and form my own opinion. But my cleverness was purely analytical; I was still too excited by learning to have found my own voice. Karl's opinion of the world was so uniquely expressed in his music that it was as if its mysteries were visible only to him.

'We all go mad in the end,' I said, my eyes aflutter as they let go of Karl's to look him up and down in his entirety. It was a hot July evening, hotter and muggier than I had expected when choosing what to wear for my friend and the men on the moon. A nice, short skirt would have been so much cooler than jeans, and my tucked-in linen blouse was another mistake; it was clinging to my body like paint that wouldn't dry, its long sleeves far too tight to roll up. I had covered up too much of myself and felt stupidly overdressed. Karl was very noticeably *under*dressed, and looking at him made me feel even hotter. He was wearing shorts, an unbuttoned denim shirt whose sleeves had been cut off, and a pair of flimsy flip-flops. Really he was quite a dish. What I could see of his body was sheer definition, a picture of athleticism altogether disproportionate to effort – being a prodigy, Karl *never* did sports. I had never seen *so much* of him before, and now I could see even more! After wriggling his fingers, Karl had brought his hands together at the back of his head and stretched his torso backwards as he yawned, exposing the hardness of his abdomen and both sides of his muscular chest.

'My God, you have such enormous nipples!' The words had spilled out of my mouth sooner than I had been able to think them, let alone hold them back. I could feel the rush of blood that would turn my ears crimson, and was grateful that I wore my hair long.

Karl seemed hardly fazed. Without moving his arms, my poker-faced friend looked down at his chest, first to the right and then to the left. 'I suppose I have,' he said.

I burst into a fit of nervous laughter, and when he *still* remained impassive, 'You mean you hadn't noticed? *Honestly?*'

Karl knitted his brows, repositioning himself on his stool as he landed an extended finger on each of his nipples. 'Is it important? Should I see a doctor, you think?' His hair, the darkest shade of brown before black, already too long before the school year had ended, was by now a disorderly mop, and clumps of it had fallen forward when he lowered his head to examine himself. There was something of the foreign aristocracy about him, I thought, but French rather than German, which I knew was absurd.

'They don't *feel* abnormal,' he said.

'If you don't stop rubbing them, they'll grow even more.'

'Ha!' said Karl without stopping.

And suddenly I was feeling territorial. 'Has someone else been playing with them?' I asked him in a manner that implied it was my business. Well, he and I were friends; we could ask each other anything.

Karl looked at me as if he hadn't understood what I meant. '*Playing* with them?'

'Like you're doing now, only harder, *much* harder, maybe even biting them.'

'*Biting* them?'

I had to roll my eyes. 'It's called foreplay,' I said.

'Ah, you mean sex.' And letting go of his nipples he cracked his fingers twice before swivelling back into place, and after staring intensely at the keys for a couple of minutes, he spread out his fingers and held his hands up in the air...

'Not *Für Elise* again, please.'

Even before I had finished, Karl had gathered his hands in his lap and was staring at the ceiling.

'You can if you want to,' I said.

'Hmm, I wonder...'

'If anyone has bitten your nipples?'

'About what you said; that we all go mad in the end.'

'We do,' I said, laying my covered forearms flatly on the piano.

'*All* of us?'

He seemed unruffled even by the prospect of madness. If his eyes betrayed any emotion, it was only curiosity and wonder perhaps mingled with a measure of pleasure - the pleasure of mocking me, probably.

'Don't...' I began.

'We mustn't tell Mami,' Karl interrupted me, holding on to my eyes as though urgently pleading with me.

His elbow on his leg and his face in his hand, he had carved himself into Rodin's *The Thinker*. His features were proportionate without being commonplace; the thickness of his eyebrows gave the sockets of his eyes extra depth, and he seemed to have been sculpted in a luminous opaqueness superior to marble. His beauty was striking, monumental...

'What are you thinking?' I remembered to ask, even mimicking his air of indifference while discarding the erotica of pseudo art-historical allusions.

'We mustn't tell Mami,' Karl said again.

'Your mother's a therapist. She makes a living out of madness.'

'She wouldn't call it madness.'

'Anyway, it isn't really true.' I gave him a comforting smile.

'We don't all go mad in the end?'

'Of course we don't.'

'Are you sure?'

'Yes, Karl, I'm sure.'

'Phew, that's a relief.' He dragged his hand across his forehead while he whistled out a sigh.

'You think you're so clever,' I said, whistling out a different kind of sigh of my own. 'Honestly, you're such an actor.' I stood upright by the piano, and while I went through the motions of wagging a finger at this boy-god who somehow always got the better of me, I felt the redness return to the tips of my ears.

What I was experiencing, quite without warning, wasn't altogether unpleasant. My mild embarrassment at being so gullible was more than made up for by the first-time excitement of my sensual admiration for Karl. How lucky I was to be able to enjoy it purely, from the safe distance of a friendship that would always be platonic, because... well, because why would Karl be interested in me?

'I was trying to make a point,' he said, getting up from his stool and offering an open hand to me. He bowed his head a little as he gave his hand a jerk to encourage me to take it. When I did, he led me away from the piano to the opposite end of the room, and we sat next to each other on the sofa, facing the TV.

'And what point would that be? That there's a God who can hear me?'

'That there's more to life than just being clever at manipulating words.' While he spoke almost mechanically,

Karl was looking at me oddly, not talking down to me exactly, but as though he felt sorry for me.

'You don't think I know that?' I knew it at that moment better than at any time before.

'And everything you read is so depressing. Mami thinks it's unhealthy.'

After a spell of reading mostly Kafka and Dostoyevsky, I had made the leap from fiction to the quicksand of pure philosophical thought – Plato, Schopenhauer, Nietzsche. But Karl was being unfair. I had not been seduced, and remained a steadfast sceptic. In the soup of postulated "knowledge", my young inquiring mind had always sought the fly of the flaw. There was no incontrovertible truth; in its many different forms the flaw was universal. But there was beauty in the poetry of manipulating words, and I was clever enough to regard what I read as mere exercises in expressing different versions of *un*truth. I had examined obsessively the lives of the men (they were mostly men) whose fictions and theories proffered an interpretation of the world. Invariably their vantage points were tainted, mired in contemporary prejudice or personal tragedy, even in lunacy. As for religion, Svidrigailov's mockingly cynical account of eternity in *Crime and Punishment* had instilled in me an absolute lack of even the most minimal capacity for faith. I was definitely not a mystic.

Karl had never before shown any interest in what I was reading. He had politely listened to me talking about *Phaedo* and *Phaedrus* and *The Metamorphosis*, and had winced at my devotion to Nietzsche. I had tried to explain that Nietzsche had been much misunderstood, and that in any case what had attracted me was not so much the letter as the lyrical energy – the raw gusto - of what he had written, but Karl had barely listened. I was interested in his music; he did not reciprocate by being interested in my thoughts. The few comments he had made had been flippant. But apparently he did have an opinion after all: his mother's.

'And what does Mami think about your music?' It was a blow below the belt. Mami didn't know about Karl's own, very special compositions. Only I did.

'Tell me what you think of this,' he had said to me one afternoon, and after picking out a sheet from the stack he had just carried from his room, he had delved into the piano with a tenderness that bordered on reluctance, as though luring to the surface the emotion he had wanted to convey by performing affectionate surgery. I had sat there dumbfounded, enraptured by the music and my friend.

'Oh my God, Karl, you wrote that?' I had asked in complete disbelief as the final few notes drifted off.

Karl, still suspended in a bow over his instrument, had turned his head slowly to look at me, and that was one of the very few times I remembered him smiling so broadly. I knew, and Karl knew that I knew, that I didn't have to know a lot about music to appreciate that what I had just heard was sublime. And now, to score a silly point, I had thrown his confidence back in his face.

'You think my music's depressing?'

'What does it even mean, "depressing"?' Puffing out a cushion and pulling a face, I tried to make light of my outburst.

Karl shrugged his shoulders. 'Dunno,' he said. 'Sad?'

'Plato isn't sad, and nor is Dostoyevsky. Kafka's *life* was depressing, but I don't think his books are. They're a bit claustrophobic, but parts of them are also very funny. And Nietzsche was as much of a poet as Plato.'

'That leaves Schopenhauer and my music.'

'That just leaves Schopenhauer. Your music may be sad but it's also uplifting. It fills you inside with...' I held the cushion over my chest, and I almost said "feathers", but that wasn't the word I was looking for. 'I'm not really sure with what, but whatever it is it's amazing. And it definitely isn't depressing.'

'Uplifting,' Karl repeated uncertainly. 'I don't feel it.'

'You don't? You *look* like you do. When you're playing.'

'Huh, then I suppose I must do.' And then unexpectedly, 'Let's go upstairs to my room.'

2

Ten Years

Attached by a common wall to my father's shop, our small semi-detached house stood at the far end of a winding dead-end street south of Camden Passage, a flea market near Angel Underground Station. It had taken me twelve minutes to walk home, idle time in which my mind had gone blank, marking my short journey not by thinking about Karl but by failing to imagine a single tomorrow. I must have looked at my watch a hundred times, as though I were a grown-up hurrying blindly to some urgent but unspecified appointment. The night of the city had completely passed me by. Having cut my way through it, I had no recollection of breathing in its air or of taking in its threat. I had experienced it only as a succession of fuzzy shafts of light – all the streetlamps where, without knowing why, I had stopped time after time to read my watch.

'So? Did you get into your boyfriend's pants?'

My father George Hareman, the illusionist, contortionist, magician known as "Mr Magikoo", made a habit of guffawing at his crudeness like an imbecile, and tonight was no exception.

It was almost eleven, and I had hoped that by now he would be in bed. Ever since *before* I was tall enough to reach the front door keyhole (on tiptoe), I had had my own key and had always come and gone as I pleased – I was a sensible girl; my father knew he could trust me. And he hadn't done a bad job of raising me, had he? I read an awful lot of books and was more or less dating a classical pianist. What better proof that rules and regulations were counter-productive, stunting children's creativity and growth... I found his camouflaged indifference almost funny.

But unfortunately he was not in bed. He was - as was so often the case whenever Mia-Mia was visiting her brother's bed-and-breakfast in Torquay - sprawled in his dilapidated chair, peering at me over *The Weekly Magic News*.

'No, I did not!' I snarled at his ridiculous toupee. 'And he's *not* my boyfriend!'

'Oh, then I suppose that *lovely* shade of beetroot is your normal colour, is it?' And roaring as he turned the page of *The Weekly Magic News*, still peering at me over it, 'No, I personally reckon it can only mean one thing. *Someone's* had his cherry popped tonight, and I'll wager he's a Kraut. Now tell your dad the truth, am I right or am I wrong?'

'You're wrong and you're *disgusting*!' Burning with rage and immobilised by shock, I was pressing with both hands against the knot that had formed in my stomach.

'Well, pardon me for *giving* a damn.'

'Don't take any notice of him, love; he's always had a filthy mouth. *Shut* it now, George, or so help me...'

I felt the familiar wetness collide with me sideways even before I had time to turn round.

'Auntie Ada!' Having made me wet with her watery sweat, auntie Ada had my face in a vice, squeezing it hard with both hands and wetting it this time with kisses. 'Mia-Mia is away,' I was able to whisper.

'I know,' auntie Ada whispered back – even her breath was full of moisture.

Every so often auntie Ada turned up unannounced with an overnight bag. If Mia-Mia happened to be visiting her brother's bed-and-breakfast in Torquay, she would stay. I loved her dearly, even more as she grew older. I had gradually become aware that her visits' primary purpose was to check on my emotional and physical wellbeing.

Mr Magikoo's Magik Shoppe had chaotically spilled over its old stock into every nook and cranny of the house, which made giving it a good and thorough clean an almost impossible task, to which for years auntie Ada was proud to have proved more than equal. But then came Mia-Mia, whose touch with housework was as magic as the best of the magic in *Mr Magikoo's Magik Shoppe*, and even more magic than auntie Ada's. Not by working around it but instead by *organising* its untidiness, she kept the house as spotlessly clean as *Mr Magikoo's Magik Shoppe*, for which feat she had got up auntie Ada's nose and very little gratitude from Mr Magikoo. Although meticulous in matters of personal hygiene, my father had otherwise always been oblivious to dirt, and would have hardly been able to notice the difference. And it was no good auntie Ada going about the house with her finger, looking in corners for dust or behind things for pockets of grime - there were none to be found. There was no getting around it. Mia-Mia was a domestic goddess. By also making all the necessary arrangements for repairs, browbeating handymen until they were practically working for free (money was tight, and she wasn't one for throwing it around), I was certain she had rescued house and shop from complete dereliction and possibly total collapse. *And* she was an excellent cook, which in the circumstances I had thought it wiser not to mention to auntie Ada.

'Beautiful! Every time I see you, you look even more like an angel.'

'Ha! Like a really chubby cherub, you mean.'

Auntie Ada vigorously shook her hands in my father's direction, as if to erase his sniggering stupidity. She and Mia-Mia were the only two people in the world I could think of who had ever said nice things about how I looked, things that I myself had never noticed. Even tonight, when

Karl had appeared to harbour amorous intentions, he hadn't made the slightest attempt to seduce me with words, as if I ought to have known to make do with his bare proposition. Although, consciously at least, I had never before thought about my friend in that way, I could have given a detailed physical description of him with my eyes closed. If anyone had asked him, would he have been able to say what shade of brown my hair was; or what length; or how strikingly my pale purple lips came to life when I smiled; or how delicately curved were my lashes and what colour were my eyes? His were an extraordinary blue that gleamed with iridescence...

'Don't you pay any attention to his nonsense. You're a healthy young girl, as pretty as the prettiest English rose. *And* you have your mother's *magnificent* eyes, may God rest her beautiful soul.'

Auntie Ada never missed an opportunity of pinpointing anything in which I differed favourably from my father. After clamping my chin between fingers made crooked prematurely by arthritis, and tearful with a joining together of sadness and joy, she stared into my eyes open-mouthed, as though filling her lungs with a gust of reinvigorating mountain air.

'George's are like painted jellied eels,' she snorted, bringing herself back to the world with a roaring guffaw not unlike that of her brother's. And with her mouth still twisting mischievously, 'Shifty, squinty, tiny and liquid,' she spat, pointing with a twitch of her nose at my father. Then tightening her grip of my cheeks, she turned back to face me, widening her lips into a smile as though to mark out the breadth of her love for me. 'Whereas *yours*, well! They take one's breath away with their brightness. Like giant wells of goodness they are, emerald jewels that sparkle like Val's.'

'Wells are full of water,' my father puffed while shifting in his chair, still behind *The Weekly Magic News*. 'And *giant* wells are even more liquid than eels.'

'It's true, auntie Ada.' After using it to rub an eye with, I held out the hook of my left index finger.

Auntie Ada let go of my face to slap with both hands the contrary evidence out of the way. 'Your eyes are *pellucid*,' she said. And then hissing at the back page of *The Weekly Magic News*, 'Whereas *his* are more like the miasma of a swamp.'

Craning over his paper, my father goggled to the best of his ability at his sister. '*These*, I'll have you know, are the eyes Val fell in love with, and she never once complained about *either* their size *or* their affliction.'

'That woman was a saint.'

'And it's an allergy. I would hardly call an allergy a miasma.'

'I was *not* referring to your allergy.'

'Come on now, the girl,' said my father as he slowly bent his head in my direction. 'I thought we'd agreed that we'd keep all our differences private, and you know it's what Val would've wanted.'

'Val was too good for you. You didn't deserve her, what she saw in you I'll *never* understand. I mean look at you, George. You're fat, you're short, you've got hardly any eyes in a face that's full of ears, nose and mouth, and as if it isn't bad enough that you're as bald as a coot, you *will* insist on wearing that ridiculous toupee.'

'I'm muscular, not fat - as I'm sure my Mia-Mia would be happy to confirm. And I could easily be tempted to remind you, Ada, my love, that *all* my friends at school without exception thought that you were actually... But no, I've no wish to be mean.'

'Thought that I was what, beaten up by hardship and looking twice my age? Well, they wouldn't have been wrong. We've been as short and as fat and as ugly as each other ever since we were kids, we've neither of us been blessed in the way God decided to put us together. But you've been blessed in a way that I haven't and you certainly didn't deserve, first with Val and now with your daughter. Forty-five and on a good day I might look like I'm sixty, what gift have *I* had to keep me looking young? I should be glad of my arthritis, I suppose! God forbid I should be accused of being ungrateful…'

'Look, Ada, let's not be raking up the past and blaming God for whatnot. You're my sister and I love you, and as I've tried to tell you already I've no wish to be mean, because I know that you're just angry that we've lost her.' And with that, my father tried to hide himself again behind the crumple of *The Weekly Magic News.*

'*Lost* her, you say!' Auntie Ada gave out a wounded growl, her stridency fired up under memory's strain. 'Ten years, George, ten years almost to the day since you killed her, that's how long it's been, and you still haven't looked your own child in the eye to beg her forgiveness, and not just for that, with her mother still barely in the grave, you very nearly murdered your daughter as well!'

'Ada, that's enough!' *The Weekly Magic News* was on the floor. Half-risen from his chair, my father loomed as though frozen in mid-motion, his legs still bent and his arms hanging loose like an ape's.

As she made a leap towards him, auntie Ada burst with violent sobs into tears, and somewhere near the middle of the distance between them she stopped, her thick frame trembling opposite my father's bending bulk. Then as she turned around slowly to make her way upstairs to the bathroom, where she would lock herself up for at least half an hour, slumping back into his chair my father disappeared behind *The Weekly Magic News.*

I remembered every one of a thousand variations of that scene like a dream: my father scowling in his chair, auntie Ada sniping angry words at him, then stomping towards him as though ready to strike him, gaining ground and then retreating. Shrinking into a corner I would watch them without ever taking part, supposing in my bookish understanding of the world that this must be what people meant by grief.

3

Otto Dix

Just a handful of zigzags away, Karl's house in Cross Street belonged to a different world. Over an expanse of beam upon beam of solid oak, the piano room was also the living room, *and* the dining room, *and* the kitchen, full of shiny bright orange Formica. The piano was old, but had once belonged to someone very famous. The rest of the furniture was Scandinavian, wooden and modern. Sliding glass doors opened out to a miniature patio so immaculately uncluttered and tidy that it looked like it belonged to a minimalist doll's house. I had never seen the rooms upstairs, but if the bare-walled downstairs was anything to go by, I imagined order and brightness and space and sharp angles. Karl lived comfortably in the sparseness of this spotlessness alone with his mother, a robust, sharp-mannered Bavarian brunette who spoke impeccable English with the faint trace of an accent I had the impression she hated. Every time she spoke, her struggle to suppress it took a visible toll on her face.

Unlike me, who in my family history found only consternation, Karl seemed to revel in his, and in his deadpan manner made a habit of relating it to me anecdotally, not in any logical order and certainly not chronologically. Frau Angela, as he liked to refer to his mother if he didn't feel like using the affectionate "Mami", was a Schmidt who had married a philandering Smith (the son of a Smith who had married a Greek) and then, when it dawned on her what he was up to, divorced him and proudly reverted to Schmidt, whereupon Karl's father, a gifted neurosurgeon, had "thrown a black stone behind him" (as his Greek half might have said), and emigrated to Australia with Sigrid, a chirpy blonde nurse from Stockholm in Sweden. Frau Angela (who was now Dr Schmidt) had then insisted on a hyphenated surname for their son, and Karl duly became a Schmidt-Smith, a tongue twister of a mouthful that the cruelty of children had in no time contracted to "Shitsmith".

"The cruelty of children" had been Karl's own expression, and in one way it was typical of his attempts to set himself apart from his stories. I had witnessed the juvenile cruelty of calling him "Shitsmith" first hand, and Karl's complete indifference to it had been so natural it couldn't have been faked. But on many other occasions, the remoteness of his stories felt more like a deliberate smokescreen.

Striking parallels ran through our lives. We had both lost a parent at around the same age, and we both blamed our fathers. In Karl's case, the parent he blamed was also the one he had lost. But the biggest difference was that most of the time I felt an uncontrollable need to *vent* my emotions. Karl seemed to want to keep his under wraps.

'What are these black stones that the Greeks throw behind them?' I wasn't trying to bait him. I was genuinely curious.

'It's just an old saying.' The gesturing had stopped, abruptly the gaze became sharp and the hint of a smile disappeared. The iron mask hadn't quite dropped, but it was clear Karl disliked being interrupted. I suspected he had carved up his life into blocks of entertainment to make it less painful, and losing their flow made his stories come apart, exposing the parts that he tried to keep hidden.

'I know it's just a saying, Karl, but what does it mean?'

'It means cutting off from the past.'

'And is that what your father said he was doing?'

He glowered at me only very briefly. 'I think he did Mami a favour,' he shrugged, his face smoothing out as he wrested back control of his story. 'You wouldn't think it to look at her, but she's actually quite brilliant.' The hands were in the air, and as the gaze became warm there was again the same hint of a smile. 'And it's not just by coincidence she's here. My grandfather had planned for his daughter to leave Germany long before it actually happened – he must have predicted not only the war but also the German defeat. Did you know his name was Karl?'

Of course I knew; in his animated, tongue-in-cheek way, he had told me the story many times before. Some years before the war had started, with Germany already in the stranglehold of Hitler and the Nazis, grandfather Schmidt, a wealthy Munich dealer who specialised in "decadent" art, had had the foresight to cut out of its frame a canvas by Otto Dix and have it sewn by his wife into the lining of her coat, together with its provenance papers. He had then very wisely handed over the remainder of his stock to the Gestapo. During the war he fought valiantly to stay alive, and succeeded, eventually surrendering himself to the British. A year after Germany's defeat, awkward in a coat that was too big, his daughter disembarked at Dover in the company of her young fiancé, lieutenant Euripides Smith.

Otto Dix bought Angela and Euripides the opportunity of a good education. When Karl was born in 1952, Euripides was at the tail end of his medical training, and Angela had been awarded a First Class Psychology degree, and then in just two years had successfully completed her doctorate on Wilhelm Reich. She wrote prolifically, contributing to many publications. Turning the predominant orthodoxy on its head, *The Interpretation of a Nightmare*, her voluminous paper on Freud, had ruffled many feathers and generally caused quite a stir.

'When they met in Munich, she fell for my father head over heels, and the bastard pretended to reciprocate, while behind Mami's back he carried on screwing every Ulrika, Astrid and Frieda. I think grandfather Karl would've probably preferred an American bridegroom, but beggars can't be choosers, apparently not even when they've got an Otto Dix up their sleeve, so in the end he made do with my dad.'

'Just as well or you wouldn't be here.'

'Which he wouldn't have done if he'd known what my dad was getting up to,' Karl went on, and before I could speak, 'yes, yes, just as well he didn't or I wouldn't be here.'

'Does he write?'

'He died a few months later. His wife had been killed in an air raid, and after bartering a painting for a new life for his daughter, which I'm sure is what he did, he must've felt that he had nothing more to live for.'

'I meant your father.'

'I was six when he moved out, just seven when he moved to Australia, but unfortunately I remember him clearly. He even introduced me to Sigrid, who's *at least* a foot taller than him, and kind of bent to one side. Dad looks like a pillar-box, and she's the leaning tower of Pisa.'

'Swedish women are often very tall,' I blurted out dumbly.

'My father's never written, but she has. Every year she sends a postcard on my birthday inviting me to visit them in Sydney. And every year she adds a postscript, to say my father sends his love. Mami says he's too ashamed to write to me directly. Personally I say he's an arsehole.'

'So you haven't written back.'

'Mami says I should, but I haven't.'

'You've thrown a black stone behind you, as your Greek part might have said.'

'Mami and I have both moved on.' I read his steely glance as a warning: I had pushed him far enough.

'And your father's mum and dad?' There were ready-made questions I knew he enjoyed.

'Dead within a year after my parents got married. Rat-tat-tat, shot by a firing squad in Greece.' Karl had made a gun by bending one arm, and moved it left to right in a rapid shooting gesture.

'Really, by *firing squad*?'

'Wrong place, wrong time, wrong side in the wrong civil war, if there's ever a right civil war.'

'That's so awful, your poor dad...'

'Greeks like a bit of tragedy, it's in their blood.'

Having got over Euripides' flight in a jiffy, Frau Angela worked hard, and her enterprise had been rewarded: her practice as a Reichian therapist was thriving. To give her son free rein with the piano, she saw her clients in a small, rented flat just a little further east towards Highbury Corner.

Tonight, Karl had made no mention of his past. Tonight, moments after he had threatened me with hell, while we squabbled over the significance of words and what I liked to read, I had looked him up and down and seen a different Karl, almost irresistibly attractive. And after my ineptly getting back at him for using Mami's words, Karl had used words that were entirely his own.

'Let's go upstairs to my room.'

4

Magic

In the house where I grew up, I felt like an illusion in a box full of horrors. I played with toys that broke when I touched them, and when I touched them again put themselves back together. One wall in the room where I slept resembled an exhibit of restraints used in torture: handcuffs, padlocked belts, spiked iron collars. Against another, a menagerie of animals squirmed in inadequate cages while their stuffed predecessors watched them with glass eyes from their perches. Everything apart from my mattress, my wardrobe and a solitary chair, served as stage props in their public mistreatment. One of Mr Magikoo's best-known tricks involved pulling a rabbit out of *two* different hats; it was a spellbinding conjuring feat in which by sleight of hand the mutilation of the rabbit was concealed.

My room itself was a windowless box that once every year was dismantled, removed, and then reassembled in music halls and theatres in a grand tour of the country, from Blackpool to Great Yarmouth to Brighton and Bristol and Bath, serving to conceal Mr Magikoo in his trick of disappearance and becoming The Invisible Man. In a lightning flash of darkness, my room would be gyrated on a crudely constructed mechanical axis, its revolution brought to a standstill by a stagehand at precisely the spot where my father would at just the right moment slip behind a curtain and fall through its door. My room would then again be very quickly rotated, so that when the curtain fell open, the audience would see just a solid blank wall. Then in another lightning flash the curtain would be drawn, my room would go around on its mechanical axis, and when it came to another standstill my father would leap out of the door and through the curtain, tumbling over as he fell onto the stage. By the time he was back up on his feet, ready in a lingering finale to pull back the curtain, the door would have again disappeared. It was comedy and mime, rather than magic, but the audiences apparently loved it.

When I was eight, even I had been a prop – stage name: Little Magik Matchstick. Had my father shown any sign of contrition, and some small degree of warmth towards the six-year-old girl whose mother he had publicly singed by electrocution, then perhaps I might have managed to forgive him. Instead, when I had barely recovered from my loss – by the good grace of a measles epidemic I had at least been spared being a witness to my mother's execution – Mr Magikoo conjured up in his sick imagination a bright new number for his Magikal Extravaganza, in which his daughter would simulate the narrowest of escapes from being sliced like a carrot into pieces. In an optical illusion that required her to be thin, Little Magik Matchstick would slither intact through an apparently impossibly small gap between two razor-sharp blades that slid back and forth across each other like a double-sided vertical guillotine – stage name: Sweeney Todd.

The routine was far from risk-free. On the stage of an old Victorian theatre in some godforsaken town, and before the blades were fitted for the terrifying number's premiere performance, I had spent several excruciating hours accustoming my body movements to the tempo of Sweeney Todd's. The way my heart was beating was telling me something was wrong.

My father squatted beside me, which he almost didn't have to (he really was very short), tugging playfully at my pigtails.

'There's really nothing to it,' he told me. If only he could *hear* how fast my heart was beating... 'It's all about getting your timing right. You know, like when you're skipping. And you're good at skipping, aren't you?'

I *was* good at skipping, but this wasn't like skipping *at all*. Slipping through a pair of moving blades was *not* the same as hop-hop-hopping on the spot over a harmless piece of rope.

'But I *hate* it, do I really have to?'

From behind my father's back, one of the stagehands cleared his throat, and when he caught my eye he shook his head with an extraordinary violence, as if to say in no uncertain terms that NO, I didn't really have to.

'If you want to be a star, yes, you do really have to,' my father told me sternly. But then returning quickly to his honey-coated tone, still tugging at my pigtails, 'And what little girl in the world wouldn't want to be a star?'

'Did mummy want to be a star?'

'*Of course* mummy wanted to be a star. And she was, she was the biggest, brightest star there ever was.'

When I looked again at the stagehand, two other stagehands had joined him. All their eyes were wide as though filled with my own fear, and with that same extraordinary violence now all three of them shook their heads. I turned around to look at Sweeney Todd, whose metallic clinking and clanking was terrifying even when he wasn't wearing blades. Then I snatched back my pigtails and lashed out at my father with both fists.

'And now she's dead,' I snivelled as I tried to catch my breath. 'I don't *want* to be a star, I don't *want* to be dead!'

How he managed to persuade me, I wouldn't have been able to say, but he did. Fear and practice made of me a piece of elastic, and for one entire season Little Magik Matchstick, clutching a theatrical bouquet of plastic daisies, wriggled to the tempo of the sliding double-sided guillotine, acrobatically defying the swinging blades of Sweeney Todd.

But this never-ending season was it, I wasn't going to do it ever again, *no way*, and before our final performance at the Magic Palladium in Croydon, I already had a plan. Starting from tomorrow I would stuff myself with sweets – cream cakes, ginger biscuits, chocolates and custard puddings, anything and everything that I could lay my hands on... If I put enough weight on, Little Magik Matchstick would hardly be Matchstick, and by no amount of bending would fit through any acceptable gap. At the thought of all those cakes that lay in store, my mouth was watering already.

After his signature rabbit trick, Mr Magikoo was taking a bow in his top hat and cape, and when the enthusiastic applause had subsided - the auditorium was bursting at the seams – he rose up to the full height of his shortness and extended his arms as though offering himself to be crucified.

'Ladies and Gentlemen, please hold your breath, for you are now about to witness an extraordinary feat. In the face of THIS!' At which point Sweeney Todd made its entrance from the wings and was pushed into place, slightly further back from the middle of the stage. 'Yes indeed, Ladies and Gentlemen, your eyes are not deceiving you, it is verily as hideous and deadly a contraption as it looks.' With a swing of his cape he had gathered his hands into fists, then with an almighty jolt he threw them both open towards Sweeney Todd. On cue the machine was switched on, and slowly gathered speed. 'It is in fact even *more* hideous and deadly than it looks, as hideous and deadly as the hideous and deadly Sweeney Todd after whom it is named. And in the face of THIS, the hideous and deadly Sweeney Todd, I present to you the brave, the heroic, the incomparable Little Magik Matchstick!'

With my bouquet of plastic daisies, I made my way to the side of Sweeney Todd and took a hesitant bow. The applause made my heart beat even faster.

'Ladies and Gentlemen, before your unbelieving eyes Little Magik Matchstick will cross in one piece, unscratched and completely unscathed, from *this* to the other side of Sweeney Todd through the horrifying Scylla and Charybdis of its overlapping blades, begging your indulgence, if I may, for my modest mythological flourish. Ladies and Gentlemen, I will now give you a small illustration of the truly mortal danger to which Little Magik Matchstick will shortly be subjecting herself. Voluntarily, I can assure you. *Happily*, even...' Here he paused for a moment while he dug into the inside of his cape. 'As you can see, I'm holding in my hand an ordinary cucumber fresh from the market. I am holding it in front of me, and I'm approaching Sweeney Todd. Now I'm poking it like *so* at the innards of this vicious machine, and I'm holding in my hand... *half* an ordinary cucumber, fresh from the market... Please, Ladies and Gentlemen, without further ado put your hands together for Little Magik Matchstick!'

'STOP! Turn off that horrible abomination *right now*, or so help me, George, I'm going to the police.'

'Auntie Ada!' I mumbled to myself in astonishment.

'This isn't entertainment, this is cruelty and abuse,' auntie Ada continued to boom, zooming down the central aisle to the foot of the stage.

'Hear, hear!' someone yelled.

'Off, off, off!' shouted another, and now *everyone* was shouting it: 'OFF, OFF, OFF!' Shouting it and stamping their feet...

A stagehand pulled the plug on Sweeney Todd, and its clinking and clanking screeched to a halt. At last it was OFF, and I let my posy drop to the floor.

Quick as always to think on his feet, Mr Magikoo was already by my side, and enveloping me with his cape, he filled the stage with fits of fake laughter. 'Please, Ladies and Gentlemen, a warm round of applause for Little Magik Matchstick, our young practical joker who had you all fooled!'

That *was* my final performance, and the last time I toured with my bedroom and Mr Magikoo. When my father was away, auntie Ada was glad to stay over – the portable bed in our pocket-sized storeroom upstairs suited her seasoned English hardiness just fine. She didn't live far – she had a small one-bedroom flat in Tufnell Park - and had few other commitments as far as I knew, other than her reasonably flexible job at the library in Kentish Town.

I was happy that the Sweeney Todd nightmare was finally behind me. But perhaps for some extra insurance, I decided all the same to go through with my original plan, and starting with a chocolate éclair and some Garibaldi biscuits the day after Croydon, I embarked on a lifetime of gorging on sweets. The effect would not be catastrophic. Yes, Little Magik Matchstick would soon be a thing of the past, but my fortunate metabolism meant that I would stabilise at just short of "plump". And indeed it would be a just-short-of-plumpness, firm and well defined, that in later life would stand me in good stead: it gave me extra curve and made me a voluptuous woman.

As well as cleanliness and French cuisine, Mia-Mia's arrival on the scene brought about a host of other changes. In the first place she forbade any more tours. After just a cursory inspection of my father's books, she informed him bluntly one evening that the tours were a drain on his finances that he could no longer afford. If he concentrated all his efforts on *Mr Magikoo's Magik Shoppe*, they might just about manage to save it. It had a steady stream of customers and quite a reputation, but suffered from inadequate accounting and shrinking profit margins.

'You've had your fun with the tours, now it's time for Mr Magikoo to call it a day, give or take the odd guest appearance. And what's this about taking your daughter's room away with you every time you've been on tour? That would *never* have happened if I'd been around, and I'm putting a stop to it right now. Why she's put up with it for so many years is beyond me. I hope you've not been bullying the girl.'

'Of course not.'

'It can't have been easy, raising her alone, but she's a teenager now. Fourteen is a difficult age.'

'Ada's been helping. Jane's more fond of her than she's of me.'

'Well I can't say I'm surprised.'

Obviously at that stage Mia-Mia didn't know what had happened either to my mother or to Little Magik Matchstick. Had she known, I imagined that she would have been even less surprised.

'And all those filthy animals you keep in her room, dead or alive they've got to go, and they've got to go first thing tomorrow.'

'But Jane might not want them to go. She's especially fond of the rabbits.'

Liar! Mia-Mia was right, I *had* put up with it for far too long, and I was glad that I had found a second ally. Had it not been for auntie Ada, who knows what hideous fate had been in store for Little Magik Matchstick! But that was the only time my father had deferred to his sister on anything related to his magic. He must have known he was breaking the law, and when auntie Ada threatened him with the police, he didn't have much choice but to give in. With Mia-Mia it was different. She had Mr Magikoo under her spell, and this was my chance to make the most of it.

'No I'm not fond of the rabbits *at all*,' I said, emerging from the darkness of the kitchen, where furtively I had delighted in my father's dressing down. 'You've only just met Mia-Mia and you're already telling her lies. You're asking her to let me keep the rabbits because you want to butcher them, not because I like them.'

'You *butcher* rabbits? What kind of magic is that?'

'It's just a trick I used to do,' my father answered sheepishly. 'It was *very* popular, and there was very little pain involved, I promise.'

'Oh yes, very little,' I said, 'only the pain of being cut into two.'

'But it was very quick. It had to be, or the trick wouldn't have worked.'

'What *was* the trick?' asked Mia-Mia.

'Pulling a rabbit out of two different hats,' my father explained.

'Stop! If I hear any more I'll be sick.' Mia-Mia had her hand over her mouth.

'Can we at least keep the budgerigars?'

'Not in *my* room,' I said.

The next day, when I came back from school all the animals were gone and the torture wall was bare. I celebrated in the kitchen with a slice of treacle tart *and* a piece of Rhubarb pie with ice cream.

Mia-Mia had been firm and decisive – manly, even. I had found her indomitable spirit inspiring. But soon she had reverted to being my father's kitten. As for auntie Ada, my father told her he had made a financial decision to give up the tours, and all the animals had been donated to a charity pet shop. I thought it strange that she listened without asking any questions. Perhaps she had guessed Mia-Mia's part in these momentous decisions, and had judged it an unflattering reflection on herself.

5

Men on the Moon

Six words that had turned my whole world upside down: 'Let's go upstairs to my room.' If they hadn't been said, my reaction to my father's crude insinuations would have been to shrug them off. But they had been said, and the evening at Karl's had not ended there.

'Let's go upstairs to my room.' Looking at me over his shoulder, he had bent his body forward and was leaning on his knees with his hands, ready to spring up onto his feet. Clearly I had heard him correctly. Any doubt had been dispelled.

Instead of answering I looked at my watch, as though I couldn't have envisaged any other impediment than time. I was petrified. Was it possible... no it wasn't... was it? Well, why not? Why *shouldn't* Karl be interested in me, even if I wasn't quite as godlike as he was? My looks were not unpleasant, my body had shape, and Karl and I stood perfectly erect at about the same height. Hadn't stranger things *actually* happened?

'And even if I *did* believe in the Bible...' The pitch of my voice on the edge of a shriek, I shrank back into silence, still embracing the cushion I had pressed against my breast after telling him his music was uplifting.

Karl narrowed his eyes. 'The Bible?'

'My father,' I managed to stutter. 'If I believed in the Bible, probably I'd hate him even more. I'd choose an eye for an eye over turning the other cheek.'

'I don't believe in the Bible any more than you do,' said Karl, snatching the cushion away from me and hurling it over to one of the armchairs – apart from the sofa (dark grey, speckled with burgundy), the living room in Cross Street was furnished with two matching armchairs, arranged around an oblong wooden table precisely at the centre of an oblong woollen rug (ultramarine, decorated geometrically in black). 'Frau Angela doesn't either but she likes going to church. Even if there isn't a God, she thinks that religion is useful.'

'I think religion is harmful.'

'I think what Frau Angela means is that it's good for business,' said Karl, and it was probably the first time I had seen him roll his eyes. But then his face was placid again, and it edged towards mine as he turned his body round until our knees almost touched. 'Forget the Bible. It just isn't fair, hating your father for something that wasn't his fault.'

'It *was* his fault.'

'It was an accident.'

'He wired my mother up in an electric chair, and then he pressed a button and he electrocuted her.'

'It was part of their act, you said they'd done it dozens of times.' His gaze had become too intense; I could feel the heat of his breath; *something* was touching my knee.

'Except this time he decided that he wanted bigger fireworks.'

'Mami says that you must let the past go. But first you need to deal with what's happened. Instead of grieving you've been blaming your dad, which is no good for either of you.'

'I tell you things in confidence.'

'I know,' said Karl. 'But every time you visit me you bring it up – out of the blue, like tonight. "Play something," you said. And the next minute we're at the piano and you're telling me how much you hate your dad.'

'And you're always calling yours an arsehole,' I wanted to say, but that would only have proved Karl was right. Hatred was too strong a word. 'I blame your mother's meatballs,' I said. 'They gave me indigestion.'

'Very funny,' said Karl. 'Now come on, let's go upstairs.'

For the second time I looked at my watch. 'You should turn the TV on, I want to see the men on the moon.'

'I've watched the whole thing live,' said Karl.

'But I haven't. And you said they'd be showing it now on the news.'

'They'll be showing it on the news all week. It'll be like the Kennedy shooting all over again.'

'You watched Bobby Kennedy being shot?'

'That was so unmemorable I'd forgotten all about it. No, I meant the President's.'

'But that was years ago.'

'1963, November 22.' The weight of his body was now against mine, and one naked arm had crept its way behind me.

'You had a TV in 1963?' I shook myself forward, and I turned to look at Karl from the edge of the sofa.

'That same one,' he said, flexing his head in the TV's direction. 'Six years ago and I remember it almost like I'm watching it now. Snap, and Jackie puts her arms around Jack. Then another snap that blows off half his head, and now he's definitely down and Jackie makes a run for it, climbing on all fours over the back of the open limousine – I mean, where do you think she thought she was going?'

'And they showed all that on TV? But how old were you in 1963, I'm surprised Dr Schmidt let you watch it.'

'Mami's very progressive when it comes to the news; we often watch horrible things. The news is real, she says, and it's good if you can see what's going on, as long as you know that they're not showing lies. I'm not sure that she's right, though. When I watch even horrible things on TV, I can't get it out of my head that I'm watching a movie, it doesn't feel like *any* of it's actually real.' And brandishing a finger at the television, 'There's something about TV that makes things seem fake, don't you think?'

Rapt with admiration, I just shook my head. 'I've only ever watched TV with you. We've never had one, dad says he doesn't approve.'

'Now *there's* a good reason to hate him.' While he stared into the distance, Karl had brought his hands down on his thighs, and the judder of the clap made me jump. 'Sorry, that was out of order,' he said, and through the denim of my jeans he was squeezing my knee – was I glad I wasn't wearing a skirt? Then with his head against the back of the sofa, still stubbornly avoiding my gaze, 'So, are we going upstairs or not?'

Just then the front door opened and Frau Angela walked in, practical handbag in one hand and bulging worn-out briefcase in the other. I thought about what Karl had said - that his mother was more brilliant than anyone might guess just by looking at her. Were all men the same, judging even their own mothers by looks?

Undeniably Frau Angela was not of the swinging '60s, and it had nothing to do with her age. She was emphatically not psychedelic; it was as if style and colour had eluded her completely, but she looked neither old nor odd in her plainness. Taken one by one her features were not unattractive, but taken as a whole they became incoherent, adding up to a contradictory impression of severity overwhelmed by excessive good health. I hadn't a clue what a Reichian therapist was, but I suspected Karl's mother was probably a good one. All the same, without knowing why, I didn't really like her.

'Another time then.' And letting go of my knee, Karl got up to greet his Mami with a kiss.

'The TV isn't on? Good evening, Jane.'

'Good evening, Dr Schmidt.'

'Please, you must call me Angela.'

'You said you'd not be home till late,' Karl said as he carried her briefcase to the dining room table. 'Jane's eaten all the meatballs, by the way. They gave her indigestion.'

'Karl! It's not true, Dr Schmidt.'

Frau Angela brushed away the air with one arm, while stretching out the other to switch on the TV.

'I cancelled my last two appointments,' she gasped as she fell into one of the armchairs, kicking off her sensible shoes. 'It's not every day we land on the moon, and as I missed it when it actually happened I'd like to watch it now.'

'You cancelled your last two appointments *again*?'

'My son is making fun of me, Jane.'

'Mami got the times wrong,' Karl explained. 'They were landing late last night, but it was almost another six hours before Armstrong came out of the capsule and actually stepped on the moon, and by then it was four in the morning.'

'July 20, they said. At a reasonable hour here in London, I thought. So I cancelled my last two appointments to get back home in time, and in the end I was falling asleep on the sofa, I couldn't even manage to stay up for the landing.'

'But yesterday was Sunday,' I said.

'My *busiest* day,' sighed Dr Schmidt. 'All the fun of Saturday is gone, Monday is looming, and suddenly the weight of the world seems so unbearably heavy. The mistake, of course, is how extremely we separate the week from the weekend; it's very punishing. One must learn to make the best of it; that's what I say to my clients. Karl also, he must know how to rest. Just *listen* sometimes, not learn but *enjoy*. And almost every Saturday we manage to find something. You should join us some time, I'm sure Karl would like that, no?' And when Karl had nodded to say yes, 'So I take the day off every Saturday, then I work in the afternoon and evening on Sundays and Mondays, then all day on Tuesday - tomorrow until ten, with the two missed appointments, and today I had to start in the morning, to catch up with *yesterday's* two missed appointments. The moon has been a scheduling nightmare. But now it's fine, we know that they are already there.'

The TV was warming up, and the buzz of the grainy black and white filled me with an odd premonition of chaos.

'How are things at home?' It was Dr Schmidt, not Frau Angela or Mami, who had asked me the question while we waited for the picture to adjust.

'I've already told Jane what you said.'

'I see.' After scowling at her son with a glare of disapproval, Dr Schmidt leaned forward in her chair to assault me with professional concern. 'What happened to your mother was terrible,' she said. 'But so was what happened to you. Terrible, terrible…'

'I'm all right, Dr Schmidt, really. It was nearly ten years ago now, I don't even remember my mum very clearly.'

'But *here* you remember, *here* you will never forget.' Dr Schmidt had spread out both her hands, and with one over the other was thumping at the side of her breast with some force. She looked like she was giving herself CPR. I felt myself erupting in goosebumps. Was this how a Reichian therapist did things? And what on earth might a Reichian therapist do next? A vague apprehension took hold of me.

'Anyway,' I said, trying to change the subject, 'dad's been very happy since he met his new girlfriend. I quite like her, most of the time. She's called Mia-Mia, and she works as a hairdresser in Chelsea.'

'Yes, Karl did mention something, and I think it's important that you like her.'

'She's lived with us since soon after they met, for more than two years now... But she goes to her brother's bed-and-breakfast in Torquay quite a lot.'

'Look!' Karl cried out. 'There's Armstrong coming out of the capsule.'

'Is that really the *moon*?' Dr Schmidt had recited the words like a child.

The weightlessness, the crackle, the blur; I thought the effect was otherworldly.

'That's one small step for man, one giant leap for mankind...'

'So banal,' said Karl.

'Karl tells me that you're reading Franz Kafka,' said Dr Schmidt. And going back to the bouncing about on the moon, 'Ach, the *symbolism*! While they slowly murder Vietnam, even on another planet they show off their flag.' Then returning to me, 'A tortured man but a *marvellous* writer, complex and yet also entirely simple. As I always say, one is never too young to be reading Kafka, and never too old to be reading him differently.'

'The moon isn't a planet,' said Karl.

'Wednesdays are my Sabbath, non-religious of course. Would you like to have lunch with us the day after tomorrow, let's say at half past two? I'm planning a *very* late lie-in.'

'I'd love to, Dr Schmidt, if Karl doesn't mind.'

'Karl would be delighted,' said Karl, winking at me surreptitiously as I got up to leave. 'And I'm also free tomorrow evening, if you're not reading Kafka.'

'Wait!' Frau Angela instructed, lifting up one arm to bar my way. I turned to Karl, but he looked as at a loss as I was. Leaning forward in her chair, his mother had her face almost rubbing with the static from the television screen. 'Richard Nixon!' she cried out, as though his likeness had jumped out from the grain. 'The man is so obviously a crook, and if he's managed to become the president of the United States, then I'm sure he's also capable of *that*! It's so *ridiculously* bad that it's almost convincing. "That's one small step for man..." Was that really the best they could come up with? Did they honestly believe they could fool us with a cliché and a B-movie set in the desert? If that is the moon, I will eat Paul McCartney's guitar.'

'But why, Dr Schmidt, why would they do that?'

'A red-under-the-bed anti-communist hysteria,' answered Frau Angela succinctly. 'In the new war everything's becoming propaganda. But lies are not a good way to fight lies. It's like throwing out the baby with the bathwater, an old German saying that reminds me very much of Confucius.'

'We have the same saying in English,' I said.

'No! What you have is the German saying translated into English. But really, Karl, I cannot bear to watch this any more. Please, turn it off.'

6

Mia-Mia

Late in the morning on the day after mankind's giant leap, Mia-Mia returned from Torquay. As though the moon had spent the hours of the night pleading with the sun to punish London for Nixon's conceit, it was a particularly scorching day, and with the windows open auntie Ada and I were sitting at the kitchen table washing down a sandwich with tea. The two giant slices of Black Forest Gateau auntie Ada had brought with her were waiting in front of us on separate plates. When we heard the front door open, auntie Ada's eyes locked forlornly onto mine...

'Have you seen today's front pages? Apparently we've conquered the moon.' Breezing in, Mia-Mia had slung a pile of papers on the table.

'They landed very late on Sunday night, and on Monday at four in the morning Armstrong came out of the capsule,' I said. 'Most of these are yesterday's papers.'

'I've not had time to look at them properly,' said Mia-Mia.

'What brought *you* back so soon?' asked auntie Ada.

'Torquay, if you must know. But this *heat*! It's just too much, I don't think I'll survive it if it goes on much longer.'

'Your hair certainly hasn't,' said auntie Ada.

'I had it cut short, don't you like it? Mia-Mia Farrow, I thought, in *Rosemary's Baby*.'

A natural silvery blonde with beautifully shaped unplucked eyebrows, when her make up was on Mia-Mia was... I would have probably said "handsome" rather than "pretty". She wasn't what they called "a bombshell", but had the gift of making excellent use of her flaws: her elongated awkwardness was ballerina-like, and by accentuating her complete lack of curve she took on the air of a confident model like Twiggy. Somehow or other she was really quite pleasant to look at. She wore fashionable clothes from trendy boutiques on the King's Road in Chelsea, where she occasionally worked as a stylist in a hairdressing salon – she was apparently very sought after, and claimed she made an absolute fortune in tips. She never wore a bra, as far as I could see. In fact, as far as I could see, Mia-Mia had very little cause to wear a bra.

'I'm *parched*, aren't you even going to offer me some tea? I'll make a fresh pot for all of us, shall I?'

'There's a good girl,' said auntie Ada.

'I've watched it all on television,' I said, puffing myself up like a peacock.

'Don't fib, we don't *have* a television.'

'But my friend Karl has,' I said. 'And I watched all *this*,' I poked with a finger at the headlines, 'with him and his mum. Karl stayed up through Sunday night and watched it live, and then we all watched it together last night on the news. We were talking and the astronauts were *there*,' I pointed with a finger at the oven, 'jumping about on the moon. You can ask her if you don't believe me. Her name is Dr Schmidt, and she's a famous Reichian therapist.'

'Ooh, a famous Reichian therapist, is she?'

'What's a Reichian therapist?' asked auntie Ada.

'She knows how to make people happy,' I said.

'No wonder she's famous.' When she laughed, Mia-Mia had an irritating habit of clapping her hands.

'Another charlatan,' said auntie Ada.

'Oh, but she's not. And she doesn't believe that any of this actually happened.' I was poking at the papers again. 'She thinks it's probably fake. Nixon's propaganda.'

'It wouldn't surprise me,' said auntie Ada.

'It's all to do with throwing out the baby with the bathwater,' I said. 'Like the Communists do.'

'If I knew what that meant, it would probably make sense,' said auntie Ada.

'Shall I be mother then? I just hope that what they say is true, and tea really does cool you down.'

'I take mine black,' said auntie Ada, after getting up to rinse out her cup. And after rinsing out mine, 'And white with one sugar for Jane.'

'Only one, are you sure? I thought she took three.' Mia-Mia looked at me for confirmation.

'Not when there's cake,' I explained.

'And why are all the windows open, there's hardly going to be a draft when there isn't any air. You're just letting all the dust in.'

'Karl's mother's German, you see. Karl's named after his grandfather, who stole an Otto Dix from the Gestapo. His grandmother on the other side was Greek and his grandfather British, and they were both shot in Greece, executed in the wrong civil war just because there wasn't a right side. Their son's name was Euripides Smith, and he'd promised old Karl that he'd marry Angela Schmidt as long as they could share the Otto Dix. They both needed money to study. But after Karl was born, Dr Euripides Smith moved to Australia to practise neurosurgery in Sydney with his girlfriend from Sweden, and Dr Angela Schmidt stayed in London with Karl to practise Reichian therapy near Angel. Karl's name's now officially Schmidt-Smith.'

'That seems perfectly straightforward,' said auntie Ada.

'And you only know the half of it,' I said.

'Who's Nixon?' asked Mia-Mia. 'Is he one of the astronauts who walked on the moon?'

'You're not serious,' said auntie Ada.

'He's the president of the United States,' I said.

'Really? I thought that Jackie Kennedy was president of the United States.'

'No, Jackie Kennedy was one of the astronauts who walked on the moon,' said auntie Ada. 'And the tea's too bloody weak.'

I couldn't help a little giggle.

'Are you two making fun of me?' asked Mia-Mia.

'As if!' said auntie Ada. 'And you've still not really told us why you've cut your visit short. George said you'd be away *at least* until Thursday.'

'I was, but I won't have my brother speaking down to me, just because he's got a poky bed-and-breakfast in Torquay.'

'Speaking down to you how?'

'It doesn't matter how. I won't tolerate being spoken down to, and especially not in this heat.' Mia-Mia crossed her arms against her chest and stared at the two slices of Black Forest Gateau. 'So I'm back, and my Mr Magikoo is *delighted* I'm back, as he made very clear when I popped into the shop to say hello. And I mean, *very* clear.'

Reminded of the Black Forest Gateau, I dug a fork into my slice and savoured the first mouthful.

'But it's not even noon yet,' said auntie Ada, 'how long is the journey from Torquay?'

'Long enough.'

'I mean, if you left Torquay this morning...'

'What is this, the Spanish Inquisition? I left Torquay when I left Torquay.'

I filled the awkward silence with mouthfuls of Black Forest Gateau.

'I think I'll be off now, home to glorious Cyprus Street,' said auntie Ada, slapping her hands on the table and half getting up.

'*Already*? I hope it wasn't anything I said.'

'Just get George to let me know when you've made up with your brother. And try not to leave it too long.'

'Really, Ada, you're welcome to come over and stay whenever you like, you know that.'

'I don't think I know that at all.'

'Well, you do now, because I've just told you. We all know how much Jane likes to see you.'

'Not quite as much as she likes to see Karl.'

'I might be seeing him later this evening,' I said.

'Might you indeed!' said Mia-Mia, sneaking me a little wink.

'But don't you know at all when you're next going to Torquay?' insisted auntie Ada.

'I should probably stop going altogether.'

Auntie Ada's mouth quivered. 'And why would you do *that*?'

'Because I've never really been all that keen on my brother, or on Torquay for that matter.'

'I'm sure the feeling's mutual.'

'Oh, don't go yet, auntie Ada.' And after scraping my plate clean and swallowing what was left of my Black Forest Gateau, 'You've only just arrived, I've hardly seen you.'

'I know,' said auntie Ada, 'and I'm also disappointed. But why not try and look on the bright side? Mia's right, the less you see of me, the more you'll see of Karl and his television.'

'The name is Mia-Mia, and I never said any such thing.'

'Here, you can have my slice too.' Auntie Ada used both hands to push her plate towards me.

'Ada, you'll make the girl fat. And I've not even been offered a biscuit.'

'But you *never* eat sweets,' I said.

'That's right, my lovely, I don't, I was pulling your leg.' And pushing the plate even further towards me, 'Go on, don't be shy.'

I looked at the slice of Black Forest Gateau, and then I looked at my watch. 'I better not,' I said. 'Tomorrow I'm having late lunch with Karl and his mother.'

'Oh, late lunch!' beamed auntie Ada, at last sounding cheerful again.

'And you might also be visiting him later this evening,' said Mia-Mia.

'My, you *are* seeing a lot of each other.'

Late one night more than two and a half years earlier my father had come home from the pub, stumbling after Mia-Mia through the door, steering her unsteady tallness by the waist as though she were a merry wounded soldier. Auntie Ada was staying, and we were both still up. It was a cold winter night, and the triple-bar electric fire was on. It gave out little heat unless you were too close, and then it dried you up. But the colour of its crackling orange bars was thrown around the room and made it more homely. With a heavy blanket over us we were huddled up together on the old two-seater sofa my father had claimed as his chair, discussing Kafka's *The Metamorphosis*.

Auntie Ada knew a lot about books. She had a good job at the library in Kentish Town, where she had started her career just one week after finishing school, earning the required qualification after several years of intensive part-time study. She often told me stories from her childhood that made my skin crawl, but never with the bitterness that always took her over when she quarrelled with my father.

Her dream of University, as a stepping-stone to writing for the stage, had been thwarted by the need to bring in an extra wage. My grandfather had died in the war, rather ignominiously mauled by a dog while pilfering wine from a farm in northern France some time *after* Mr Hitler had expired in Berlin. According to auntie Ada, he had not been greatly mourned. My father, who was six years her junior, had been the apple of their mother's eye since the day he was born, and my grandmother had always been determined that her dreams for her son would be fulfilled even at the cost of sacrificing totally those of her daughter. "A good marriage", in other words a marriage that she wouldn't feel relieved to be delivered from by a dog, ought to be ample for her Ada. It did not befit girls to be too clever. If anything, it damaged their prospects.

My father's dreams for himself, firm and more resilient than his sister's, had formed when he was still a young boy, and did not correspond in the slightest with those that his mother had been harbouring on his behalf: University as a stepping-stone to a middle ranking job in the civil service. Life had stunted her imagination, even reining in her ambitions for her favourite child. But fortunately for my father he was gifted with a *wild* imagination, and the dexterity to conjure sleights of hand that defied the laws of nature.

'After everything I've done for you, you want to be a *magician*?'

Those few words, said auntie Ada, were my grandmother's last. She and young George had watched the symmetry of their mother's face contort as her central nervous system meted out the various symptoms of a stroke, so massive she could never have recovered from it. Within forty-eight hours she was gone.

'So first he killed his own mother and then he killed mine. And I'd have been next, if you hadn't put a stop to Sweeney Todd.'

'It's a miracle that *either* of us survived,' said auntie Ada, and no sooner had a chuckle escaped her than we both broke into spasms of quite uncontrollable laughter.

'But seriously, auntie Ada, did you never feel angry, not even a little bit? I think you'd have been brilliant as a playwright.'

'I think I've been quite brilliant enough as your auntie. And I'm not sure I'd have been even half as brilliant as a playwright as you imagine. I'd have lacked the violence of John Osborne's language or the exuberance of Orton's bad taste. I'd have even lacked the brilliant titles of Williams and O'Neill… No, I'd have been too polite, a sentimental feminist, mediocre at best… you see how I can't help babbling on?'

'At least you'd have tried.'

'Oh, but I did, no one could've stopped me from trying.' Auntie Ada spread out the blanket to cover my feet, and snuggling up to her I had my arms around her neck. 'My friend Edith from the library came over every Tuesday after work and we'd read what I'd written, trying to act it out like we were actors rehearsing. And Tuesday after Tuesday what I'd written was so bad that neither of us could keep a straight face. Every week we'd be in stitches, and poor Edith would be embarrassed, and I'd end up feeling rotten for putting her through it. So to put us both out of our misery I stopped, and everything went in the bin. You know what Edith said? "Ada, you're selfish," she said. "Those Tuesday nights were *precious* to me." Apparently she wasn't embarrassed at all. She was just too exhausted from laughing. "I've not had so much fun in all my life," she said, "and now you've gone and stopped it without giving how I'd feel a second thought." "Edith," I said, "our Tuesday nights were precious to me too. If we put our heads together, I'm sure we can figure something out." And we did. Every week I wrote a sketch about one of our Tuesdays, this time trying to be deliberately funny. Well, it turned out that I was terrible at comedy too, only not in a way that made either of us laugh. And that was the end of my Tuesday nights with Edith.'

'That's so sad. Is Edith all alone now?'

'All alone with a husband and five children, except on Tuesday nights.'

'But I thought you said...'

'*Our* Tuesday nights are over,' chortled auntie Ada. 'But Edith's Tuesday nights have just begun.'

'Is she having an *affair*?'

'With Bingo, and her husband blames me.'

'So you definitely didn't give up writing because of what happened to mummy?'

Auntie Ada's breast rose sharply. 'Even my evenings with Edith were over by then.'

'How come you never married, auntie Ada?'

'Oh my... where did that suddenly come from, I wonder.'

'I'm sorry, that was a *horrible* question to ask.'

'Life,' said auntie Ada, as though she hadn't heard me.

'Life... What does that even *mean*?'

'We really are asking big questions tonight,' sighed auntie Ada. 'Let me see how I can put it... Men weren't exactly chasing after me, for obvious reasons, and I didn't have the time to be chasing after men. I had a life too full already.'

'Too full already with what?'

'With theatre and wonderful books, and with answering my even more wonderful niece's impertinent questions.'

I loved listening to auntie Ada, especially her fairy tales. They weren't the ordinary fairy tales that everyone knew, but dark, melancholy, *scary* ones. Auntie Ada called them "psychological". These grown-up fairy tales, which she started without knowing how to finish, had somehow had the effect of passing on to me auntie Ada's love of reading, and perhaps even the seeds of a longing to write.

From auntie Ada's fairy tales, the leap to *The Metamorphosis* had been but a short one. I had read it one evening from start to finish, then I had turned to the beginning and read it again.

'I lay in bed wide awake in that horrible room and I felt...'

'Like a bug?'

'It's not funny, auntie Ada.'

'Maybe Kafka was a bit premature.'

I sat up abruptly, gripping auntie Ada's hand as she made to pull it back. 'No!' I said. 'I don't think I've read a more beautiful story. It made me feel like I had Gregor inside me, just here, at the centre of my tummy, where I can sometimes feel Karl's music. But I wasn't the bug that Gregor's trapped inside in the book. My room was the bug, and we were both trapped inside it.'

'Dear God!' said auntie Ada. 'Uncle Freud would have a field day. And this Karl?' It was the first time I had mentioned his name.

'Karl's my new friend who plays the piano. Everyone thinks he's a genius.'

'Your new friend or your boyfriend?'

'Oh no, just my friend. I think I'm too young for a boyfriend.'

Outside the night had been still, but now the eerie whistle of a gust of wind had wrapped itself around the house as though in a frantic attempt to uproot it. When I looked up at my aunt, what I saw was not the usual face of reassurance.

'What is it, auntie Ada? I'm scared, it sounds like something evil.'

'It's just a gust of wind, I'm sure it'll pass in a minute.'

But it didn't pass, nor was it a gust of wind. The catastrophe that was approaching was human.

'It's not an act of God, it's your father.'

'It's *partly* my father,' I said. 'The whistling is his, but those spine-tingling giggles are definitely someone else's.'

'A *woman's*.' Stiffly upright on the sofa beside me, auntie Ada had drawn up the blanket to just below our eyes, and was holding it scrunched up with her fists. 'I'm scared,' she said, 'it sounds like something evil.'

And when the door opened and the slender Mia-Mia wafted in unsteadily ahead of my father, his squat bulkiness protruding either side of her tallness as he steered her in a zigzag by the waist, auntie Ada and I simultaneously and spontaneously screamed...

The excitement of my evening with Karl had brought it all back. On that cold winter night, none of us had made the best impression. Mia-Mia was the first woman my father had brought to the house since the "mishap", and some small degree of shock would have been normal. But our unwelcoming reception had betrayed something far beyond a small degree of shock. I interpreted our scream as a reflex reaction to the vast discrepancy – it was really nothing short of a chasm - between this rather conspicuous newcomer and the simple, understated memory of my mother. "Chalk and cheese" was nowhere near close; it did not even *begin* to cover it.

But with time, I had become accustomed to this vast discrepancy. In fact, I was glad of it. If there was going to be a new woman in my father's life, the less that woman resembled my mother the better. How lucky, then, that

Mia-Mia resembled her not in the least. And hadn't I been taught (by Kafka and auntie Ada) not to judge by appearances? Wasn't it ironic that Mia-Mia had made her entrance seconds after our discussion of the bug in *The Metamorphosis*? How could anyone tell, far less judge, what kind of Gregor Samsa - decent, caring, *ordinary* – might be trapped behind that high-heeled armour of extravagance that rocked from side to side as Mia-Mia?

Auntie Ada was a different story. Resolutely she remained the proverbial immovable mountain: whatever might have been the first impression that had made her join me in a scream, she seemed to want to cling to it forever. Mia-Mia really wasn't that bad. She was a loudmouth, undoubtedly, but auntie Ada had a big mouth too, so it couldn't have been that. Was it perhaps a sense of unshakeable loyalty to my mother? Many years had passed since the "mishap" she had never forgiven her brother for, the "mishap" I had never forgiven my father for, the "mishap", I suspected, my father had never forgiven *himself* for. If my mother hadn't lost both her parents before I was born, no doubt they too would have been added to the people who had never forgiven George Hareman.

I wanted to tell Karl that he was right. Grief was at the heart of all that circular lack of forgiveness. I had already lost my mother. By blaming my father, I risked losing him too. Yes, he was selfish, and cruel, and a fool without being dumb, which was actually worse than being dumb. But mightn't that *also* be grief? I found it difficult to judge him without judging myself, and I wondered if the same mightn't be true of auntie Ada. If it was, then auntie Ada was judging herself far too harshly. Nearly ten years, and no one had recovered from my mother's death. This last thought filled me with an almost unbearable sadness.

No one need compare Mia-Mia to the woman everyone had loved, and who everyone had suffered from losing. Auntie Ada had perhaps suffered, and also sacrificed, the most. Whereas my father had found solace by withdrawing into Mr Magikoo, auntie Ada and I had found solace in each other. But I was a child with a long stretch of life still ahead of me. Auntie Ada was now a woman whose life belonged to me; it was as if her own had all but ended. For anyone's life to move forward, we *all* of us needed the chain to be broken, and by setting off a domino effect Mia-Mia might just manage to break it. For the sake of this distant possibility alone, I thought that she at least deserved a chance.

I had never *really* disliked her. And I had grown to like her more and more since she moved in.

'She's not that bad, auntie Ada.' On a crisp Saturday in October, almost two years since Mia-Mia's first appearance and our scream, auntie Ada and I had just got off the bus and were on our way to see the Parthenon marbles at the British Museum.

'Oh, I think she's actually worse than "that bad".'

'Is it because… you never find any dust?'

'Of course not, what a thing to say!'

'Is it because… she doesn't have a proper job?'

'Hairdressing *is* a proper job.'

'But she only works part-time.'

'So do I these days. And I'm sure she makes more money than I do. Why all these questions, are we playing a game?'

'Yes,' I said, skipping forward two steps, then returning to auntie Ada and clasping her arm as I walked on beside her. 'Is it because… she never wears a bra?'

'No, it's not because she never wears a bra.'

I was running out of words to put in her mouth.

'Does it have anything to do… with how she dresses, and all that make up she puts on?'

Aha, the first hesitation.

'Is it because… she's so unlike mum?'

Auntie Ada stopped dead in her tracks. 'Your mother was a saint,' she said, and turning to face me she held me in place so that we could look at each other head-on. 'So no, I could never blame anyone for not being like her.'

We walked silently through Russell Square. The previous night's rain had seeped through the earth and brought to life its colours, giving an exaggerated magnitude to every sensation. Fresh, bright, revealing, days like this were to be savoured, and I was taking in the purity of the air in deep breaths. Even people looked sharper, more defined in their movement, invigorated as they cut through the chill.

When we were back on the grey of the pavement, I tugged at auntie Ada's arm.

'But doesn't it have *anything* to do with how she looks?'

Now a second hesitation, and after a more temporary halt and a sigh, 'It has something to do with who she isn't.'

'But you said...'

'I don't mean your mum.'

'If not mum, then who?'

'Or *what*,' answered auntie Ada. And surging forward as she shook both her hands in the air, 'You're too young to understand. Now come on, before the Greeks descend on the museum to claim their marbles back.' And as an afterthought almost, 'It doesn't really matter what either of us thinks of Mia-Mia. I don't think she'll be staying for very long. Her sort never do.'

I didn't have a clue what she meant by "her sort". I had never heard her speak like that before.

'But she's nice to me, auntie Ada.' This was only true up to a point. Mia-Mia liked to tease me just a little bit more than I liked to be teased, but she did it without thinking, as though she were performing to a crowd. I didn't really mind all that much. 'I actually like her,' I said. In fact I liked her a lot. And contrary to auntie Ada's prediction, she did stay around.

As I became more independent, busy with reading and homework and Karl, auntie Ada's visits to the house grew scarcer. Occasionally we would still take the bus to the centre, to eat cakes together and browse around the bookshops in Charing Cross Road, as often as not on our way to an exhibition or the very special treat of a matinee performance at the theatre. Only rarely did we go and watch a film; auntie Ada for some reason disapproved of the cinema. She thought it generally dumbed people down.

'I'd say it was time for Mr Magikoo's well-earned aperitif, wouldn't you?' Mia-Mia would purr affectionately as she whirled her viscous tongue around my father's ear the minute he had walked through the door, where (unless she was away at her brother's bed-and-breakfast in Torquay) she greeted him at eighteen hundred hours precisely every evening, weekends included – the proximity of the shop promoted in the household a culture of strict punctuality in certain routines from which I was excluded.

'How well my Mia-Mia can read my mind,' my father would then answer in that very high-pitched voice he couldn't help when he felt horny, which he evidently did as he pinched Mia-Mia's bottom at just a few seconds past eighteen hundred hours every evening, weekends included.

Through the gap between *Beyond Good and Evil* and Volume II of *The Brothers Karamazov*, I would carry on peeking...

'Any news from Torquay?' my father often asked with a squeak while he carried on pinching.

'Early days,' Mia-Mia always answered.

'But you *are* making progress.'

'Mm!' Mia-Mia would mumble in vague reassurance, and I would wonder what progress she could possibly be making in Torquay.

Mia-Mia's bottom must have been the blue of a permanently irritated bruise. My father's daily pinches, which I witnessed from the dining room table, buried in philosophy and fiction and homework (my own room, being a box, was too small for a desk), consisted of prolonged and fanatical clamping and twisting. Far from ever complaining, Mia-Mia moaned with pleasure to the rhythm of the heavy-breathing clock on the wall behind the dining room table. Or perhaps it was my own throbbing heart that I could hear as I snooped from behind my barricade of abstract thought.

Through obstinate spells of Schopenhauer bleakness, a Nietzsche fascination that bordered on a crush, and ultimately a Buddha frustration that enlightened me by practically driving me mad, every evening without fail I pretended not to watch, unable not to notice Mia-Mia staring back in my direction with a luminous glint in her eye. Not content with being pleasured by my father, she was also pleasuring herself by imagining that she was pleasuring me. But what I found *even* more disturbing was that I was actually being pleasured. Mia-Mia was imagining correctly.

'Pas devant les enfants,' Mia-Mia would then remember to utter knowledgeably in French.

'Jane?'

'Studying.'

'In her room?'

'Behind you.'

'That's my girl!' my father would exclaim, and then he and Mia-Mia would disappear behind the flimsy hollow door of the only decent bedroom in the house.

Not even solid oak could have muffled that cacophony of animal sounds emanating from the other side. My father, who was slightly hard of hearing, clearly liked to listen to himself talking dirty; he wasn't so much talking as shouting, and I would wonder if it hadn't crossed his mind that I could hear.

'You like that, don't you... mm? Go on, say how much you like it...' It was that kind of thing, only smuttier.

And on and on it went, Mia-Mia's affirmative guttural grunts punctuating the obscenities of Mr Magikoo's piercing falsetto until nineteen hundred hours precisely, when one last unearthly screech would signal its final crescendo. Behind my barricade I remained stock-still, like one of those religious statues that bleed or shed tears. But instead of either weeping or bleeding, I'd be wet with the reeking perspiration of hormonal adolescence, and palpitating wildly. So loud and distinct were my rapid heartbeats that had I leaned any part of my breast against the door, I might as well have pounded on it with my fists. What I felt in my total incapacity to move out of earshot until *after* my father had climaxed, was a culpable mixture of excitement and shame. I was disgusted by the thought of my father having sex, but there was something about Mia-Mia that aroused me. And it wasn't because I was attracted to women.

It was all rather confusing at my age.

7

Uneasy Dreams

We were walking hand in hand along the sand of a deserted beach. The air was damp, and the water still and quiet. We came across a jetty that went far into the sea, a corroded mass of metal with fragments of dark, sodden wood. Battered by the waves, the primitive monochrome structure imposed itself upon the landscape in a brutal but inevitable way, its long winding frame hunched over the sea like the fossil of a melancholy pathway. Now Karl let go of my hand and climbed onto its backbone. He moved effortlessly while I stood at the edge of the water and watched him. Then I was with him; now with him and now watching him from where I was standing, unable to move, unable to be with him holding his hand. He moved further and further away, and I tried to call out to him, 'Karl! Karl!' But my words had no sound. I was with him as he reached the end of the jetty, far, far into the ocean, but when I saw him turn to look at me, once more I stood heavy at the edge of the water, my arms stretching out. 'Karl!' But again there was silence. He turned away from me and gazed ahead into the sea for a moment or two. Then almost comically he held his nose before he plunged into the water, his body a perfect vertical to its horizon. I tried to call again, 'Karl!' And again there was nothing. I felt the water freeze Karl's body as he sank through it; I felt the terror Karl was feeling as he drowned.

'Karl!' As I finally managed to call out his name, I woke up. Lying flat on my back, I felt cold in the dark, as cold as I had felt in my dream at the moment when Karl had hit the water. 'I must have thrown off the covers in my sleep,' I thought. I continued to stare at the ceiling waiting for my eyes to adjust, for the blackness to turn grey as it did every morning. Although my room had no windows, enough light seeped in through the edges of the ill-fitting doorframe to break the total darkness, which I wouldn't have been able to bear.

But this wasn't my room. I had kept my eyes wide open and the darkness had remained undiminished, preventing me from seeing even the outline of the light bulb that hung over my bed, and *because* I couldn't see it I knew that this wasn't my room. And if this wasn't my room, then it followed that this wasn't my bed, nor could the warmth that I now felt beside me be Karl's, unless Karl had only drowned in a dream...

'Karl, is that you?'

'No, no, no,' said a voice that wasn't Karl's.

I felt the warmth draw closer until it was burning, while somewhere in the distance I heard laughter – my father's?

'It's me, silly,' said the voice that wasn't Karl's. 'Here, let me show you.'

A crushing weight bore down on me until I was sinking, sinking through this unfamiliar bed as though it were quicksand, its thousand million grains of fire searing my body...

Again the laughter rumbled in the distance.

'But why won't you pinch me?' asked the voice that wasn't Karl's. 'If you pinch me, you'll know who I am.'

'I think I know who you are already.'

'You may *think* you know,' said the voice. 'But you won't know for sure unless you pinch me.'

'That's just foolish,' I said. The warmth had given way to the coolness of stone. We were lying on the floor under the bed. 'And I do know for sure. I recognise the smell of your breath.'

'Of course you do, I'm your mother,' said the voice of my mother.

'My mother's dead. She's dead and you've stolen her voice.'

'Then how would you know if I haven't also stolen someone's breath?'

'Stop trying to confuse me,' I said. 'Please, I'd like to go back to my room now.'

'But wouldn't you like to see the device first?'

'The device?'

'Your father designed it himself. It's *very* elaborate; I'm sure you'll like it.'

'Is it far?'

'We're actually lying on it now.'

'We're lying on the floor under the bed.'

'Ah, but we're not, we're lying on a *bed* under the bed.'

'Is that what the device is? A bed under the bed?'

'Manufactured to precise specifications. It has to be adjustable, you see.'

'It's not particularly comfortable, is it? It doesn't feel at all like a bed.'

'It's not supposed to be particularly comfortable,' said the voice. 'As a matter of fact, the longer you lie on it, the less comfortable it becomes. And if you lie on it too long, you disappear. It's designed to stop people from hiding.'

'But no one really hides under the bed.'

'Oh, you'd be surprised.'

'You're still trying to confuse me. We're not *really* on a bed under the bed.'

'I can prove it to you if you like.'

'How?'

'Try and pinch me and you'll see.'

'I know you're Mia-Mia.'

'I *used* to be Mia-Mia,' said the voice of Mia-Mia. 'And you're right, I still have her breath.'

'Very well then, I'll pinch you,' I said, and after I had groped this way and that in the space under the bed, I felt right beside me the cold, slightly shivering hardness of the shell. Even before I had run all across its smooth surface the tips of my fingers, before I had felt underneath it and almost cut myself against the sharpness of its limbs, and long before it had begun to squeak, I knew it must belong to a giant bug.

I sat up with a start, and when I looked up at the ceiling, I saw very clearly the outline of the light bulb that hung above my bed.

I had, in the end, given in to the second, even larger slice of Black Forest Gateau - the mistake had been to look at it again after I had spoken to Karl.

As always, saying goodbye to auntie Ada had made me feel sad, and I was hoping Mia-Mia might cheer me up. But when the telephone rang, Mia-Mia was already at the top of the stairs on her way to the bathroom, no doubt to have a shower and freshen up after her ordeal at her brother's bed-and-breakfast in Torquay.

'Jane?

'*Karl*?'

'Try not to sound so surprised.'

Of course I was surprised. We'd had each other's numbers for years, but it was always me who called. This was the first time Karl was calling me.

'Has something happened?'

'I'd say so, wouldn't you?'

No one could see me, so why should I have cared what colour my face was?

'Yes,' I said.

'I'm calling to say sorry.'

It had all been a mistake, he would say. We were friends, that's all, and if he'd given me the wrong impression by asking me upstairs to his room...

'Nothing happened,' I said, dredging up the sound from somewhere deep.

'Are you angry?'

'There's nothing to be angry about.' My voice had now completely lost its breath.

'Oh, but there is,' said Karl. And after an eternity, 'It was late. I should've walked you home.'

I felt the emptiness inside me filling up.

'Mami was *furious* when she realised I hadn't gone with you.'

'Tell Mami I wouldn't have let you. I like walking home by myself.'

'If I'd thought of it you wouldn't have been able to stop me.'

'But you've never walked me home.'

'Last night was different.'

'I know,' I said. 'And I wanted to call you.'

'You did?'

'You were right about my dad, I don't want to be angry all the time.'

'I thought you weren't listening,' said Karl. 'I thought maybe you were feeling distracted.' And when I made no reply, 'Are you coming round later? I'll be home after 8.'

'I might do,' I said.

'I've been thinking about you a lot. Last night I couldn't sleep, and first thing this morning I needed to go out for a walk, to try and clear my head. I walked from home to Angel, then all the way to Old Street and then further east, but I wasn't taking anything in. And suddenly I realised that people were giving me looks. Honestly, Jane, it's like

Dickens down there, from one street to the next it becomes a different world, run down and noisy and *poor*. Unsafe even in daylight, or at least that's how I felt. So I put my shirt back on, and I ran most of the way back to Angel. And can you guess what I did next? I got lost. You know *how* I got lost? Looking for your house. I was going to buy some tricks for a party, so you gave me the address for *Mr Magikoo's Magik Shoppe* and you said you lived next door, you remember? Anyway, I found it in the end. I'll come and pick you up if you like. Tonight, I mean. If you're not reading Kafka.'

'It's fine, I'll make my own way if I'm coming,' I said. 'Like I always do.'

'Any time after 8.'

Exhausted by his roller-coaster call, I had walked straight back into the kitchen like a robot. And sitting colourfully erect on its plate, showing off its layers of exquisite bliss, its glazed scarlet cherry radiating on top, auntie Ada's slice of Black Forest Gateau had screamed at me, 'EAT ME, EAT ME!' I had not even attempted to resist, and had paid a heavy price for my greed. Instant indigestion had led to self-disgust even before the last mouthful, the few crumbs of leftover evidence staring at me sneeringly from not just one but *two* empty plates. After doing the washing up, I had quietly retreated to my room. Mia-Mia was still in the bathroom.

Being a windowless box, on a hot day like this my bedroom was actually cooler than anywhere else in the house, and I had lain down on my bed intending to distract my guilty conscience with Kafka. In the circumstances of that afternoon, *In the Penal Colony*, which the second part of my dream had merged with *The Metamorphosis*, had proved an unfortunate choice. On this particular occasion Kafka's brilliance had not had the desired effect. It had added to my indigestion a churning knot in my stomach that had threatened to make me throw up. The monotonous detail in which the Officer described to the Traveller the torture apparatus of bed, inscriber and harrow by which the waiting Condemned Man was about to have the words of his sentence cut into his body had repulsed me; probably it had reminded me of Sweeney Todd. And at the point where the Officer revealed to the Traveller that the Condemned Man was ignorant not only of the nature of his sentence but also of the fact that he had been condemned, the book had closed in my hands as though of its own volition, and I had lifted myself up to turn off the light. Some time after that I must have fallen asleep, and my dreams had indeed been uneasy.

I remembered reading somewhere that dreams that had been dreamt had already served their purpose, and that attempting to interpret them was not only futile, it was actually counter-productive. Or perhaps I hadn't read it; it might have been Karl who had told me, in that deliberately roundabout way he had of telling me things that made me feel stupid. Everything he said sounded plausible enough, sometimes even profound, but at the same time he often seemed to have drawn his apparently self-evident conclusions from nowhere. I could never tell for sure if he was pulling my leg. And after confusing me, in the next breath he'd be chiding me that there was so much more to life than just being clever at manipulating words. Well, I didn't need to interpret my dream, or to imagine what the purpose of that part of it had been in which I had been helpless to save him from drowning, to know that I was thinking of Karl far too much. And I also knew why. 'Let's go upstairs to my room.' After his phone call I knew he would ask me again. Did I *want* him to ask me again? Would I go? And if I did, how could I be sure what might happen? I wouldn't know the answer to any of these questions unless we were together alone in his house. It was not yet half past five, and I would not be reading any more Kafka. What I needed was a shower. And after having a shower, I would take a little longer to decide what to wear.

I stumbled out of bed and I emerged from my dungeon-like room to the tropical brightness of the rest of the house. The air was still heavy with moisture, and as I made my way upstairs to the bathroom feeling sticky in the clothes I had fallen asleep in, I wondered how on earth I would get dry after wetting myself in the shower. Thinking already of the pink cotton blouse I would probably pick from my wardrobe, and how it might look with the blue and white polka-dot Bermudas Mia-Mia had bought for me on one of her trips to Torquay, with my towel thrown over my shoulder I barged into the bathroom almost falling through the door, which I hadn't thought to knock on even though it had been shut.

Shut but not locked. Mia-Mia must have felt sticky too, and had obviously just had another shower. Reaching down to dry her feet, her long, lean figure was bent forward towards me, not very far from the door. In slow movements, she let the towel drop as she stood up, then crossed her arms over the smoothness of her chest and clutched at her neck as though about to strangle herself. It had already registered that I ought to have knocked, and that Mia-Mia was naked. But then I had become transfixed, as transfixed and mute as Mia-Mia, whose gaze I felt caressing me with kindness. A moment she had probably dreaded had passed. And I was still in the room. I hadn't even screamed.

'Oh my God, Mia-Mia...' I finally managed to gasp.

'So now you know I have a penis,' said Mia-Mia. Her voice was different now, more natural, but not only because it was very slightly deeper.

'Yes, a penis,' I said.

'Quite a specimen too, don't you think?'

'I've not actually seen one before.'

'Well, then. I think it's good you've seen a friendly one first.'

'Yes, I suppose so,' I said.

'You can't imagine what a nightmare it's been trying to hide it, expensive *and* painful. I mean, look! The bulge it makes isn't exactly discreet. But now I think you've seen enough.' And picking up the towel and wrapping it around her waist, 'Come, let's go have a glass of something cold.'

As we sat opposite each other drinking lemon squash with lots of ice, I still couldn't get my head around the wet and semi-naked Mia-Mia. She reminded me of David Bowie, a young British singer whose picture I'd seen in one of the music magazines Karl's mother had subscribed him to, and whose brand new song I'd listened to on the red transistor radio auntie Ada had given me last Christmas. It was called *Space Oddity*, and it probably wasn't a coincidence that it had just been released, a few days ahead of the Apollo 11 launch that had landed two men on the moon. Even Karl had described him as "quite interesting, if you like that sort of thing", and although this David Bowie was definitely a boy, he had a slender, tender boy/girl look not dissimilar to Mia-Mia's. And unless there was something the world didn't know about David Bowie, they were also both endowed with a penis.

There were a million questions I wanted to ask, but although I no longer felt embarrassed to look, because Mia-Mia was more beautiful than ever to look at...

'You're miles away, aren't you?'

'Oh my God, Mia-Mia...'

'Are you trying to make me show you my penis again?' Her smile was full of warmth. 'You and I, we can be friends now if you like. Or would you rather not be friends with a freak?'

'But you're *not* a freak.'

'I do feel like one sometimes.'

'Well, I think you're beautiful, like David Bowie.'

'I'm sure even David Bowie sometimes feels like a freak.'

'I liked to watch while dad pinched your bottom. I even liked to listen while the two of you made noises in the bedroom.'

'We should've been more careful,' said Mia-Mia. 'Don't worry, I'm sure you were just curious, and there's nothing more normal for a girl who's growing up than being curious.'

'I thought you knew. I was sure you'd seen me watching.'

Mia-Mia shook her head to say no. 'It's no excuse, I know, but I've been too distracted.'

'By my father, you mean.'

'Not *just* by your father.'

She smiled again as she reached over the table. Her hands seemed more fragile even than the rest of her somehow, but when her fingers moved, their elegance reminded me of Karl's. I let go of my glass, and as our two pairs of hands came together, they tightened round each other before flattening themselves in a pile.

'I like it, you see, this peculiar dangling thing between my legs. And apparently I shouldn't, because otherwise I'm nothing, and everyone needs to be something.'

'How can anyone be nothing?'

'That makes two of us who don't understand. So I don't think I'll be going back to Torquay, which is actually this hell in Shepherds Bush where they're supposed to try and help you be yourself.'

'Oh my God, Mia-Mia, do they want you to get rid of your penis?'

'I'm sure they'd chop it off themselves if I let them. They're so angry that I won't say I hate it. "Hate it? It's part of me and it's a thing of beauty, so why should I hate it?" That's what I told them. "Then you're neither a man nor a woman," they said, "and how can you expect us to help you if you're still in denial?" They're doing that, you know, in the States, making women of men by taking a snip at their penis. And if that's *really* how you feel, like a woman, then I don't suppose you'd want to have a penis. But it isn't how *I* feel *at all*.'

'Then why did you ever go to such a horrible place?'

'It's complicated,' said Mia-Mia.

'Oh my God, Mia-Mia... It was my dad, he made you!'

'I told you it was complicated.'

'I mean, does he know?'

'Obviously he knows about my penis, and he hates it. Every time we... let's just say I do my best to keep it out of the way.'

'But does he know...'

'What he doesn't know is what I'm telling him tonight. That occasionally I like dressing up as a girl, that at work I still enjoy being Mia-Mia, but I'll always be a boy.'

'A boy!' I repeated the words with enthusiasm. 'Does that mean you shave? And your body, it's so hairless.'

'It's simple enough to get rid of the few hairs I have in the places where I'd rather not have them. And I'm twenty-five, so I suppose that must make me a man. A man who likes to sleep with other men, and wake up with them too.'

Mia-Mia pulled her hands out of the pile and ran them both together through the little that was left of her hair. 'And there's really nothing wrong with that. It's hardly something new, and it's not even illegal any more.'

'And my dad?'

'He just wants to be a man, who can't admit he's fallen in love with a boy. And to be fair, he didn't know I was a boy when we met. He saw me with the girls at the pub after work, we flirted, I gave him the number at the salon, we met a couple of times, and when he tried to kiss me I told him. Well, it didn't stop him kissing me, or inviting me back. And he almost talked us both into believing Mia-Mia was a girl, and that this thing between her legs was unnatural.'

'This afternoon I fell asleep while I was reading. And I dreamt of you. First I dreamt of losing Karl, and then I dreamt I was with you under the bed. I could only hear your voice and smell your breath, and you were telling me this place under the bed was an elaborate device designed by my father, and if you lay in it too long you disappeared. And when I tried to pinch you, you weren't really you any more.'

'Please don't tell me that you dreamt I was a boy.'

'I dreamt you were a bug, like the cockroach in *The Metamorphosis*.'

'I don't think what Kafka had in mind was a cockroach. All these books you've been reading, maybe you should leave them for later. It might not be time for them yet.'

'That's what auntie Ada said three years ago.'

'And she might've been right.'

'But why, I think my dream was amazing. It's like I knew that you were really someone else. It was only a coincidence, of course. I always have strange dreams when I've had too much cake.'

Mia-Mia jolted forward, coughing back into her glass the sip of lemon squash that had almost made her choke.

'Really you're too much, and I mean that in a nice way. A young, teenage girl with a head full of books, but still only a young, teenage girl - and I also mean *that* in a nice way.'

'You sound so different now. I mean the way you speak, not just the sound of your voice.'

'Less brash, less trashy, altogether more classy?'

'I never thought you were trashy.'

'The way I see it, life is research. After I finished my degree...'

'You have a *degree*?'

'I have a very *good* degree in English,' giggled the flat-chested Mia-Mia.

'Oh my God, Mia-Mia!'

'And I'm also a fully qualified hairdresser, as well as a very convincing dumb blonde.'

'Was my dad research too?'

'Oh no, no, no, your dad was life researching *me*.'

I shook the half-melted ice in my glass until there was more liquid, but there wasn't enough, and I ended up crushing the ice in my mouth.

'You think auntie Ada knows you're a boy? You think that's why she's funny with you?'

'Ah yes, your auntie Ada. She really doesn't like me, does she? Well, she's not stupid, so it's possible she's guessed – she might even have noticed my crotch when I haven't quite managed to hide it, which is an art form, believe me, and I'm sure I've not always got it right.'

'I'm not stupid either, and *I* never noticed your crotch.'

'You're not stupid at all, but nor are you suspicious by nature, at least not as suspicious as your aunt. And if she's guessed, she's probably thinking, "How do I explain to this child that her father, who she thinks is responsible for killing her mother, is now having sex under our noses with a man?"' Mia-Mia fell back in her chair, before returning to lean against the table on her elbows. Resting the side of her head in the palm of one hand, she looked piercingly into mine from a depth behind her eyes that had never before been revealed. Karl's were a boy's eyes. They had reminded me of hawks in a nest, preparing for their predatory journeys. But Mia-Mia's had deceived me completely, the dimness of their delicate green an illusion of movement. 'I hope one day you'll both be able to forgive him, it's the only chance he has of forgiving himself, even though he knows that it wasn't his fault.'

'Is that what he told you, that it wasn't his fault?'

'It was in all the papers at the time, he's shown them to me, "one in a million freak accident" they called it, a strike of lightning at just that one moment.'

'A strike of lightning… But doesn't auntie Ada know this?'

'It's like he *wants* to be blamed, and Ada wants to blame him, so… And then there's Little Magik Matchstick, which I don't think he'll *ever* be able to forgive himself for. He puts it down to a kind of madness, "a possession" he calls it, that took complete control over Mr Magikoo.'

'If it hadn't been for auntie Ada, and then you putting an end to the tours, I'd either still be doing it, or I'd be fatter and probably dead from stuffing down too many cakes.'

'But you're not, you're neither fat nor dead, you're a gorgeous, sensitive, intelligent girl about to fall in love with a bright and talented boy. And now you also know, more or less, what his penis is likely to look like.'

'You think if he asks me I should agree to have sex?'

'Do you want to have sex?'

'I don't want to get pregnant.'

'And you won't, if you're both careful. But really, if you're not sure, you should wait until you're older.'

I nodded, as though Mia-Mia had been reading my thoughts. And then returning to auntie Ada, 'She thinks you won't be around for very long. And if she doesn't like you it's because she doesn't know you. I disliked you too at the beginning.'

'And now we're friends.'

'Friends forever,' I said.

'I hope so.' Her smile now was fainter, more tentative, as though suddenly it wasn't all as simple as that. 'Let's just wait and see what your father says, now that there's no more Mia-Mia. If I'm going to be staying, at least within these walls I'd like to go back to being Jack.'

'Jack. I like it.'

'Jack with the enormous penis,' said Jack, and the two of us, or perhaps even the three of us, stood up and hugged each other while we laughed.

'Did you really think that Jackie Kennedy was president of the United States?'

'And that Nixon had walked on the moon?'

'I knew you were probably teasing.'

'You talked a fair amount of gibberish yourself, I seem to remember.' Jack pulled away and made me look at him by lifting up my chin with his finger. 'I think someone was overexcited,' he said. 'What *was* all that nonsense about Communist babies and Nixon's propaganda?'

'It's apparently a famous German saying. "To throw the baby out with the bathwater." Dr Schmidt thinks that Nixon's a crook, and the landing on the moon was a lie to fight Communist lies with. She's convinced it didn't actually happen.'

Jack rolled his eyes and kept his eyebrows arched. 'I know the saying,' he said, 'and I wasn't aware it was German.'

'Dr Schmidt said so, she was very insistent.'

'Oh, was she indeed! Well, you can tell this Dr Schmidt that the Germans lost the war and it's *our* saying now.'

'I honestly don't mind that you're a boy, or a man,' I said, when we had both stopped laughing. 'And I'll say so to auntie Ada.'

All thoughts of an evening with Karl had disappeared. I was seeing him tomorrow for lunch, and there would be plenty of other evenings when I wouldn't be reading more Kafka, or delving into Schopenhauer's strictures, or reciting from my favourite Nietzsche, although now and again I might still have a flicker through Plato. All the events of this eventful afternoon – my dreams, the surprise of my new thoughts about Karl (I wouldn't yet describe them as feelings), then the bigger surprise of the penis in the bathroom, and especially my conversations with Mia-Mia (who had now come out as Jack) – had united to make life, lived now in the present, infinitely more exciting than stories. "Stories" was the way auntie Ada and I had dealt with the past, but today had already belonged to the future. And it still wasn't over.

8

Daddy

It was far from over.

At eighteen hundred hours precisely, when my father came in through the door, Mia-Mia was not there to greet him. Damp, bare-chested and with nothing but his towel wrapped around his waist, Jack was still in the kitchen with me, drinking a second glass of lemon squash with lots of ice. With only flimsy walls, and no door, separating the kitchen from the dining area where I did all my studying, and just the few pieces of furniture – a pouffe, my father's chair, a glass-top coffee table - comprising the rest of the living room leading to the little hallway where Mia-Mia should have been waiting, I had heard the door open, and now I heard it shut.

'I'd say it was time for Mr Magikoo's well-earned aperitif, wouldn't you?'

'It's not funny,' I said. 'He'll know you've told me if he sees you like this.'

Jack stood up from the table, and hesitated over me, squeezing my shoulders. 'I want him to know,' he said.

'Mia-Mia?'

'He's still at the door,' I said. 'He doesn't sound happy.'

'Hello, George,' said Jack in his new voice as he made his way through.

For a few long moments there was silence.

'What's this?' I heard my father ask. 'Where's Ada?'

'Ada's gone.'

'And I suppose Jane's with that German boy again. So what's this all about, the voice and that towel, and you looking like the cat's dragged you in?'

'Your daughter's in the kitchen.'

'Okay, you've had your bit of fun now, so how about you put something on and make yourself normal.'

'Really, she is. We've been drinking lemon squash.'

For a few longer moments there was silence again.

'She walked in on me in the bathroom, you see.' And before there was time for more silence, 'She's seen me - *all* of me, George. So there we are. Cat's out of the bag, as they say.'

I heard it: the crack as something hit something else, my father striking harshly against the side of Jack's face with his hand, Jack not making a sound. I got up from the table, held on to the back of the chair...

'And while we sat at the table enjoying our lemon squash, your daughter and I both agreed that there's more than one way to be normal. That *this* is normal, and that *my* way is the only way, at least for me. So there won't be any more visits to my brother's bed-and-breakfast in Torquay.'

'You should cover yourself up, if Jane's really in the kitchen.' My father's voice had deepened too. It was hoarse, as though speaking implied an impossible effort. 'Then you can pack up your things, and by the time I get back I want you gone. *None* of this is normal, but if you're happy to be a pervert good for you.'

'I can go and be a pervert somewhere else.'

'Yes, somewhere else,' my father repeated.

'But not in this house, not in your bed.'

'No.'

'That was a mistake.'

'Yes. A mistake.'

'A mistake that went on for almost three years.'

'And now it has to end.'

'Nothing's really changed, George.'

'What's changed is that I want you to go.'

'Because I'm queer and you're not.'

'We're not about to have a discussion.'

'Because there's nothing to discuss.'

'Just make sure that you're not here when I get back.'

'Dad, don't be stupid.' I was standing with my back to my books, not hiding behind them. I had seen Jack pick up the towel from the floor and wrap it again around his waist. I had seen him stand upright, still within my father's reach. And as though I were invisible, I had listened to their dull staccato voices as they exchanged a rapid volley of words.

My father turned sharply towards me with his body.

'Please, just go to your room,' he said without looking at me.

'Jack's right, nothing's changed.'

'It's Jack now, is it?'

'It's always been Jack,' said Jack.

'Then you're both right, nothing's changed, and it's all been a mistake from the start.'

'And so you've hit someone you love,' I said.

'Love? Don't make me laugh.' But as he turned back to face Jack, my father wasn't laughing. '*You* did this,' he said. 'You *planned* for her to see you, and then for me to come and find you half naked with her, drinking lemon squash and telling her I'm queer and it's normal. First I kill her mother and now this, something else she won't be able to forgive me for. And I'm supposed to feel *proud*?' The word "proud" had nearly choked him, his sharp intakes of breath no longer able to hold back the violence of his sobbing.

When Jack touched the side of his arm he didn't flinch, and when I fell on him and clasped myself around him, through his sobbing he kept muttering, 'I'm sorry, I'm sorry, I'm sorry.'

But it was still far from over.

I led my father by the hand to the kitchen. Jack had motioned to me to go ahead, that he wasn't leaving, that he would join us after putting on some clothes. Still unshowered in what I had fallen asleep in, after less than fifteen minutes I sat with them around the kitchen table, Jack barefoot in his faded blue jeans and plainest white T-shirt, a boy's change of clothes I hadn't seen him wearing before, my father in slacks and a navy short-sleeved shirt that he hadn't tucked in.

He was short and muscular, with small dark brown eyes surrounded by prominent features. But auntie Ada was wrong when she said he was ugly. The bony structure of his face made him primitively handsome. I had never examined my father so closely before. He looked like he had lived a hard life, but in spite of it looked younger than just under forty, and younger still when he was not wearing his toupee. His head had a shape that suited his face, and every second morning he would stand over the sink and run his barber's clippers all around it, giving it a Zero crop that was always fastidiously even. If anything the Zero crop made the hard-edged coarseness of the toupee look even more fake ("like a hairy omelette", according to auntie Ada), but evidently fakery wasn't an issue. My father was so attached to his hairpiece that even Mia-Mia had failed to wean him off it. Once, in the days that had preceded Mia-Mia, he had tried to shave his head with a razor, in the hope, I suspected, that a Yul Brynner look might have taken the edge off his complex. Instead, he had taken the edge off his head, cutting into it so badly and in so many places that for two weeks he refused to step out of the house. A moonscape of infection made the toupee too painful to wear, and *Mr Magikoo's Magik Shoppe* was given an extra vacation.

Somewhere on that teetering journey between the front door and the kitchen, the toupee must have either fallen off or been discarded, and in the bare vulnerability of my father's expression I saw a reflection of Jack's. The two men – it had only just struck me that I now thought of Jack as definitively a man, not a boy – really couldn't have been physically more different. But my father, stocky and stern in his baldness, and Jack, a wisp in his Mia-Mia Farrow short haircut, seemed at last to share a more essential sameness that went beyond appearances and lies. Yes, Jack could make my father happy, much happier than Mia-Mia could have made him if Jack had been forced out of her completely. But perhaps it was all wishful thinking; what did I know, a child between two adults? Even if I didn't know enough, it was worth it to pretend I knew something.

'Daddy,' I said, 'you're throwing out the baby with the bathwater.' It was the first time I had called him "daddy" since that night long ago when daddy had come home and sat me on his knee to put on a musical voice and say to me that mummy had flown off to heaven to be with the rest of the angels. 'Daddy, what does that mean? Does it mean mummy's dead?' To which my father had replied with a single rapid nod of his head; that was the only other time I had felt his body shiver as he sobbed. As though that had in fact been his sign of contrition, I felt retrospectively the warmth of his shiver. Perhaps my father's "possession", as Mia-Mia had described it, had been an outlet for the guilt that had consumed him. Tonight seemed like the right time to tell him I forgave him. Even if he hadn't been to blame, which would counter any need for forgiveness, I thought we both needed to hear it.

I felt stupid as soon as "the baby" had slipped out of my mouth with "the bathwater". In spite (or perhaps because) of all the heartbreak unfolding at home, I was still finding roundabout ways to fill my mind with Karl, and no sooner had I imagined his smile, not unusually ironic in the circumstances, than I felt a rush of blood wetting my face as it worked its way up to the top of my head. Sweaty and red, but invisible again; my father and Jack, sitting opposite each other either side of me, both clutching at the glasses of iced lemon squash they had waited for me to prepare, were cooling their hands but not drinking, their gazes averted to separate corners of space far apart. It was as if I hadn't spoken, and my stupidity had gone unnoticed even by Jack, who had earlier claimed the baby and the bathwater for England. And in that empty silence, just for a few seconds I allowed my young mind to drift all the way to the moon.

But now it was time to put babies and blushes and Karl and the moon to one side.

'Auntie Ada said it didn't matter what she thought of Mia-Mia, because her sort never stayed around for very long.' Looking down at my hands, neatly intertwined on the table beside my glass of iced lemon squash, I had just become aware I might be leading up to more than just asking my father a question.

'What would Ada know about my "sort"?' When I snapped him a glance, Jack raised both his hands, as though to take back his words in order to let me go on.

'What would Ada know?' my father said differently, his tone as sad as Jack's but more strident.

'She said not liking her had something to do with who Mia-Mia wasn't, or maybe *what* she wasn't, but that I was too young to understand what that meant.' I paused, as much to reconsider where all this might be going as to wait for my father to speak. And when he didn't, I prompted him by letting him know that the unfamiliar word I had already spoken had not been a slip of the tongue: 'Daddy?'

'Are you asking me a question?' my father replied, and I felt the gravity of his features as he turned his head slowly to face me, his eyes like liquid stars that barely gleamed far away.

'Something else I'd not be able to forgive you for. Is that what auntie Ada told you? Did she think Jack wouldn't stay because she knew that in the end you'd make him go?'

'Ada loved your mother like a sister. And she's been like a mother to you, she's always known how to love you much better than I have.'

'But that isn't what I'm asking you, daddy.'

'It doesn't matter what anyone knew.' My father stood up from his chair as though he were about to leave the room, but then he bent forward to lean against the table with his fists. He stayed in that position for only a matter of seconds, and when I touched his elbow, he drew back his fists and sat down.

'He's right,' said Jack. 'It might have mattered before, but no one has to guess how you feel any more.'

I shook my head from side to side, but slowly, to give myself time to think what I wanted to say, and how I should say it. And then I spoke the words exactly as I had thought them. 'No. I think you're both wrong. For things not to matter they need to be spoken, they can't just stay hidden forever. And, daddy, I think you need to hear how I feel.'

My father George Hareman, the illusionist, contortionist, magician known as "Mr Magikoo", fell back in his chair, gathering his arms across his waist. He was twisting and bending his fingers in turn, and it struck me as a wonder that these thick, ungraceful protrusions were as capable of magic as Karl's.

'How you feel is just words,' my father told me, 'but the world out there is ugly, and it doesn't let you feel just with words.'

'But I don't,' I said. 'I don't feel just with words. None of us does, it's not true.'

And now his heavy shoulders gave an almost imperceptible shrug. 'I'm feeling that I'm sorry,' he said. His voice was so leaden that it made me think of "one small step for man". 'But it's no good just being sorry, it isn't enough.'

'You still want me to go,' said Jack.

'It's got nothing to do with wanting.'

'Wanting's what got us into a mess in the first place, isn't that right, George?'

'Please, Jack,' I said. And then with a deliberate movement I returned to my father, craning as I hunched in his direction, trying to claw back his gaze from the floor, smiling when I had it in my grasp. 'How I feel about Jack is that I'd like you to want him to stay. But you knew that already, I think. Now I also want to tell you how I feel about you.

'I remember enough of the time before we lost mum to know how much you loved her and how much she loved you – how much you loved *each other*. And I've not forgotten, either, all the many things the three of us did together. Happy things I thought I didn't *want* to remember, because ever since we lost her you've allowed auntie Ada to blame you, even though she's always known it was unfair. So I blamed you too, but not only because of auntie Ada. I just couldn't make sense of mum not being here any more, and I wish you'd been able to put me on your knee and let me feel your pain *every* night, not just on the day she was gone. Jack's told me about the "one in a million" strike of lightning, and I know you and mum were both happy doing your magic together, so if I say I don't blame you, it just means that now I know you weren't to blame. But because I think you need me to, I'll say I forgive you, because I understand now that *everything*, even Little Magik Matchstick, was part of the madness of grief. Mine on one side, and then yours and auntie Ada's, which you said was like a sister's but I think was like yours.'

I waited, unsure if what I had just said had been clear. It didn't seem to have been clear to Jack, who perhaps had been too moved by my almost unconditional exoneration of my father to have even heard, let alone interpreted, what I had attempted to imply about auntie Ada. He was smiling at me fondly, as if to say that even if he and Mia-Mia and my father were all destined to part, some good had already come out of the truth. But what I wanted to know was whether there were parts of the truth that were still being withheld. Regret, gratitude, relief had all passed through my father's eyes while I spoke; they had brimmed with every emotion at once. But then, at the end of my last sentence they had clouded, becoming illegible again.

'What you and auntie Ada felt, was it the same?'

'Your mum, she was so full of kindness. No one would've known that she suspected. And it made Ada happy.' My father looked suddenly lost in the past, as though snapped into it by those few extra words. 'She made so many sacrifices, she deserved to be happy.'

'And that's the secret you've wanted to keep. But did you owe auntie Ada a favour? Is that why she still can't forgive you?' And when my father's eyes had narrowed into slits, dark like wet silverfish, I found the courage to ask him. 'In the past, before mum, did you stop auntie Ada from loving someone else?'

'I don't understand,' said Jack, who had again crossed his arms over his chest and was clutching at his neck with the squirm of his twitching long fingers. 'So we think Ada suspected Mia-Mia was a man, and we know she was fond of your mum. But how did we get from the "one in a million" to this?'

'Stop her?' My father looked at Jack as he echoed my question, as if to say that it had all gone beyond how we had got there. He ran the fingers of one hand over his baldness, slowly, like he was trying to read the answer in the grain of the stubble on his head.

'Did you?' I asked him again, wondering if I was pressing him too hard; if I ought to have pressed him at all; if raking up too much of the past was a mistake. I would try and explain to Jack later that I wasn't really sure how we had got from the "one in a million" to this; that I had heard words I hadn't known were there until they had been formed and I had given them sound; that these words were faster than my feelings; that my feelings were still holding back, unformed or half-formed in the pit of my stomach; that if they surfaced too quickly they might interfere with the truth; that the truth must have something to do with why auntie Ada, who was not a heartless woman, had lied so heartlessly and for so long.

My father lowered his eyes, and after bouncing them off Jack he looked at me sideways. 'I always told her to be who she was, that there was no other way to be happy,' he said dully, as though to neutralise his words and divest them of meaning, while the fire of the past still smouldered in his eyes.

Jack's arms were untangled, and his hands rubbed back and forth against his jeans. He had pulled his chair back (I hadn't noticed when) and seemed to me so rigid that even the shrill of another harsh sound might break him. It was *too* hard trying to stay impassive at one corner of a triangle I myself had cut into, pulling one side or another in different directions, away from Jack as likely as towards him. Was I doing this for Jack and my father, or was I doing it for myself? Had I even for a moment thought about consequences, or had this been a pent-up unleashing, one I hardly controlled, of a mere irresponsible child's impulsive curiosity to find out the truth at all costs? Was there even such a thing as "the truth"? But now that I had started, from this point that we had reached, however we had got there, we needed to reach a conclusion.

'But did you tell her that because there was someone?'

'I always used to tease her, when *I* was a kid and she was too much of a grown-up...' Again my father stopped, as though compelled to return to his reverie and let it run its course, where if anywhere the answers to my questions might be found. 'With dad away, mum couldn't bear to part with us, she said, so all three of us stayed in London through the war. It was me she couldn't bear to part with, of course. Well, trying to spoil your child in the middle of a war wasn't easy, but it was just that bit easier with Ada there to help, by bringing in an extra wage and going without.' As though weighed down by the burden of memories I hadn't foreseen, my father bent his head, so deeply that the surface of his baldness reflected the light from the lampshade that hung low over the table. When he lifted it again, I pushed his glass of lemon squash a little closer. He smiled and took a swig. Then he nodded, once, twice, four short nods in all, as if he were readying himself to go on. 'It wasn't how I saw things at the time,' he said, 'if that counts as any kind of defence.' And when I had returned his four nods with a more emphatic nod of my own, and Jack had reached half way to touch him but stopped, 'Then came the end of the war, dad was dead, and so were Ada's dreams. And I was still the same brat she was picking up from school every day, working for, washing for, always going without for, fattening me up for the grandiose plans your grandma was imagining for me, after imagining nothing for Ada. The same brat who was too much of a coward to tell his idiot friends to quit making fun of his sister as soon as they saw her, just because she looked so old and hadn't really learned how to fit in. And to smash their faces up if they didn't.'

'Kids are cruel,' I said like a grown-up, 'but they don't necessarily mean any harm. They call me names too, because they think I'm different from them, but I don't really care, and I can't imagine auntie Ada did either.'

'What names?' my father snapped.

'Silly names,' I told him, 'like "bookworm" and "clever clogs" and "Einstein".'

'I wouldn't mind if someone called me "Einstein",' said Jack.

'Karl says they think I'm super-clever, but I'm not, and I'm terrible at science. I just read a lot, that's all.'

'After today, I think we should all call you "Sherlock",' said Jack. 'How old are you again?'

'In December I'll be seventeen.'

'So sixteen,' said Jack.

'Does he look out for you, this Karl?'

'We look out for each other.'

'Then you're both lucky.' While he tapped his fingers on the table, my father's eyes were fixed on Jack's outstretched arm. 'You were right before, when you said I'd hit someone I loved. The only person in my life I've ever hit and it had to be him. But it still doesn't change how I feel.'

'How you feel?' If Jack hadn't asked it already, I would have asked the same question more bluntly. At the heart of what my father had just said lay a brazen contradiction.

'How I feel about the future,' he answered. 'We've both got to move on.'

'You and "him", whose name you can't say,' said Jack.

'Me and you,' said my father, raising his gaze to meet Jack's. 'We've both got to move on, whoever we are.'

'But auntie Ada… Was there someone or not? Was that what you teased her about?' I interrupted their exchange in the hope that the past might yet salvage even more of the present. Already it had transformed my own feelings for my father, and my perception of him was now marred only by his stubborn refusal to give in to his feelings for Jack, even after admitting he loved him. If there had been no other way to be happy for his sister, why couldn't *he* be who he was?

'There was someone, yes. But no, that wasn't what I teased her about. I used to think she was too shy, with men I mean, and I teased her a lot about that, but she wasn't really shy, she was just indifferent. Which I realised when I saw how she was with the woman she'd fallen in love with. I never teased her again after that, she was so miserable that I wouldn't have wanted to add to her hurt.'

'Did the woman know?' I asked.

'Of course the woman knew, they were as head over heels as each other. They met at the theatre, an amateur performance of *Macbeth*…'

'"Unsex me now!"' Jack spoke the words dramatically, before apologising with his undulating hands.

'And afterwards they had a drink, then to some posh hotel where the woman was staying. When Ada came home, she couldn't help herself, she told me everything. Your grandma was dead by then, and it was just the two of us in that house off the Seven Sisters Road, before I met your mum and we sold it, to buy this house and Ada's flat in Tufnell Park. But you know why she told me? Because she expected me… because I think she *wanted* me to tell her she should stop being so disgusting.'

'But you didn't,' I said.

'I didn't, of course not. And later when we all went out for dinner and I saw them together, I told Ada she'd be a fool to break it off. So she carried on seeing her for almost a year...'

'And did she have a name, this woman?' No comparison or bitterness had seemed to colour Jack's question. He had said "this woman" affectionately.

'Yes.' My father looked at him head on. 'It was Jane.'

'So you called me Jane after her.'

'When Ada suggested it, Val fell in love with it, and I was glad. I was glad that the woman who had made Ada act on her feelings, who'd loved her and offered to give everything up so they could share their lives together, would be acknowledged by at least being remembered.'

'Imagine if her name had been Dorothy, or Mildred, or something equally awful, like Gladys,' said Jack, after signalling to me by lightly tightening his lips that my father was in danger of being irretrievably lost to the past.

'I quite like Dorothy,' I said.

'Well you would, wouldn't you?' said Jack.

'Val would still have agreed, if she thought it was what Ada really wanted, and so would I.'

'I was joking, George.'

My father raised his head, like in an uncompleted nod. 'She was famous, you know, your namesake.' And half-letting go of his sombreness, 'Not as famous as your dad, of course; in his heyday, no one was as famous as Mr Magikoo.'

'Mr Magikoo and his assistant,' I said.

'Who took the country by storm,' said Jack. 'You should get your dad to show you all the clippings.'

'And they're not telling fibs. We *did* take the country by storm, year after year. We kept the show fresh, thanks to your mum. She was as full of ideas as I was, always pushing me to try different tricks – "flights of fancy" we called them in those days - researching the old greats for inspiration. Wherever we travelled, we always had you with us, and we *loved* having you with us, it made us feel complete. And you'll be glad to know Val *loathed* my rabbit trick. She thought it was a cruelty to use animals at all.'

'So did Mia-Mia,' I said.

'Yes, so did Mia-Mia,' said my father. He rubbed his eyebrows with a forefinger and thumb, kneading them like they were dough. 'You might as well know, I suppose. Those blades Sweeney Todd had, they were only plastic. You were never in danger. But you had to believe that you were, you had to be afraid, or no one else would have believed that they were blades made of steel, and that Little Magik Matchstick was the bravest little girl in the world. A star, just like her mother.'

'But you used to slice a cucumber in half, I remember.'

'That was just one small section, much higher than your height. But that's all beside the point. It was cruel to make you frightened, the cruelty was exactly the same, so please don't think I'm trying to make excuses.'

'Even I didn't know that,' said Jack.

'It's not beside the point that I was safe.'

'Safe means not being frightened,' said my father.

'Let's not talk any more about Little Magik Matchstick and the blades of Sweeney Todd, tell us more about Jane,' I said. 'How was she famous?'

'She was a writer of some sort, an *intellectual* Ada said. I'm not really sure what her books were about, but anyway that's not why she was famous. She was a wealthy American who'd married very young into British high society, got lucky and lost her brute of a husband in the war, inherited a second fortune and indulged herself by buying modern art. She even took Ada to Paris once or twice, to look at things that she was thinking of buying, told her that she valued her opinion. And she's a fast learner our Ada, from one day to the next she knew who was who and what was what in modern art, had quite an eye for it too, apparently. Didn't like to feel like a freeloader, she said, so she needed her opinion to carry some weight. Anyone would think she'd have been happy...'

'Yes, anyone would think she'd have been happy...'

'But she wasn't,' I said faintly, wondering if interrupting Jack again meant that I was now taking sides.

'I know what he's implying.' My father too had spoken only faintly, almost to himself, as though turning thoughts around in his head. But then he swung round in his chair to address Jack directly. 'You're saying that if this is what I think about Ada, then why can't I be happy with you? And that may sound like it's fair, but it's only fair if you're comparing like with like, and I'm telling you you're not. You and me, we've always been a lie, and I'm not saying it was anybody's fault. But it was different with Ada and Jane, they were more like me and Val.'

'Ah,' said Jack.

'You know why? Because we shared the same beginning, which was new, and not the end of something else that hadn't really ended.'

'Three years, George, almost.'

'And it's time I don't regret, even if I know it's come to an end.'

'You *can't* know that, daddy, you can't. And if you don't regret it, then it can't have been a lie.'

'Then I'll not say it was, I'll just say it can't go on. Because tonight's brought us back to the beginning, which still feels like the end.'

'Can't you at least also say that for almost three years you were happy,' said Jack.

'Maybe. And that's more than I could say for our Ada.'

'So why couldn't she be happy?' Too afraid of the present, was I wrong to keep returning to the past?

'Ada? Oh, the usual. Other people partly. But mostly herself, not being able to accept who she was and be happy with it.'

'So much for "anyone would think she'd be happy",' said Jack.

'Times were very different back then, she just couldn't get it out of her head that it was wrong, that this life wasn't really for her, that she could never give Jane what she deserved. So she wrote her a letter to end it, and the next day a package arrived. It was a small, tiny sculpture of a stretched out female figure almost as thin as a matchstick, standing on a lump of plaster that dwarfed her even more, gazing ahead and looking completely bereft.'

'I've seen it. Auntie Ada has it on her mantelpiece. But I've never really looked at it properly.'

'Well, you should,' said my father. 'That piece of nothingness is by a fellow called Alberto Giacometti. Jane bought it because Ada had fallen in love with it, and she wrote to Ada saying that if it hadn't been for her she might never have noticed what Ada had seen in Giacometti's work. I managed to talk Ada out of sending it back. "You'd be adding insult to injury," I said, "and Jane deserves neither. At the very least you can allow her a gesture." And then when you were born, she said one day it'd be yours. It's a tiny thing, but apparently it's worth quite a bit, Giacometti died a very famous man.'

'And Jane?'

'Went back to the States, Ada said. Has a wing of her own in some fancy museum in Philadelphia, with all the art your auntie Ada helped her choose. Gave it all away in the end, all except the Giacometti on Ada's mantelpiece.'

'But they haven't kept in touch,' I said.

'There were a few letters from Jane at the beginning. But Ada never wrote back, and I think at some point Jane gave up. Once she realised that Ada wasn't changing her mind, the last thing she'd have wanted was to add to her distress. She's not been mentioned in years now, not since I met Val. She and Ada hit it off straight away, your mum obviously reminded her of Jane, and being close to another woman was a way of reliving the past. But then at some point she forgot about Jane, you could see it in the way she looked at Val.'

'And mum knew?'

'Your mum was an angel... or a saint, as Ada likes to remind me, as if I needed reminding. She knew – if I knew, then she must've known too, by my silences mostly. Very occasionally she would ask me a question, but for the most part it wasn't really something we talked about. And I doubt if Val and Ada ever talked about it either, even though they spent a lot of time together – doing all the things you and Ada like to do, and thank God it's your mum you've taken after, not your philistine dad. When Ada first told me that she'd got a Giacometti from Jane, I'd never even heard the name. "So what's a Giacometti?" I said. "As I doubt Jane's only given you a biscuit, I suppose he must be a jeweller and she's given you a ring." Val knew what it was as soon as she first saw it, and when she asked her, Ada said it was a copy she'd picked up from a flea market in Paris. But your mum was like you. Nothing escaped her. "That's no copy, George, it's a genuine Giacometti, believe me," she said. "Ada's lying, someone's given her that sculpture. If she'd bought it herself she'd have told me." I bit my lip and kept my mouth shut.'

'It's funny. There's a painting at the heart of Karl's family history, and a sculpture at the heart of ours.'

'I think your auntie Ada's made much better use of her sculpture than the Reichian therapist's made of her Dix, if you'll pardon the pun.'

'You've really got it in for Dr Schmidt, is it because she goes to church?'

'I've a general aversion to therapists, I didn't even know she goes to church.'

'What's a "Dix"?' asked my father.

'Otto Dix is a German painter,' I said. 'Hitler thought he was degenerate, so a lot of his paintings were destroyed, but at least he survived. Karl thinks he's still alive.'

'So what is she, a Catholic?' asked Jack.

'She's not actually religious. She just thinks that religion is useful. Karl says going to church is good for business.'

'Ah,' said Jack. 'She must be a very *practical* Reichian therapist.'

'I'm not really all that keen on her either,' I said.

I was getting flustered. This wasn't the time to be bringing up Karl and degenerate painters, or Hitler, or church being good for business... But my father, who had been so downcast, was now almost smiling.

'And what's a Reichian therapist?' he asked.

'Someone else who makes a living out of theories,' said Jack. 'Another parasite if you ask me. A *charlatan*, according to Ada – your sister doesn't mince her words, I'll give her that.'

'No... no, she doesn't.' My father seemed absent again, but after stretching out his arms and taking a breath he recovered himself. 'I'm sorry I put you through that, and for imagining I wanted you to be someone else, not yourself.' He was touching Jack's arm, and many more words danced around in his eyes than he managed to speak. 'I thought that if... but no, that was definitely a lie. And you went, week after week, *for me*, even though the sickness wasn't yours.'

'The sickness was theirs,' said Jack, 'but at least after going there so often I know myself better. I even like myself better, I think.'

'You should,' said my father. Then he took a second breath and turned to me. 'She'll always be there for you, Ada. You're all she has now.'

'But I've got *you* to be there for me,' I said, and if my father hadn't looked at me so miserably, 'You and Jack,' I would have gone on to say.

I stood up and spread my arms around him. He turned in his chair and pressed his head against my shoulder. 'Nothing's changed,' I found the courage to say one more time, but my words met only with a stiffness in the expanse I was embracing and a stillness in the weight against my shoulder. In the suffocating silence that had almost filled the room, Jack stood up behind his chair and pushed it in until the back touched the edge of the table.

'I think I should go now,' he said, while his arms flailed again across his chest. This time his hands had disappeared behind his shoulders - like a contortionist's, I felt stupid for thinking. 'There's no place for me here any more, I feel like I've become an intruder,' Jack went on limply, and now his whole body was swaying, as though he were about to collapse in a heap on the floor.

My father looked up at him, staring woodenly at the young slender body as it reeled on the spot, but then all at once he was up from his chair and standing behind him, gripping him from under his arms and manoeuvring him out of the kitchen, past my books on the dining room table, into the chair he always sat in to read *The Weekly Magic News*. I was right behind them, wanting to help but not knowing how.

'A glass of water,' my father said.

'I'm fine now,' said Jack, when I was already on my way to fetch the water. And after he had drunk it and handed me the glass back, 'Thank you,' he smiled, first to me and then to my father. 'I just felt dizzy for a moment, it's probably the heat.'

'Do you feel strong enough to walk?'

'Daddy, he isn't.'

'He needs some fresh air, you both do. And I need just an hour to myself. We all need a breather to take in what's happened. What's the time now?' And after looking at his watch, 'It's almost a quarter past seven, take Jack somewhere nice for some food.' He took out his wallet and handed me some notes. 'Jack?'

'Anything you say, George. If Jane doesn't mind.'

'Of course I don't mind, if you're sure you're all right.'

'I'm fine now. And I wouldn't mind some food.'

'I'll stay here while you get yourself ready,' said my father. 'Have a shower first, if you like. You look like you've been wearing those clothes for a week. Here, I'll take the glass in case Jack needs more water. Now go!'

In the dim light of my box room, after my five-minute shower I threw on my pink cotton blouse and blue and white polka-dot Bermudas, slipped into my sandals without undoing the buckle on the side, and after just a quick glance at myself in the mirror on the door of my wardrobe I made my way anxiously back to where Jack and my father were waiting exactly as I had left them – Jack holding hands with himself in the chair, and my father standing awkwardly beside him, holding Jack's empty glass.

'Doesn't she look lovely!' said Jack.

'She does.'

'You should tell her more often, instead of always teasing her.'

'You tease me too,' I said to Jack.

'He's right, I should,' said my father.

'And you should break up that box you make her sleep in, open up her room to how it was, with a window she can actually open, instead of having it behind a piece of board.'

'But I like my box room. It's like no other room in the world.'

'I should've let you have my room,' said my father.

'I don't think Mia-Mia would've slept with you in that box room,' said Jack.

'The box room is *mine*,' I said. And after doing a girlish twirl, 'These are the Bermudas Jack brought me from Torquay,' I tried to joke, but my humour fell so flat on the floor that it might as well have been my father's toupee.

'Right, we should leave your dad alone before he asks us for his money back.'

'You better put some shoes on first,' my father said to Jack. 'Stay there, I'll fetch you your pumps.'

'Oh dear, I don't think I'm allowed back in the bedroom,' Jack sighed under his breath. And when the pumps arrived and he was putting them on, 'Your Bermudas are actually from Carnaby Street, so I think that officially makes you a hippy.'

'I'd like just five minutes with Jane,' my father said. 'If Jane doesn't mind.'

'I'll wait outside,' said Jack. 'Take as long as you like.'

'Jane?'

How my eyes must have sparkled with joy. My day had been too full, first with Karl and Mia-Mia and then with Jack, and lastly with attempting to keep up with "the truth" and its unstoppable momentum. At the heart of the new future I dared to imagine, my father was the threat that might prevent it. But the way he had just spoken my name was full of all the affection and warmth I had craved since that moment on his knee when the whole world we had shared had collapsed, and I knew at last that even if everything else was uncertain, our feelings for each other were not.

When Jack had shut the front door behind him, daddy lifted me up off the floor and lowered me into the depths of his chair. He sat beside me on the pouffe, and I saw my hands being dwarfed as he took them into his.

'I'd like you to know that I'm sorry,' he said. 'I'm sorry about Ada and I'm sorry about Jack. I'm sorry I haven't been a better father, and I'm sorriest of all about what happened to your mum. It's no excuse that we were young, or that we encouraged each other to do stupid things. We had to think of you, we didn't have the right to be stupid.'

'It was an accident, daddy. A one in a million chance of something that had never crossed your minds.'

He smiled and brought the nest of hands to his mouth, unfolding mine briefly to kiss them. 'You're so much like your mother,' he said, 'and I've always loved you as much as I loved her. I wanted to tell you tonight, because there's a chance that tomorrow... Well, who knows how we're both going to feel?'

'*I* do,' I said. 'I promise I'll still love you even if you ask Jack to leave.'

'Let's see,' said my father. 'Sometimes how we feel, and how we need to *protect* how we feel...' He broke off a sentence he didn't seem to want to decide how to end. And after just a quick squeeze of my hands that felt like a heartbeat, 'I also wanted you to know, in case it makes a difference, that when I've not been away there's not been a night when I've not come to your room and kissed you good night. Mia-Mia would be snoring like a man and I'd slip out of bed and listen at your door to make sure you were asleep. Then I'd hold my breath and tiptoe to your bedside, and I'd sneak you a little kiss just there... or sometimes there... depending on which side you'd fallen asleep in.' He broke the nest of hands to touch first the right side of my forehead then the left, and his finger as he touched me was trembling. 'But there's no way I can prove it, and I couldn't say I'd blame you if you thought I was making it up.'

I threw myself out of his chair and I saw his quiet tears as I kissed first the right side of his forehead, then the left.

'Our secret,' I said. 'I want it to belong just to us.'

When a short time that couldn't have been counted had passed without unnecessary words, daddy got up and made me giggle as he whisked me off to the door.

'How you've grown,' he said as he was setting me down.

I looked back from the last of the five shallow steps that led down to the gate where Jack was waiting. I smiled and daddy smiled back.

'Nothing's changed,' he said, and after blowing me a kiss we all waved goodbye, then he stepped back inside and shut the door.

9

Encounters

Jack and I held hands as we zigzagged away from the house. An unremarkable turning was the only point of exit from the labyrinth of narrow alleyways and cul-de-sacs that snaked around it. On the map, stripped of all the buildings that at least gave it some character, our neighbourhood looked like a plate of spaghetti.

'The second time your dad called to invite me for a drink he made me come all the way from Chelsea to Angel. And when he asked if he could kiss me and I told him that I'd love him to but I was actually a boy, he didn't bat an eyelid, I swear, he just went on and kissed me like I hadn't said a word.'

'You think he'd guessed already?'

'Or maybe he was trying to keep me quiet. That kiss just wouldn't end; it must've gone on for at least half an hour. People were staring; someone even whined that we should get ourselves a room. None of it bothered your father one bit, I had to push him off in the end, or the landlord would've shown us the door.'

Jack would raise his arm now and then, and mine would rise with it, and we laughed as we carried on walking hand in hand without slowing our pace. I could feel Mia-Mia's invisible presence beside us, an inseparable part of the boy and the man my father had fallen in love with.

'Imagine if they'd got an inkling I was actually a man,' Jack carried on, reminiscing about the beginning of something that already might have come to an end. 'You'd think your dad would be more mortified than I was, but he was too much like a boy in the middle of falling in love, even more than *I* was, and his whole world at that moment was that. "Just as well I live round the corner," he said, then he put his arm around me and I followed like a lamb, circling round these creepy little streets and thinking to myself, "This is it, my last night alive on this earth, any minute now he's going to strangle me and dump me in a ditch." But then we turned a corner, went up those little steps and there we were, safe and sound and being screamed at by you and your aunt.'

'In all those years since dad… since we all lost mum, it was the first time he brought anyone back - a woman I mean, except he'd actually brought back a man…'

'He brought back Mia-Mia,' said Jack. 'And we've just taken her away from him.'

'I was thinking just the opposite. You were a part of Mia-Mia and she's still a part of you.'

'Yes, well, I'm not sure if that's good enough for George.'

'When we talked, I told him I'd still love him even if he asked you to leave.'

'I should hope so.'

'But he loves you, he's admitted that it wasn't all a lie. He even said you made him happy, so why would he ask you to leave?'

'And he can't take all that back *whatever* he decides.' Jack tightened his grip of my hand as we slipped out of the plate of spaghetti. 'What I've never understood is how people find their way to the shop.'

'But they do,' I said. 'There's never been a day when it hasn't been busy.'

'That's magic for you, I suppose.'

We were on Upper Street now. A light twilight breeze was cooling the air and making the evening feel fresh. There wasn't much traffic, and the people who were out were mostly clustered in orderly queues at the bus stops, waiting to get home after a hot day at work. Suits stood apart as overalls mingled, and women looked glum in their tight office skirts and monochrome blouses. Dotted here and there, almost always in pairs, the most colourful girls were also the most cheerful, causing boys to gawk as they swanned their way past them.

'Jack, are you sure you're all right?'

'Don't worry, I'm not about to faint on you. George was right, all I needed was a bit of fresh air.'

'And some food. I haven't seen you eat since you got back from your brother's bed-and-breakfast in Torquay.'

Jack leaned down to knock my shoulder with his. 'Aren't you the funny one, eh?'

'It can't have been easy for you, all that pretending.'

'I'd say parts of it were hard, but some parts were actually fun.' Jack spoke slowly, as though dwelling on the parts that had been hard, and I dragged on his arm to slow him down. Just then a group of dirty children ran across us, chasing after a ball. When it hit a shuttered window and bounced back, Jack let go of me to tackle it by turning it around, and all in a single deft movement was keeping it steady on the ground with his foot. The boys and one girl had all gathered round, looking eager to play with this stranger who could handle a ball.

'Come on then, come and get it,' said Jack, but as I moved to one side he did a little dance around the ball and then lobbed it with a kick at the biggest of the boys, who hit it with his chest and made it drop to his feet.

As the whole group cheered him on, Jack picked up my hand and we got out of their way. 'Good kids,' he said, turning to give them a wave. He took in the air in a long deep sigh, and as he breathed it out he pushed both our arms as far into the sky as he could without lifting me completely off my feet, and then he lowered them again after holding them still for just a few seconds. 'It wasn't the pretending I minded so much, or even the limited wardrobe forced on Mia-Mia by having to keep that preposterous bulge under wraps. What really got me down was George's constant fear of being found out.' The way he spoke now was more purposeful and brisk, almost carefree. 'And yes, Shepherd's Bush was hell, but at least all the newspapers were free, and I'm grateful that I haven't got a brother in Torquay who puts me down. Oh, and I did have a sandwich while you were dreaming.'

'That was hours ago,' I said.

There were so many questions I wanted to ask. If he didn't have a brother in Torquay, did he have another brother somewhere else? Were his parents still alive? Did they know? I wanted to ask about his English degree, about where he had studied, what books he had read, who had been his friends, if there had been someone else before my father... I wanted to know about the first time he had fallen in love, how it had felt, how he had known. I wanted him to tell me how I could be sure if the same thing was now happening to me. If all the strange sensations I was feeling meant that I was falling in love, would I know it? And could I only know if Karl felt the same if he told me?

'How about you, are you hungry?' At the sound of Jack's voice I came to.

'A bit,' I said.

'You like fish and chips?'

'I don't think that's what dad had in mind. He gave me twenty pounds.'

'What time is it now, eight o'clock?'

'A few minutes after.' I had been looking at my watch nearly every five minutes, but perhaps not as discreetly as I'd thought.

'Wasn't Karl expecting you tonight?'

'Nothing was arranged, I just said I might go round.' I didn't want to mention Karl's phone call. Remembering it there was something about it I hadn't enjoyed, but I didn't want him judged by repeating words spoken in over-excitement — really nothing more than "a fair amount of gibberish" like mine.

'Will the Reichian therapist be there?'

'Not before ten, she's working late.'

'And don't they live close by?'

'In Cross Street.'

'That's where Ada's flat is.'

'Auntie Ada lives in Tufnell Park.'

'Is there another Cross Street in Tufnell Park?'

'12F *Cyprus* Street,' I said.

'It sounds quite similar,' said Jack.

'I suppose so.'

'But Karl is definitely in Cross Street, which is less than five minutes away.'

'Yes.'

'So what are you waiting for?'

'I don't want to leave you.' In a window as we passed it I saw our reflection, two passing figures like so many others, all with secrets of their own. The lights inside were on, and although the yellowish tinge of our outline in the glass made us seem more united, what I had just said to Jack was only partly true. No, I didn't want to leave him alone, but I did want to see Karl. To spend half an hour with him would be enough.

'I'll wait for you somewhere. And then we'll make our way back together.'

'Let's eat first, and then I'll decide if I want to see Karl. Where's the fish and chips place?'

'On the way,' said Jack. 'Come on, we haven't got all night. The Reichian therapist looms…'

'Salt and vinegar in both?' asked the man behind the counter.

Jack and I both nodded.

'In or out, open or closed?'

'Let's at least sit down,' I said.

'In,' said Jack.

'Open is fine, if you don't have plates.'

The man looked at me blankly.

'Open,' said Jack. 'And we'll also have a couple of Fantas.'

'I'm paying,' I said, and already the man was taking money out of my hand.

Captain Cook's Fish and Chips was "authentic" according to Jack. Auntie Ada had spoiled me, and I would have described it as a little bit better than "basic". It had some tables at the back, it was clean, and it wasn't very busy. But it was too brightly lit. The pickled eggs in the jar on the counter looked like biological specimens, and the bubbling golden oil gave an aura of radiation. Too brightly lit and also too green: the walls were green; the plastic tablecloths were green; the floor tiles were green; made of thin shiny metal, the chairs were like mirrors filled with green… A little bit better than basic as long as you didn't mind green – the glare from the fluorescent strips swept the greenness off the floor and off the walls and made *everything* green. I was gaping at our spread of fish and chips. It was as green as our side of mushy peas, and so was Jack.

'What's wrong? You don't like the fish? Mine's delicious.'

'Mine's delicious too, but it's *green*. Everything in here is green. *You* look green. I'm sure *I* do too.'

'Now you mention it, you do look a little bit peaky,' Jack said, and we both tried to muffle our giggles. 'Now come on, eat up. The sooner we're finished, the sooner we'll be out of here. And while you're visiting Karl, I'll wait for you on a bench in Islington Green. Turning green with envy.'

We were very good at giggling but terrible at muffling, and the small crowd of atomic Martians were all staring at us. I dug into my food self-consciously, abandoning the useless plastic fork for my fingers, easily breaking the rigid battered fish into pieces and eating them like popcorn, while occasionally slurping from my bottle of Fanta. Jack, who hadn't even bothered to pick up a fork, was holding up his fish horizontally, rotating it and biting into it as though it were corn on the cob. And when eventually it broke into two, he used what was left on either side to scoop up at least some of the forgotten mushy peas.

'It wasn't so delicious after all,' Jack nodded at my leftover fish.

'Well, well, well, what have we got here then, mm?' A burly posh-sounding boy, too smartly dressed for a fish and chips shop on a hot Tuesday night in north London, had appeared out of nowhere and was standing over Jack, looking down at him sideways with his back half-turned to me. 'We know each other, don't we?' He was loud and aggressive, like he was trying to make a show out of looking for trouble.

'I don't think so,' said Jack.

'*Course* we do,' the boy shot back.

I had pushed my chair away from the table, to have a clearer view of Jack and at the same time of most of the shop. The three people at the table next to ours made a noise getting up, and the boy took a bow as they hurried around him on their way to the door, walking out without looking behind them.

'*Course* we do,' the boy repeated, picking up his rant where he'd left off. 'But in case you need reminding, I've seen you in here before, had your arm round this old guy, plebby type as I remember, with this lopsided rug on his head. Your sugar daddy I'm guessing, am I right? But wait a minute...' He paused to scratch his head, darting glances at the two younger boys who were watching his performance from the counter and were probably his friends. 'Yeah, it's all coming back to me now. A hooker with her pimp, *that's* what I thought at the time. And don't get me wrong, I'm an open-minded guy, live and let live as they say, but only up to a point, and *way* beyond that point is *this* here sorry excuse for a male of our species, a queer today, and tomorrow an even *worse* kind of queer when he kits himself out as a bird, like he did last time I saw him, sitting at this very table with his sugar daddy perv...' While he thrust his finger back and forth, pointing at Jack as though about to jab him, he had swung his body around to face the counter, but every two seconds he would turn to look at Jack, almost spitting the words in his face.

When I turned around too, the whole shop had come to a standstill. The last two customers were hesitating at the door; the man who had served us had two open bags in one hand and the big pot of salt in the other; arms akimbo, the woman beside him was looking defiant; insipidly the two boys looked on without making a move.

Jack now had his elbow on the table and his head on its side in his hand. He gave me a wink before slapping his gaze at the boy – he was big, but no older than fifteen or sixteen. I knew his type from school; young kids who imagined themselves to be clever and hard – so much cleverer and harder than they actually were.

'Have you finished?' said Jack in his manly voice.

'Have I *finished*? I haven't even started!'

'No, I think you've finished,' said Jack.

'Come on, Mike, just leave it,' said one of the boys at the counter.

But it was too late for Mike to just leave it. Mr Captain Cook of *Captain Cook's Fish and Chips* already had him by the scruff of his neck and was manhandling him roughly as he showed him the door.

'And don't show your pretty face in here again,' Mr Captain Cook was barking at him as he pushed him outside, 'or I'll have my wife deep fry it with the fish, and then I'll serve it personally to the dogs. As for you two shrinking violets,' he howled, turning to the boys who stood frozen by the counter, 'I suggest you have a think about the company you keep, before that psycho gets you both into trouble. Now go on, take your fish and chips and skedaddle.'

He shut the door and locked it, turned the sign around from OPEN to CLOSED, and as he approached us he gave a big shrug of his shoulders.

'To think we've put a man on the moon,' he exclaimed at the sky. 'And we *still* can't teach our kids right from wrong. You know what really bugs me? How the spoiled ones, who've never lacked for anything, are usually the worst. How are you, Miss Mia-Mia? I thought you looked familiar when I served you, but my brain just didn't click. And your friend is she okay? First time in our restaurant and *this* had to happen.'

Mr Captain Cook had pulled up a chair and was turning now to Jack and now to me, all the time wiping his hands on the sides of his apron.

'Yes, I'm okay,' I said. 'Thank you.'

'We're both fine, Frank, really,' said Jack. 'But I'm Jack now.'

'Oh I see, Mr Jack, yes of course.'

'Just Jack, Frank,' said Jack.

'And Miss Mia-Mia, she won't be coming back with Mr George?'

'No,' I said, 'but Mr George might be coming back with Jack.'

'This is Jane,' said Jack. 'Jane is George's daughter. Jane, this is Frank, and over there behind the counter is his lovely wife Norma.'

When Norma waved hello I waved back.

'Well, it's a shame we won't be seeing Miss Mia-Mia, but I'm glad we'll be seeing more of Jack.'

'And of Jane,' Norma shouted from her place behind the counter.

'Now if you're sure you're both okay, I think we've got some customers waiting outside,' said Frank, and he got up to shake hands first with me and then with Jack.

I walked out of *Captain Cook's Fish and Chips* to a world that felt bigger, harder, more unwieldy, where opposites constantly collided and people got hurt, not just strangers but people I was actually close to. The world I had built for myself was no longer self-contained and shielded from danger; "my own world" had always been a temporary fiction. The way I had experienced the loss of my mother was different. Today there was nothing that I hadn't understood. Everything that happened from the moment I walked in on Mia-Mia in the bathroom was part of "real life", encompassing fear, and anger, and outrage, but also pride, and resolve, and affection. But these were all easy feelings. The night could so easily have had a different outcome, whose immensity I knew because I had experienced it before. But this pervasive uncertainty was just another part of "real life", and if it made it seem unbearably precarious, it also made it feel more exciting. My father's words rang in my ears: 'The world out there is ugly, and it doesn't let you feel just with words.' I thought of Karl's fear as he hurried away from the unfamiliar world he'd strayed into, and of how naturally Jack had played ball with its children. Human action took innumerable forms, and gave rise to a vitality that went beyond making everything certain.

I had my hand around his arm, and it struck me again how physically fragile he was. But Jack's stride was steady and firm, and he was leading me in the direction of Cross Street. My legs were short compared to his, and I almost had to run to keep up, with Jack and with a night that had not yet run its course.

'Shouldn't we go home? I think we should,' I said, but I said it without trying to slow him down.

'Why? Because of what happened?'

'You nearly got beaten up.'

'Nothing happened, and I didn't nearly get beaten up. Believe me, I should know. I've been beaten up enough times before. That was just an idiot showing off, a bigmouth, that's all. If he really wanted to beat me up... no, let me rephrase that, if he was going to beat me up he'd have had his fish and chips and waited for me outside. Violence likes the dark.'

'Who was beaten up, Jack or Mia-Mia?'

'Oh, we've both been beaten up. But not for a while now, with time I've got better at slipping away. God knows I've had a lot of practice. And that was one thing about being with your dad, I always felt safe.'

'I hope you went to the police,' I said, and when Jack started to laugh and wouldn't stop, 'But why's that so funny? Isn't that what people do when they get beaten up?'

'Yes, *people*.'

'I don't understand.'

'Well, nor do the police. There's precious few Normas and Franks in this world, and precious *none* of them have joined the police.'

'That's not possible,' I said, and already we had passed the telephone box on the corner with Cross Street, just ten houses separating us from Karl's.

'So, show me where your genius boy lives.'

'But it's a quarter past nine.'

'Let's hurry then,' said Jack.

We could now hear the music, not exactly pouring out but rather wafting freely through the open ground floor windows. There were eight steps to the door, wide, deep and high, really quite majestic, and I had run up and down them a thousand times before, but at the thought of climbing them tonight I felt nauseous.

'Beethoven. Piano Sonata No. 29 in B-flat.'

'You know everything,' I said.

'I know Beethoven,' said Jack. 'Dad was a fan. Still is, I imagine.'

'He likes to play this a lot. I think it's too sad.'

'What is joy without sadness?'

'You really think that's true?'

'What I think is that there's no time to be getting philosophical. If you go in now, you'll have him to yourself for at least half an hour. Come on, I'll take you to the door and I'll even ring the bell for you, and then I'll wait for you at the top of the street by the telephone box. He's good, your boy. He's *very* good.'

Jack had walked with me up the steps, and when the bell had been rung, I felt his breath whispering 'Good luck!' in my ear, before he flew like a feather down the steps and disappeared. The music had stopped, but the evening was now drumming in my head, as though remonstrating with me for an act made more selfish by everything I hadn't said to Jack. So much was hidden in the things he had told me, begging many questions I ought to have asked.

'You came,' said Karl, pulling back from the door to open it more widely.

The first thing Karl did was to telephone his mother, to laugh about Chopin and say that he needed the house to himself for an extra hour.

'I can't stay long,' I said. 'I need to get back home to my dad.'

'But you hate him, what's the big rush?'

'No I don't, when you called me...'

'I know. You told me you were tired of being angry. And that's good, I'm happy for you.'

'It's because of what you said.'

'See? So tonight let's be happy together.'

'I can stay for half an hour. But then I have to go.'

He was standing so close to me I couldn't see the whole of his face, but I knew he wasn't smiling.

'I really like you, I wouldn't be like this if I didn't,' he said, and already he was starting to kiss me. First my neck, then my mouth, while touching me only lightly in places I would rather not be touched - not tonight, not so soon. But the kisses were so coy and the touching so light that I didn't resist. And now I was kissing him too, running both my hands through his hair.

'Let's not stay standing,' he said. 'Let's go upstairs to my room.'

I had thrown myself out of the door, then I had bolted down the steps, and now I was running, running as fast as I could, shaking as I ran in the middle of the road, holding back my tears, choking on the scream I held in for as long as I had to for Karl not to hear, blinded by headlights that instinct alone made me swerve to avoid, drawn at last to the shadow, slender and tender and tall, unmistakably the shadow of Jack, who had swayed like the wind into my path so that I could fall into his arms.

I sobbed and I sobbed and I sobbed, and as I sobbed I felt the surge of violence in Jack's chest, which I knew I would have to but wasn't yet ready to quell. My scream had died in me before I found the strength to give it sound, and for some time it was all I could do to breathe in and out in short, snivelling, hiccupping gasps, my breast rising and falling at the suffocating speed of that same shallow rhythm. With one arm around me Jack held me tightly in place with a strength that I couldn't have imagined, while with barely the tips of his fingers he was stroking my hair to one side and keeping it out of my eyes.

When I loosened my grip by a notch, Jack did the same, and our eyes met as I lifted my head up away from his chest, to let it fall back in the cusp of his hand.

'I have a handkerchief,' he said, and when I blinked as I nodded, he let go of my head to dig into his opposite pocket. 'Here. Dry your eyes first, then blow into it as hard as you can. You'll feel better after that, I promise.' Holding onto it by a corner, he had given the handkerchief a jerk to unfold it, and when he handed it to me it was so big that I wished we could hide under it and conjure ourselves somewhere else. 'It's your dad's,' said Jack. 'I've always liked to borrow his.' I fell away from him a fraction more, bringing both hands to my face, to dry my eyes first, and then to blow into the handkerchief as hard as I could, following Jack's instructions to the letter, his clutch now unfastening little by little as my own strength returned. The muscles in my legs had again become tense, almost supporting my weight by themselves.

'Better?' Even as our bodies drew apart, held together only by fingers spread across the small of my back, I still felt enveloped by him.

The light from the streetlamps was pale, diffusing as it fell to the ground, to spread dimly across the pavement until it dissolved. I could see a long line of smaller and smaller bright circles, and they reminded me of being in the spotlight, defying the plastic blades of Sweeney Todd. A passing car whooshed by, cutting into the muted yellow haze with headlights that the driver hadn't dipped, and when Jack saw my face in the brightness he answered his question himself.

'No, you're not better,' he said, but when he tried to move closer, I placed my open palms against his chest, holding firmly on to the distance between us.

'I don't know how to tell you what happened.'

'Did he hurt you?' Jack's words sounded broken – as hard and uneven as the beating I could feel inside his chest.

'I don't want to go home yet. Dad mustn't see me like this, he must never find out.'

'Jane, you're making me frightened. Should we go to the police?'

'And say what? That when he kissed me I let him? That when he asked me to I went to his room? He even called his mother first to ask her to be late. He told her he was going to play the piano for me, some difficult pieces by Chopin he'd never tried before, could we have the house to ourselves for an extra hour? I heard his mother's laughter pouring out of the receiver, and Karl was trying to muffle it by talking more loudly. I think Chopin was a signal, he's *always* playing Chopin so what was so special about Chopin tonight? His mother knew. She knew what he had planned; she knew why he'd asked me to go round. She knew and she thought it was funny.'

'What happened when you went to his room?'

I was in no state to be pacifying Jack, what I wanted was to let it all out, and I did.

'The kissing and the touching got rougher and rougher, and when I asked him to stop he just wouldn't. "Stop it," I said. "This doesn't feel right, I think I should go now." But he didn't. He wouldn't. He said that I didn't really want him to stop, that girls were all the same and liked to play games. I said it wasn't true and I wasn't like that and I didn't play games, he was the first boy I'd kissed and if I'd given him the wrong impression I was sorry, but now he had to stop and let me go and I'd still be his friend. It was too late to be sorry, he said, and if I wanted to be friends, then why not just relax and have some fun. But he wasn't just talking, he was holding me too tightly and rubbing against me, trying to keep me still so he could kiss me again, getting rougher the more I resisted, too rough with his hands and those delicate fingers. I wanted to scream, I wanted to so badly but I couldn't. Then he grabbed me by the wrists and pushed me onto his bed and fell on top of me, and for a moment I felt dizzy and I lost all my strength...'

'Jane, I think we need to go to the police. Unless you're hurt, if you're hurt then we should call your dad first, and then we'll stop a cab...'

'I'm not, I'm not, I promise you I'm not hurt. When he let go of my hand, trying to undo his shorts, I punched him in the face and then I punched him again, again and again and as hard as I could, until he rolled off the bed and fell squealing on the floor, whimpering that I was crazy and I'd broken his nose. I stepped over him and he was yelling at me to get out, and I did, I got out, but before getting out I walked back to where he was and I kicked him. And as I kicked him, I was wishing I was wearing proper shoes.'

Jack used both hands to hold my face, and in the kindness of his gaze my disgust felt like a burden, something ugly I had borrowed from a stranger. 'I'm so sorry this happened,' he said. 'I blame myself, if I hadn't insisted you wouldn't have gone.'

'I went because I wanted to, not because you insisted. And if I hadn't gone tonight, he'd have invited me again and I'd have gone, because I liked him, I liked him a lot.'

Jack bent down and kissed me twice on my forehead. 'I'm so proud of you,' he said, 'and I think you should be proud of yourself. But I don't think you should just let it go.'

'I'm not letting it go, I'll *never* let it go.' I fell again into Jack's arms as another car sliced through us with its headlights and then drove past us slowly. I heard the laughter pouring out from inside it and felt it like a shiver of needle upon needle puncturing the surface of my body.

'We can't stay in the street. We need to go somewhere. And later when I've taken you home, if you'd like me to I'll come back.'

'What for?' I almost pushed him as I pulled too hard away from him, and standing one step back I held on to myself with my arms across each other and my hands around my neck, in a gesture I broke out of as soon as I remembered it was Jack's. 'Why would I want you to come back?'

'To talk to Karl's mother, to confront them both, to at least make sure she knows that her son tried to rape you.'

The word made me flinch. 'But I don't know them,' I said. 'They don't even exist, they were just a bad dream.'

'You and Karl, you're at the same school. Come September you'll be seeing him every day.'

'No,' I said. 'How can I see him if he doesn't exist?'

We did stay in the street, walking past St Mary's Church to the triangle of Islington Green, and then instead of turning left and entering the plate of spaghetti, we crossed to the other side of Upper Street and walked back in the direction of Cross Street. When we crossed the road again, I wasn't sure if I was following Jack or if Jack was following me. It was as if by some unspoken understanding we had reached the decision together to go back to Cross Street and look at Karl's house from the opposite side of the road, pausing for no more than five seconds before walking briskly on, turning into Florence Street and following it round to the end, where it veered its way back onto Upper Street.

The ground floor lights had been on and the windows still open, but Beethoven was no longer wafting out into a night that had now become more still, with fewer indoor lights on and hardly any traffic at all. It wasn't yet eleven o'clock, so the extra hour Dr Schmidt had promised her son hadn't passed, although a telephone call might have brought her home sooner. The absence of more music at this hour had signified nothing, but I wished Karl had been back at the piano, making up with sound for what I hoped had been a lapse — a temporary moment of madness. Briefly we had shared it, but then Karl had gone too far. And now that he no longer existed, I already knew I would miss him.

'Do you think he's okay?' I asked Jack as we again walked past the top of Cross Street, now more steadfastly in the direction of home.

'Do we really care if he's okay?'

'Yes, I think we do. He's only a little boy.'

'I'm sure the little boy's just fine. Who knows, you might've even taught him a lesson.'

'I wish we'd heard him playing the piano.'

'Ah, so that's why we went back.'

'He always likes to play when he's upset.'

'He's probably in bed with an ice pack. And it's too late to be playing the piano.'

'I feel sad,' I said.

'Of course you do,' said Jack. I had my hand around his arm again, and he squeezed it right into his ribcage. I could feel the shape of his bones with my fingers.

'I mean for Karl.'

'The same Karl who doesn't exist.'

'Yes. The same Karl whose horrible taste is still in my mouth.'

'The same Karl...'

'Please don't say that word again.' Still clinging onto Jack as he fell silent, I shut my eyes tightly, keeping them shut while I took in gulps of air that filled me with the sharp metallic tang of the night. I thought of my father waiting at home, unaware of everything except his own confusion, grappling with his demons while Jack and I wandered the streets. Across the road an ambulance flashed past, its siren blaring as it sped to or from yet another dramatic unfolding of "real life". It was definitely time to go home.

Jack tripped and lost his balance, surging forward with such force that when his arm unlocked the grip of my hand, it gave me such a jerk that it almost dislocated my shoulder. He stumbled far ahead, nearly tumbling over more than once, but somehow as he wobbled he stayed standing. When he came to a stop, still crouching he held out his arms away from his body, and used a lamppost as a pole to swing around and face me. I almost laughed, with relief more than anything else, but then I saw the rage in his gaze at something behind me, and that was when I knew that he hadn't just tripped.

'Hello again,' I heard the familiar mocking voice, and before I could turn, I was pushed out of the way with a shove by the boy who hadn't finished with Jack in *Captain Cook's Fish and Chips*. 'I promised my mates that you'd have your face punched in by the end of the night, *guaranteed*. See, I just *knew* you'd still be roaming our streets, seeing as your sugar daddy's probably dumped you. And I told the lads you needed to be dealt with *tonight*, or we'd have a fucking queer roaming our streets with his tart every fucking night of the week.'

'Yeah, fucking queer,' parroted one of his mates from the shadows. I recognised the two shrinking violets. They were still keeping their distance, cheerers-on too cowardly to heed Frank's good advice.

'But don't worry, no one's laying a finger on your tart,' said their leader as he circled Jack. 'Tonight we'll just do you.'

'I've lived here all my life and I've never seen you around,' I said. 'So how are these your streets?'

'If we say they're our streets, they're our streets,' said the bolder of the two shrinking violets.

I remembered the head bully's name. Maybe if they all knew I remembered... 'So, Mike, what's all this *really* about? Can't you find yourself a girlfriend?'

'Or I'll give her just a slap or two to keep her quiet,' said Mike.

'If you so much as touch her, I promise you her dad will find you and he'll kill you,' said Jack. 'So I'd strongly advise you to leave her alone and try your luck with me.'

'I mean, how many Mikes can there be, roaming *our* streets with a couple of stooges? And the people in the shop know your faces. It shouldn't be too hard for the police to track you down.'

'Mike's dad *is* the police, you stupid bitch,' said the same shrinking violet.

'Shut your fucking face, you fucking idiot,' said Mike.

'Come on, Mike, just leave it,' said the other shrinking violet, but again it was too late for Mike to just leave it. Before he knew what had hit him, Jack had spun around the lamppost again, and then had swooped down to head-butt him twice.

I reached for Jack's extended arm, and as I passed over Mike's squirming body, sprawled across the pavement and howling as the blood from his nose seeped through his hands, I would have stamped with all my might on his face if Jack hadn't managed to pull me away.

'That makes it a broken nose each.' Jack's voice crackled with the effort of running, and while we ran there was no sound of footsteps behind us.

As soon as we had entered the plate of spaghetti, I let go of Jack's hand one more time, to be sick on the side of the road. And finally I was able to scream.

10

Home

At last we were home, but would it still be home for Jack? In every conceivable way I was exhausted, even more so under the pressure not to show it.

'Nothing happened tonight,' I had said to Jack, just before I turned the key to open the front door.

'Imagine if anything had,' Jack had smiled without relish.

And as soon as we had come into the house and closed the door behind us, I knew that no amount of barricading could have kept the night outside, that it had followed and would stay with us, its implacable burden made heavier by the effort of pretending to my father that nothing had happened. But the vastness of the untruth in which I had made Jack complicit was essential, or the selfishness with which I had perverted the course of the night would contaminate the part that had remained, and which more than any other part did not belong to me.

When my father gave me money and asked me to take Jack somewhere nice for some food, neither he nor Jack, nor even I myself, could have imagined how completely my desire to see Karl would have thwarted what had been a simple plan: to provide a breathing space in which my father and Jack would share an equal opportunity to gather their thoughts, before reaching either separately or together a final decision concerning the future. But really I had taken Jack completely for granted, as though he had no choice but to acquiesce in whatever was decided by my father, particularly if he asked Jack to stay.

Only now that we were back, and I felt glad and relieved to be home because it was safe, did it strike me how precarious Jack's position was. 'Nothing happened tonight,' I had commanded, as though the many things that *had* happened tonight had all revolved entirely around me. As though it would be safe for Jack to be cast out into the night by my father, because the night was tonight, and nothing had happened tonight.

I turned the light on in the hallway. The bedroom door was shut.

'I'm thirsty,' said Jack, and we both walked to the kitchen.

The table was as we had left it.

'Would you like a glass?'

I nodded, and when we both had drunk our water and put our glasses down, 'What I said wasn't fair,' I said. 'Dad needs to know you were in danger tonight. He can't just turn you out.'

'I'll be fine,' said Jack. And bending his fingers, he rubbed the back of them against my cheek. 'Really, I will be. Whatever we decide.'

So it wasn't just up to my father, Jack also had a claim to the decision. Even if my father asked him to stay he might not. Perhaps the night had made him more determined. Perhaps it had made life seem too short to be wasting it on half-hearted offers. Feeling proud of Jack, I felt sorry for my father. Thoughts of Karl had receded, shrinking into a small and self-contained compartment of sadness locked away at the back of my mind.

'And you and I will always be friends, just like you promised.'

'Just like I promised,' said Jack. 'And now I think we need to find your dad.'

When I knocked on the bedroom door no one answered.

'He's probably fallen asleep,' said Jack, so I opened it slowly. The two bedside lamps either side of it were on, soaking up the colours of the room to give the empty double bed an orange sheen.

'He hasn't packed your things,' I said, while we both stood at the doorway surveying the room. 'Maybe he's gone out for a walk.'

'Stay there.'

'But why, what is it?' I was pinching on his T-shirt, trying to hold him back.

'Just stay there, please,' Jack insisted, his voice now more grave than the voice that had already alarmed me, and I let him break away, watching as he walked the few steps to the head of the bed. He stooped over the lamp on that side as though to hide it from view, and then still with his back to me sat down on the edge of the bed, only to get up again and stride back towards me. As he reached me he pulled me by the hand and closed the door behind us.

'Stay there. Promise me you'll stay there,' he said to me intently, and before I could answer he was already at the top of the stairs.

'Is auntie Ada here?' I managed to call out, but Jack had disappeared, and when I didn't hear voices, when I only heard the sound of frantic rummaging, I was unable to wait any longer. I hadn't promised, and I couldn't just stay there.

The bathroom door was open. Still wearing his underpants my father lay in a bath full of water, looking very peaceful with his eyes shut, and for a reason that I couldn't understand Jack was on his knees, breathing rapidly as he used something torn to tie up a towel he had wrapped around my father's right arm. And then I saw the blood.

'Daddy? Daddy?' It was a low, wooden repetition, stifled by incomprehension. My mind, until then too full of how I myself had experienced the night, was now crowded with my ignorance of how my father had spent the same time, moment by moment, in a sequence whose inevitable culmination had been the enactment of the scene that lay so starkly before me.

Jack flew up from his crouching position and stood in front of me, touching my forehead with his. Holding on to my shoulders, he spoke to me quickly and loudly. 'You must go back downstairs and call for an ambulance. Will you do that? Dial 999 and ask for an ambulance.'

When I nodded he let go of my shoulders, but before moving away I tried to stand on tiptoe and take another look at my father. Could he really still be alive?

'Jane, you have to go downstairs right now.'

Jack gave me a nudge and I turned around and ran down the stairs to where the telephone was in the hallway. I called 999 and asked for an ambulance, but whoever I was speaking to wanted to know who the ambulance was for and what was the problem, and I said that my father was upstairs in the bath, and he seemed to be asleep but there was blood on the floor, on the floor and in the water as well, and that Jack had wrapped his arm in a towel. Halfway through the call I had started to sob, and I was trying to get the words out as fast as I could but they were getting tangled up with my sobs and catching at the back of my throat, and as I tried to dredge them out I was fighting for breath. When the call was over, I leaned against the wall and let my body slide down to the floor. Then I saw that the receiver was still in my hand, and I made myself get up, to hang up so I could run back upstairs and be with my father and Jack.

'Is the ambulance coming?' Jack's voice resounded in the house, but the loudness was just a disguise and I hadn't been fooled.

'Is he dead?' I called back from the bottom of the stairs, but the urgency had left my voice too. I might as well have asked if Jack thought I should make a pot of tea.

'Is it coming?' Jack asked me again, and when I told him that it was, the same loud voice, now a practical voice, was asking me to call auntie Ada. 'Just tell her that we've had to call an ambulance for George and I'll be going with him, so someone should be here to stay with you. And tell her to hurry.'

In a small way this return to a sense of urgency was comforting, and the same was true of having to perform another task. My father's life and death were uncertain, and certainty would come only when the ambulance arrived, but really what I hoped for wasn't certainty at all, certainty could mean just one thing.

'Auntie Ada?' I interrupted whatever auntie Ada had answered. 'Jack says that we've had to call an ambulance for dad, and that we need you to be here and please can you hurry.'

'Is Jack Mia-Mia?'

'Jack's upstairs...'

'But is he Mia-Mia?' auntie Ada asked again.

'Yes, yes he is.'

'I'll be there as quickly as I can. Jane, are you okay?'

'No. I mean yes, yes, I'm okay. But hurry!'

'I'm on my way right now. And, Jane...'

'Yes?'

'I love you very much.'

I put down the receiver, and this time I *did* run back upstairs to be with my father and Jack. What confronted me was raw: Jack sitting on the floor at the edge of the bath, his head to one side touching my father's, two men finally at peace at a terrible price. Any uncertainty was gone. The rigid coldness of my father's colour was blatantly the colour of death.

Without moving his head Jack looked up at me. His eyes were dry but full of pain, just like mine, wet and then dry, dry and then wet, in a cycle that had now become random, as though alternating of its own accord.

'Just having a minute,' he said. I was expecting him to ask me to go back downstairs, but he either lacked the strength to or it wasn't what he thought I should do, and when I went down on all fours and crawled to lie beside him, he put his arm behind me and drew me up so close that my head touched my father's through his. And after we had both had a minute, very quietly and without the slightest movement Jack spoke again. 'Earlier in the bedroom... There were letters. I expect the police would want to see them, if they knew they existed. For the moment they're hidden.'

'Are they addressed to the police?'

'One's addressed to Jane and the other to Jack.'

'Then I think no one else needs to read them. Was there nothing for auntie Ada?'

'Jane, I'm so sorry, this is all my fault.'

I made a fist of my hand and was punching very lightly at his chest, picking up the rhythm of his heart, which was either very slow or too faint. I was shaking my head, and then I started to sob, not knowing what to say, not knowing what to do or even what to think, except that my father was dead.

'This is all my fault,' Jack said again. 'Try not to be angry with your dad.'

I could hear him but I didn't understand what he meant. I didn't feel angry, and how was this his fault? I was crying more quietly now. I took the handkerchief out of my polka-dot pocket and clutched it near my face. And looking up at Jack, 'Can I keep this?'

'It belonged to your dad, so it's yours now.'

'If I hadn't gone to Karl's…'

'Don't,' said Jack. He had turned around and moved both his knees up. 'Listen to me, Jane. Going to Karl's made no difference. I'm sure it was already too late.'

'But when, when was it already too late? And *why* was it too late?'

'I don't know. And I don't think the letters will make any difference.'

There was the sound of the ambulance arriving, its siren going quiet when it stopped. Then the doorbell began ringing insistently. Jack helped me up and we both went downstairs. At the bathroom door, I had turned around to look at my father again.

Jack had led the way upstairs, and the ambulance crew – two young men who had said very little coming in, communicating with each other almost entirely with nods - were with him in the bathroom when the doorbell rang again. I had stayed downstairs, and had stepped outside briefly while the two paramedics gathered their equipment. The flashing of the ambulance lights made the house switch on and off with the colours of the sign over *Mr Magikoo's Magik Shoppe,* a scene more otherworldly than the crackle on the surface of the moon. It was hardly a surprise that auntie Ada hadn't used her own keys to let herself in.

'Jane Hareman?'

'Yes?'

'Police. May we come in?'

I hadn't caught the two plainclothes policemen's names, nor had I been able to read what was written on their badges. The one who had been standing in front of the other had flashed his in and out of my face as though deliberately twitching to the rhythm of the ambulance lights, and I hadn't paid attention as the one who came in second followed suit. But vaguely I remembered that one was an Inspector, and that both of them had called themselves detectives.

'They're upstairs in the bathroom,' I said.

The two detectives looked at each other, and then one of them took out a notebook.

'There's nothing here about an ambulance, sir.'

'It's my father. Isn't that why you're here?'

'Is your father unwell?' asked the detective who had spoken at the door.

I shook my head in short violent jerks, like a child refusing to own up to something naughty.

'Maybe we should have a word with your mother,' said the second detective impatiently.

'My mother died when I was six,' I snapped back at him, and turning to the first detective, 'Are you an Inspector?'

'Detective Inspector Cambridge,' he smiled.

I liked him. He was so impeccably dressed that I thought he looked more like an actor. And really he was very polite.

'May I just call you Inspector?'

'Only if I can call you Jane,' the Inspector smiled again. 'And maybe while we're chatting DC Prior should take a look upstairs.'

'That's a good idea, sir,' said DC Prior, and we watched him take the steps two at a time.

'My father cut himself,' I said to the Inspector. I was hearing the words as if they were written and someone was reading them coldly. 'He died before the ambulance arrived. I think he was probably dead when we got back, but Jack tried to save him.'

'You mean you think your father killed himself,' said the Inspector.

'Yes.'

'Is Jack still upstairs with him?'

'Yes.'

'And he's definitely dead?'

'He's definitely dead, sir,' said DC Prior from the top of the stairs. Unlike the Inspector he was dumpy and badly dressed, his clothes at least one size too small.

'I'm really very sorry for your loss,' said Inspector Cambridge. 'A young child when you lost your mother, and still a child now, with your father upstairs...'

'You knew about mum's accident?'

'I did, yes.'

'But why weren't you told about the ambulance? Why else would you be here, I don't understand.'

'Well, I know you must be very upset about your dad, but there's been a complaint of assault...'

'Against Jack?'

'Jack?'

'Because it's Jack who should've made the complaint.'

'Was Jack involved in the assault?'

'How did you know where to find us? Were we followed here by one of Mike's friends?'

'We were given the address by the lady who made the complaint.'

'So this isn't about Mike.'

'I'm not sure if I know who Mike is,' said the Inspector.

'He's nobody,' I said.

'I see. Well, as I was saying, the lady who made the complaint was also very upset, and that means I need to ask you some questions.'

'But what kind of questions, questions about what?'

'About an incident involving her son.'

'You mean *Karl*? Karl's accusing *me* of assault?'

'Not Karl himself, but his mother is. I shouldn't really… I was hoping that your father could be present, you see, but obviously that's out of the question. Is there someone else, another close relative that we can contact? Or would you rather I came back another time? My inquiries aren't really urgent, not in view of what's happened and how upset you must be. Yes, I think another time would be better.'

The doorbell was now ringing for the third time.

'That's probably my aunt,' I said to the Inspector. 'Auntie Ada, my father's sister.'

All my emotions were numbed. I could only feel a hollow gladness as I went to the door. And it was auntie Ada, but she wasn't alone.

Rattled by his presence in the house, which clearly they hadn't anticipated, the two uniformed police officers, one of them a constable and the other a sergeant, offered the Inspector sheepish excuses for arriving so late.

'We were delayed unexpectedly, sir. Couldn't have been helped, I'm afraid.'

'I'll be the judge of that, sergeant, if you don't mind,' the Inspector chastised him.

'We encountered an urgent incident, sir,' the constable offered in support of his sergeant.

'Did you indeed? And what was it exactly, this urgent incident that you encountered?'

'It involved young Fairchild, sir,' said the sergeant. 'The Chief Inspector's son.'

'Ah, the Chief Inspector's son,' said the Inspector.

'That's right, sir.'

'Again.'

'I'm afraid so, sir.'

'Remind me of his first name?'

'It's Mike, sir.'

'Mike, of course. And what incident was Mike involved in this time, may I ask?'

'We found him in the street with a badly broken nose.'

'Ah, a badly broken nose.'

'All he'd say was that some queer guy and his tart had got their just deserts, sir.'

'I see,' said the Inspector, and as he took me into his gaze, 'Well, young Mike won't be our problem for much longer.'

'Sir?'

'Promotion, sergeant.' The Inspector had turned to face the sergeant again. 'Our Chief Inspector Fairchild's moving on to pastures new. Somewhere very far, I believe.'

'I see, sir. That *is* good news. For the Chief Inspector, I mean.'

Auntie Ada was silent. As soon as she had stepped through the door, she had pulled me towards her and held my face still while she smothered me with kisses. I had looked at her impassively, and even now I felt almost uncaring, only distantly embarrassed that I hadn't been able to show more emotion when I told her that her brother was dead. On the day my father died, on the day I had lost Karl, on the day when I would probably also lose Jack, my sadness came and went, washing over me as though it had no substance. The cluttering of strangers made everything seem more confusing; nothing would seem real until they had gone and had taken my father away.

'Hi, Ada,' said Jack in his masculine voice.

The two uniformed officers had joined the paramedics upstairs, and Jack must have been asked to leave. He was pale, and his wet T-shirt was patchy with stains whose earlier scarlet brightness was gone. They were crimson now, with a pale yellow halo around them, the stains of blood lost and then gone bad.

Without letting go of me, auntie Ada heaved herself in Jack's direction, and he let her take him into her embrace, without the need for words, or for wailing, or for any sounds at all, the three of us in a cluster that excluded the rest of the world. And then, like a wave that had broken only to quickly return, we fell back from each other but stayed close, holding hands in a circle of silent unspeakable grief.

When the telephone rang, auntie Ada lifted my hand to her mouth and gave it a kiss before acknowledging the Inspector for the first time as she made her way around him to pick up the phone.

'Hello,' she said, after taking a big breath and then clearing her throat. 'Sorry, who? One moment, please.' With her hand over the speaker, 'I think it's Karl's mother,' she said, 'but I'm not sure what she wants, she's speaking too fast. Does Karl know about your dad?'

'May I?' the Inspector asked auntie Ada as he put his hand forward to claim the receiver.

'She's a Reichian therapist,' muttered auntie Ada. 'Her son's a talented pianist, destined for greatness according to Jane.'

'Is he indeed?' the Inspector answered stiffly, while he and I exchanged an awkward glance.

'And he's Jane's closest friend.'

'I see. Thank you,' said the Inspector, when finally auntie Ada had passed him the receiver.

'Her closest friend, my arse,' Jack said loudly, but the Inspector quickly gestured an order of silence.

'Detective Inspector Cambridge speaking, is that Dr Schmidt? We spoke earlier, yes… Ah, a misunderstanding… Your son was confused, I see… And he realised this *after* you had made the complaint... Oh, he didn't *know* you had made a complaint... So let me get this straight, Dr Schmidt, your son told you there had been an assault, then you made a complaint, and then your son owned up to *why* there had been an assault... No, I know that isn't *quite* what you said... Jane? Yes, Jane is here. No, I'm afraid you can't, I need to speak to her first... Yes, that's right. Not yet, no... It may be necessary to ask him some questions myself, depending on what Jane has to say... Yes, you'll hear from me shortly, just as soon as I've been able to establish the facts... Goodbye.'

'Establish what facts?' asked a perplexed auntie Ada. 'A complaint of assault against who?' And when the Inspector waved away her question, 'Jane? Why is that woman calling you in the middle of the night? Are you and Karl not friends any more?'

'Daddy's dead, auntie Ada.'

'Dead, my own brother...'

'Oh, Ada,' said Jack.

'Sir?' It was the sergeant, red-faced from the heat in the bathroom. 'The paramedics are ready...'

'Right you are, sergeant, tell them to give us a minute and then we'll be out of their way.'

'The kitchen,' said auntie Ada.

'We could all do with a cold glass of water,' said the Inspector.

'Yes, water,' said auntie Ada.

'There's whisky, if anyone would like some,' I said.

'I wouldn't say no,' said Jack.

'No, nor would I,' said auntie Ada.

'If you don't mind, I should take a look around first,' said the Inspector. 'Then I'll join you in the kitchen.'

11

Questions

When eventually he joined us in the kitchen, Inspector Cambridge also joined auntie Ada and Jack in a small glass of whisky. But when already I was refilling theirs, he politely refused a second by placing his hand over his glass.

'Let's get it over with, Inspector,' I said. 'Auntie Ada is my closest relative, in case you still needed to ask me some questions.'

'I think you may have gathered for yourself that the circumstances have now changed. It's now more a matter of whether there's something you'd like to tell me.'

'You should,' Jack egged me on.

'There's nothing to tell. Nothing happened.'

'I would hardly call it that,' said Jack.

'I was there and it was nothing. Just a silliness that went too far.'

'And would've gone further, if you hadn't...'

'Please, Jack. I know Karl, and I'm sure that he's already learned his lesson.'

'He's learned it so well that he accused you of assault.'

'It was his mother who accused me, not Karl.'

'But what was it, this silliness that went too far and would've gone further − if you hadn't done what?' auntie Ada demanded.

'I think we're more or less clear about what Jane did,' said the Inspector. 'What we're *not* so clear about is how far the silliness had gone *before* Jane had to do what she did.'

'Far enough,' said Jack.

'Oh, dear God!' said auntie Ada.

'Not very far at all,' I said. 'I've already told you, Karl's a little boy, he probably thought we were playing a game, and that was how we were supposed to play it. But all he really cares about is playing the piano, it was probably Mami who told him it was time he started playing with little girls.'

'Mami?'

'His mother, Inspector,' I said.

'The Reichian therapist,' said auntie Ada.

'Is that like a chiropractor?' asked the Inspector.

'A chiropractor for the soul,' said Jack.

'A *charlatan*,' remembered auntie Ada.

'Ah, like a Freudian,' said the Inspector.

'But different,' I said. 'Karl says his mother has no time for Freud.'

Our muffled, semi-droll conversation was proving an inadequate distraction from the strained and jarring sounds that were coming from the stairs and the hallway. They would stop and then start again, as though pausing every now and again as a mark of respect. One minute the atmosphere was heavy and funereal, and in the next we would carry on jabbering nonsense. Then another noise would remind us that my father's cold body, probably on a stretcher, probably encased in a black body bag, was making its way to an ambulance that wouldn't need to turn its siren on as it drove him on his journey to the morgue. And my mind would run ahead and I'd try to imagine as faithfully as I could what kind of funeral Mr Magikoo might have asked for if the subject had ever come up.

'Would anyone mind if I smoked?' The Inspector had taken a packet of cigarettes out of one pocket and was hesitating before digging into another, probably to take out his matches.

'Go ahead, Inspector,' said auntie Ada. 'If you don't mind killing yourself, why should the rest of us mind, we don't even know you.'

'Auntie Ada!'

'My wife's just the same,' said the Inspector. '"Go on, give yourself cancer, don't mind about us," that's what I hear every day when I light up my first. "Don't worry, love," I said to her this morning. "In five years' time cancer will be curable, no worse than having the flu. If they can send men to the moon, then I'm sure those tobacco companies will help them find a cure for cancer."'

'Just as long as the Russians are looking for one too,' said Jack.

'Hmm, I hadn't thought of that,' said the Inspector, 'but then nor has the wife, so I think we're all right.' And to auntie Ada, 'It'll just be the one, I promise.' He eased a cigarette out of the packet and lit up. 'Mm, nothing like it,' he said, after a long inhalation. 'Now then, Jane, the ladies' garments in your father's room... Who should we say they belonged to? You see, they're rather too modern to have been your mother's.'

'Is that really relevant?' asked Jack.

'Of course it isn't relevant,' said auntie Ada.

'Not to my inquiries, no,' said the Inspector as he paused for an even deeper puff. 'But to the sergeant's, well, if he takes the view that they're part of the overall picture... I think you get my drift. I don't know them well, the sergeant or his constable, but I'm sorry to say that it hasn't been unknown for details of cases like this, particularly when more prudish minds than ours might consider them sufficiently salacious, to find their way into the hands of the least agreeable parts of our press. And Mr Magikoo, he wasn't just any Joe Bloggs. I mean, he was famous, an illusionist extraordinaire and by all accounts our greatest magician. Certainly that was my own experience.'

'You've seen my father perform?'

'1963, November 23, Saturday night at the Magic Palladium in Croydon, I still have the programme.' The Inspector loosened the knot of his tie, as though his trip to the past allowed for an additional degree of informality.

'He usually only performed in the summer,' I said. 'If you'd been there two summers before, you'd have seen me hopping through the blades of Sweeney Todd.' And turning to auntie Ada, 'The blades were made of plastic, I was never in danger.'

'I *was* there two summers before,' said the Inspector, 'and it never even crossed my mind that the blades might've been real. You were a charming little girl with your posy, Jimmy had a crush on you for weeks after your hop – he's my youngest by the way, and as big a fan of Mr Magikoo as his dad.'

'You must've been there on the Friday,' I said, 'or you'd also remember auntie Ada.'

'Yes, I heard about that,' said the Inspector. 'And Jimmy and I have always considered ourselves *particularly* lucky to have been there for Little Magik Matchstick's last performance.'

'Shame on you, Inspector,' said auntie Ada.

'Oh, but he's paying me a compliment,' I said. 'Thank you, Inspector, I'm glad you and Jimmy enjoyed the show.'

'And we did, very much, but that Saturday in '63, that was something really special. It was a charity do for a very worthy cause as I remember, but if your dad hadn't been billed as the night's main attraction, I'm sure half the people wouldn't have turned up. It was the day after Kennedy was shot, and everyone was feeling out of sorts, like we'd all lost a loved one. It was a miserable audience, but your dad did such a blinder that after just five minutes he had every single one of us literally rolling in the aisles. The man was a one-off, no doubt about it. Honestly, I shouldn't be surprised if *Mr Magikoo's Magik Shoppe* becomes a kind of shrine. So you see, already there's a story to be told, and all of you must brace yourselves, some very unpleasant people are likely to be falling over each other to tell it...'

'As luridly as they possibly can,' said Jack, after slugging down the last of his second glass of whisky.

'I was going to say "colourfully",' said the Inspector, 'but then I've always been prone to understatement. I will say this, though. We're talking *big* amounts of money being dangled...'

'Are you trying to blackmail us, Inspector?'

'He's not, Jack, I think he's trying to warn us,' I said.

'He's a policeman,' said Jack.

'And I'll admit that we have more than our fair share of bad apples in the force, but believe it or not, we're not all the same.' The Inspector took another long puff on his cigarette before putting it out in the cup I had offered as an ashtray. 'For some of us at least, joining the police is a vocation.'

As they became more recognisable, the sounds from the living room, in whose direction no one in the kitchen was turning, also became more intrusive. My mind was drifting. What hadn't I already seen tonight, that I should now prefer imagining to seeing?

'We should go and say goodbye,' I said, leaping up from the table. 'We can't just pretend he's not here any more. He'll be gone soon enough, and then we won't need to pretend.'

'Don't worry,' said the Inspector, 'I've already asked the sergeant to call us to the other room when it's time.' And when I had reluctantly sat down again, 'We don't have long, may I speak frankly?'

'My niece is just a child,' said auntie Ada.

'My feeling is that Jane is more sensible than all the rest of us put together,' smiled the Inspector. 'All the same, it's not my place to say if she ought to be present. But in my own experience knowing about the unpleasantness that's out there does help one to guard against it.'

'Jane isn't going anywhere,' I said.

'Go on, Inspector,' said Jack.

'My poor little lamb,' said auntie Ada.

'You must all be wondering why I'm still here. Well, after an earlier conversation with Jane, and then the sergeant's account of why he and his constable were so late arriving, I thought it best if I stayed, to have a quick look around and a word with just the three of you in private. Now, as you probably know, just two years ago there was a change in the law. Since then, and as long as they're conducted in private, certain acts between male consenting adults are no longer criminal. And I'm sure you also know that in spite of its limited scope not everyone was pleased with this change, to put it mildly - a slippery slope and all that. Any story that panders to prejudice you can be sure would make headlines, and be plastered on many front pages.'

'If this is about Mia-Mia's...' Her hand already over her mouth, auntie Ada's whiteness went pink. She took slow sips of whisky, before suddenly declaring: 'Everything that isn't George's in that wardrobe is mine.'

'I see,' the Inspector said. 'Do you mind me asking what size shoe you take, Miss Hareman?'

'4, if you must know,' answered auntie Ada.

'All the shoes in your brother's wardrobe, all the *women's* shoes I mean, are size 10. All the men's shoes are size 7. And the clothes have the opposite problem. I don't think any of them would fit you. Not by a long chalk. And they're also rather... now how shall I put this... rather more glamorous than one might expect? But perhaps that's too conservative... Ah, yes, I think I've got it. I believe the word in vogue at the moment is "groovy".'

'Well, certainly I can't be accused of being *that*.'

'What I'm most afraid the sergeant might surmise is that the women's clothes belonged to a man. But of course it doesn't matter what the sergeant surmises, just as long as there isn't any evidence to back it up.'

'Forgive me for still being suspicious, Inspector, but you do seem rather over-keen to help us,' said Jack.

'And you can't imagine why.'

'I can only imagine that perhaps you have another son.'

'About the same age as you.'

'Ah,' said Jack.

'Can't we just say that George had a big-footed girlfriend who left him?' auntie Ada suggested.

'Without taking *any* of her stuff?' countered the Inspector.

'But daddy took his own life, what's it matter what there is in his wardrobe, or if he had a girlfriend or not?'

'The press,' said Jack.

'And if by any chance there was a note,' the Inspector went on, 'are we absolutely sure it won't be found? Obviously I mean by the sergeant.'

'There was a note?' asked a flustered auntie Ada.

'No,' said Jack. 'We didn't find a note.'

'We looked everywhere,' I said.

'Did you look everywhere the sergeant might look?' asked the Inspector.

When I looked at Jack uncertainly, 'I'm pretty sure we did,' he said.

'Sergeant Morris does seem quite ingenious. It might even occur to him to have a little forage through the shop.'

'There wouldn't be any point leaving a note in the shop, I never set foot in it. And daddy wouldn't leave a note where I wouldn't find it.'

'Unless of course he wanted Jack to find it.'

'Don't worry, Inspector,' said Jack. 'Wherever he might look, the sergeant would be wasting his time.'

'I see, so we have the note covered.'

'We do, we have the notes covered,' said Jack, and I tried not to wince at his slip of the tongue.

The Inspector pounced on it at once: 'Now *that's* the kind of thing the sergeant will be looking for, you see.'

'We have the note covered,' said Jack.

'Good. And what about the girlfriend?'

'What girlfriend?' auntie Ada asked.

'The one whose clothes are in the wardrobe,' said the Inspector.

'Oh, you mean the one who left George one good morning and never came back?'

'That's the one, Miss Hareman, well done,' said the Inspector. 'Any idea why she might've left without taking her clothes?'

'Fresh start, Inspector,' said auntie Ada. 'It's the only consolation when something ends badly.'

'I think earlier you mentioned a name.'

'Her name was Mia-Mia,' said Jack. 'Lots of people saw them together.'

'Ah yes, Mia-Mia,' said the Inspector. 'And her surname?'

'Farrow,' said Jack. 'As in Mia, the actress in *Rosemary's Baby*.'

The Inspector had arranged for everyone except the family and Jack to step outside the house just before my father was taken away, giving us a short private moment in which to say goodbye.

His face had been uncovered, and the three of us had stood over my father in silence before touching his coldness and giving his forehead a kiss. And when the ambulance had driven off and the Inspector had left with DC Prior, we had followed the sergeant on a tour of the house, and it had ended where it had begun: in my father's bedroom. The two policemen paced about the room looking glum. The search of the rest of the house had yielded no secrets - perhaps more ingenious than the Inspector had given him credit for, very wisely the sergeant had not expressed the slightest interest in *Mr Magikoo's Magik Shoppe*. If the house was a maze, he must have known the *Shoppe* was certain to be a walk-in nightmare. But he had not quite given up yet. I could see the carving of thinking lines snake across his face – not at all an unpleasant face in other respects, in contrast to that of his weaselly constable. Had the Inspector not put us on our guard, probably I would have trusted Sergeant Morris with my life. As it was, I was one of three "suspects" sitting next to each other in a row at the foot of the bed. 'If only beds could talk,' the sergeant was probably thinking, as he flitted his gaze from one pillar of guile to the next.

Other pieces of furniture were unfortunately proving more cooperative. The wardrobe's three doors were all open, exposing potentially lucrative secrets. Unlocked from the centre, the first two doors opened together, one to the left and the other to the right. On a rail on the left side hung all the different costumes of Mr Magikoo. Above them, on a shelf that ran the whole width of the wardrobe, were his hats for all occasions, and in a row at the bottom his shoes.

My father's everyday clothes hung on the same rail on the right side, with his jumpers on the running shelf above. At the bottom the line of shoes continued - brogues, brogues, winkle-pickers, and finally another pair of brogues. It was the third door that had opened to reveal Aladdin's cave – the explosion of flowery colour that had been Mia-Mia, and the telling incongruity between the slimline batik tops and flowing see-through gowns, the bell-bottomed mini skirts and baby doll dresses, and on the other hand that ultimately unfeminine high-heeled collection of rather astronomical footwear.

The frills and thrills of the Victorian chest of drawers had revealed only an absence of bras, but this was '69, the tail end of the decade of sexual liberation, and if I knew that, then so did the sergeant. In any case it was an absence that the rather large collection of tight elastic slips sufficiently made up for. As I kept a steady eye on his thinking lines, I was reminded of the light bulb in cartoons: the sign of a moment of sudden revelation. I saw nothing like that in the cloud that followed the sergeant, floating just above his head, into which he occasionally seemed to peer for inspiration. His thinking lines had once or twice been flexed, but they had not been ironed out by anything he or his constable had come across so far. They both fortunately seemed to lack the Inspector's intuition and his really quite spectacular powers of deduction.

'In case there's ever anything you need,' Detective Inspector Cambridge had whispered in my ear, when already by a conjuring trick of his own he had squeezed my hand around his card. It was still in my pocket.

'So these all belonged to a girlfriend who left him, you say.' The sergeant had poked his nose again inside Aladdin's cave before turning around with his question.

'Mia-Mia Farrow,' said auntie Ada. 'George was quite relieved to see the back of her, he told me so himself.'

'Mia-Mia Farrow,' the sergeant repeated while his constable struggled to keep a straight face.

'That's correct,' said Jack.

'I don't mean to be impertinent, sir, but how did you say you were related to the family?'

'Jack's a very good friend,' I said.

'And his surname would be...'

'Spencer,' said Jack.

'Jack and I met at the theatre,' auntie Ada jumped in. 'At a fringe production, I think.'

'*Look Back in Anger*,' said Jack.

'Or was it *Entertaining Mr Sloane*? It was years ago now.'

'Nearly three,' said Jack. 'And very shortly afterwards I met George and Jane.'

'Mine's still Hareman, in case you were wondering,' said auntie Ada. 'I'm not ashamed to say I'm a spinster.'

'And your address, sir, what might that be?'

'Oh, here and there, mostly people's sofas,' said Jack.

'And most frequently mine,' said auntie Ada. '12F Cyprus Street in Tufnell Park.'

'Lovely part of London,' said Jack.

'So of no fixed abode,' said the sergeant.

'Until I get myself settled.'

'While he's trying to decide what to do with his degree,' I said.

'Mia-Mia Farrow, hmm...' Holding it aloft, Sergeant Morris had picked out of the wardrobe one of Mia-Mia's most extravagant shoes and was examining it from all angles in the manner of a curious archaeologist. Clearly the shoes and the clothes must have belonged to the same woman –

why else would they have all been in the wardrobe? But would the sergeant have made the mental leap that as a matter of fact they might just as likely have belonged to the same man? Women with enormous feet did exist, but so did men who liked to dress up as women. I scrutinised the sergeant's expression. No light bulb had discerningly lit up in the cloud above his head. Nor was there any sign yet that one mental leap had led to another, and that any moment now he would be asking Jack to play Cinderella.

'I'm trying to imagine myself in Mr Magikoo's shoes,' said the sergeant pregnantly, handing over the shoe to the constable as though it were a priceless and very fragile artefact.

'George's feet were too small for that shoe you were holding,' said auntie Ada.

'I was speaking metaphorically, miss,' said the sergeant.

'And you saw him. Those clothes,' auntie Ada went on, pointing at Mia-Mia's side of the wardrobe, 'they obviously wouldn't have fitted him either, he was far too big for them.'

I felt the warmth of blood racing in my veins while at the same time the coldness of sweat oozed through every pore on my face. Auntie Ada had just handed the sergeant the first mental leap on a plate. Would he see it?

'Oh,' he said. And then, 'Oh,' he said again. 'Yes, yes I see now what you're getting at. That perhaps this mysterious Miss Mia-Mia...' The carvings on his face had deepened, and the cloud was lighting up.

In the middle of the row at the foot of the bed I was suspect No 2, with my hands in my lap. Discreetly I gave auntie Ada a nudge with my elbow, while at the same time I felt Jack using his to nudge me. I had always been prone to nervous laughter in tense situations where silence was called for. But since offending Karl on two separate occasions by exploding into giggles at the way his fingers moved as he gave himself over to Beethoven's *Moonlight Sonata*, I had managed to develop a technique that snapped me out of my propensity and nipped the slightest titter in the bud. It was simple enough but it worked: all I had to do was conjure up death, specifically the death of my mother, far more grisly in my mind than I knew it to have been in real life, and instead of dissolving into laughter I would be choking back my tears. Certainly Karl had found it very affecting. And tonight I didn't even need to imagine. I had looked at death squarely in the face.

'Let me recapitulate,' the sergeant went on. 'You're saying that because of the size of the shoes you think that these clothes may have belonged not to a woman but to a man, and that this man couldn't possibly have been your brother because neither the shoes nor the clothes were his size. But even if they *had* been his size, personally I would find it very hard to believe that Mr Magikoo led a secret double life as a transvestite, it's a *preposterous* idea...'

'Ah, sergeant,' said Jack, 'if the world conformed to everything you didn't find preposterous, what a dull place I imagine it would be.'

'And I was saying no such thing,' said auntie Ada. 'I'm pretty sure I'd have known if my own brother's girlfriend was a man, if that's honestly what you're suggesting. Sergeant, it's late. And we're bantering about the clothes in my dead brother's wardrobe when his body's barely arrived at the morgue. Can't we have some time alone with our grief? Surely we can have this absurd conversation tomorrow.'

'But there's no need to speculate, I saw *all* of Mia-Mia in the bathroom,' I said, and my positive corroboration appeared to have clinched it.

'Hmm, very well then,' mumbled the sergeant. 'And what about the note?' he then asked us abruptly, as though to catch us out.

'There wasn't a note,' I said.

'We're sadly all as mystified as you are about my brother's suicide,' said auntie Ada.

'This is a magician's house,' said the sergeant. 'There must be a thousand secret places where a note could have been hidden.'

'And what would be the point of a note that was hidden where no one could find it?' Jack asked the sergeant.

'None,' the sergeant agreed. 'Unless... unless of course it was a place where only *someone* could find it.'

'But why would it be hidden at all?' I said.

'We wouldn't know the answer unless we found it,' said the sergeant.

'And of course we'll let you know if we do,' said auntie Ada.

'I'm sure Jack and I would've found it already. But I have the Inspector's card if we need to get in touch.'

Our instinct for privacy might have prevailed while the sergeant and his constable were there, but as soon as they were gone, worn out by our stonewalling tactics, it was as if the full weight of the night, kept at bay until then by our effort to heed the Inspector's advice in order to fend off the sergeant, had finally descended from the heavens to crush us. Auntie Ada hadn't moved from her perch on the edge of my father's double bed. Head down, she wailed almost inaudibly. Jack was standing by the door, half on the inside and half on the outside, as though uncertain of the future or of where he belonged, just as I imagined he had always felt. My sadness and my tiredness and my grief had knocked the stuffing out of me completely. I hadn't the strength to comfort auntie Ada, and I lacked any words of reassurance for Jack. I longed for only one thing – to sleep, and then to wake up from *this* nightmare too.

'The notes,' said Jack. 'After all that lying I almost forgot they existed.'

Her wailing hadn't made auntie Ada deaf. 'Notes? Were there really more than one?'

'There were two. One for Jane and one for me.'

'But where are they, who found them?'

'The sergeant was right,' said Jack. 'In a magician's house it's easy to hide things.'

'I don't understand, why would George have wanted to hide them? And how did you know where to look?'

'George didn't hide them, I did.'

'I asked him to,' I said.

'They were just there, against the wall behind the lamp.' Jack had taken one step forward and was pointing.

Auntie Ada had pushed herself wearily off the bed, and looked around to follow the line of his finger to where it was pointing.

'Behind the lamp,' I said, 'that's why I didn't see them.'

'That's where we always left notes for each other,' said Jack.

As she wavered in the middle of the room, all hunched up and looking at a loss, squinting at where Jack had found the notes, her eyes small and wet like her brother's, it struck me more vividly than ever before just how old auntie Ada looked, so much older than she ought to at her age. Forty-five was young, but my father had been even younger, and my mother younger still. Numbers and death were crowding my head. My father was dead before he was forty, just shy of ten years after my mother, who had not yet turned thirty when she flew off to heaven to be with the rest of the angels. 1959 and 1969 - years that belonged in different decades but had only a decade between them, ten years of colour, and change, and faraway deaths. I had read every issue of TIME magazine since the first time I visited Karl, always one week late, as soon as Dr Schmidt had received the new edition. Borrowed news that I was urged not to believe because it was all propaganda.

Well, I would not be reading TIME magazine any more. Overcome all at once by the littleness of life and the enormity of my loss, I felt painfully alert, my sadness and my tiredness and my grief at last giving way to a kind of retrospective nostalgia. A tall chest of drawers blocked the secret upstairs door that connected our house to *Mr Magikoo's Magik Shoppe*. Without my father knowing, I had often stepped on tied up ancient bundles of *The Weekly Magic News* to rummage through its drawers. In one of them I had discovered photographs of Mr Magikoo and his assistant performing impossible feats, their smiles so wide as they leaned against each other or held hands that they might as well be taking a bow after conquering the world. I had seen with my own eyes and held its grainy proof in my hands, but only now was I able to feel grateful and glad on my parents' behalf for the magic of those few ineradicable years. And I wished I could have shared my gratitude and gladness with my father. But I had left it too late; my father was dead and my wishes could not bring him back. I would ask for Jack's help to scour every issue of *The Weekly Magic News* and to sift through all the clippings that I hadn't known existed. And I would share with auntie Ada my father's black and white exoneration. To move forward, she and I both needed to find a peaceful place for the past in our hearts. And when this night had played out, it too would be part of the past.

'We should read the notes tonight,' I said.

Jack walked quietly to the bed, sat where he had sat while I waited at the door all those hours before. And when he touched the solid headboard somewhere just a little further up, a small drawer sprang out from its side at about the same level as the top of the bedside table. I wasn't behind him this time, but I still couldn't have found the exact spot Jack had pressed if he hadn't reached out for my hand and made me run the tip of my right index finger back and forth across a shallow bump no larger than the head of an ordinary drawing pin.

I could see the notes - or rather I could see two envelopes folded together unevenly. And when Jack let go of my hand I squeezed myself beside him on the bed and waited for him to take them out.

'There are also some things of your mother's in there. George thought I should know in case something happened to him.'

'Just the notes for now,' I told him, and with the same dexterity with which he had hidden them he now took them out. He straightened them as best he could before handing me the one addressed to *Jane*. Then he placed the second in his lap, the side with *Jack* on it face up, as though to remove from auntie Ada's mind any shred of suspicion that perhaps he hadn't told us the truth.

'Val's jewellery,' said auntie Ada. When I looked up at her, startled by the sudden closeness of the shocked disbelief in her voice, auntie Ada was standing over us staring at the magic secret drawer and covering her mouth with her hands.

'There's a brooch George said he'd like your aunt to have.'

'A brooch?' muttered auntie Ada through her fingers.

'You'll remember it, he said. It's a "V" in the shape of a heart.'

'So you knew,' I said to Jack.

'Just that your father wanted Ada to have it.'

'Val's most cherished thing and he told *you*.' Auntie Ada was whistling her words almost angrily now.

'He told Mia-Mia,' said Jack. 'And he was going to tell Jane on her seventeenth birthday. Or earlier if he had to, if something happened to Mia-Mia. I made him promise.'

'*You* made him promise. It's been ten years since we lost Val. How long have *you* been around?'

'It's unfair blaming Jack, it was daddy's decision.'

'Ada's right,' said Jack. 'George should've told her. But he found it too hard. It never stopped being raw, what happened to your mother.'

'And we blamed him, auntie Ada. We blamed him for something that wasn't his fault.'

Auntie Ada stood as upright as she could, her eyes looking wild even as the light from the bedside table lamp made her squint. 'It's his fault that he's left you; I can blame him for that. Or is *that* unfair too?'

'I don't know, I don't know what's unfair...'

'Ada, we've lost him,' said Jack. 'And that's what's unfair, there's no need for blame.'

'"So you knew," Jane said to you, what did she mean?'

She had heaved her heavy gaze onto Jack, and when Jack didn't answer she swung round to loom over me as I cowered on the bed. 'I've every right to know,' she said, 'tell me what you meant.' Her voice was hushed but full of thorns. '*What* did Jack know? What's George been saying?'

Stop and start, stop and start, Tuesday afternoon had jumped into the evening, the evening had burst into the night, the night had now careered into the morning. It was already a different day, a pile-up of the whirlwind succession of events that in less than the hours of a day had revealed, unravelled and then hidden again truth after truth after truth. And somewhere in that heap lay the body of my father, for whom the burden of the truth had proved too much to bear.

The truth. It wasn't all the same, a single indivisible good that ought always to be told. Yesterday I would have argued that it was, and in that respect at least, as in so many others, yesterday had been a better day. But shorn of all the lies, it had taken my father away. Lies had been told and then retracted, and smaller truths had been concealed – Karl had told a truth and omitted another, which later he must have confessed to; Mike would never have owned up to being beaten by a queer; coached by the Inspector we had all lied to the sergeant. Which of all the truths did auntie Ada deserve? Should she know that the many truths she had been hiding were no longer secret? That her brother, who could no longer speak for himself, had betrayed her? That he had told me auntie Ada had once been in love with my mother? That I knew she had not told me the truth about the "one in a million" because grief had made her cruel and unjust?

'Well it's true, it's true...' As though unable to withstand the heavy silence in which I was weighing up the merits and demerits of telling the truth, auntie Ada had punctured the air with a shriek. And when both Jack and I leapt up to try and comfort her, she broke away and threw herself face down onto the bed, to finally weep out into her brother's pillow all the truth she had been keeping bottled up. 'It's true, it's all true.' She was fighting to get the words out while she sobbed without lifting her head, gasping for air she refused to breathe in. I sat beside her and was stroking her hair, as afraid for her as I ought to have been for my father.

12

Explanations

The early hours of the morning had given way to dawn, and as its grey light began to spill in we were still in my father's bedroom. Behind the fading velvet the window was open, but that trace of evening breeze had again fallen flat. With no air to let in, it was all I could do to at least keep out the sun, and I made some small adjustment to the badly drawn curtains.

The bedspread's neutral beige was made warmer by the light from the two bedside lamps, whose pale cream shades had unevenly yellowed because of the heat from the light bulbs. In the absence of natural light, the room's muted redness gave the bed its orange sheen. In this lonely artificial glare, Jack and I sat beside each other on the bed to read our notes.

'Are you sure these were the only two notes?' auntie Ada had been asking Jack insistently. 'Have you looked behind the bedside table? Maybe one of them slipped down the back.'

'The police would've discovered it, Ada. Before they stripped the bed and turned the mattress over, the first thing they did was move those bedside tables to the middle of the room.'

'Your note was the brooch, auntie Ada. Can you think of anything more precious?'

'The brooch belongs to you.'

'And it comes with daddy's wish that you should have it. In fact I'm going to get it for you now.'

To mollify auntie Ada, before the envelopes were opened I spread out on a pillow the contents of the magic secret drawer – two small boxes and just a few loose pieces of jewellery that were making sparkling doodles on the ceiling. In the first box were my parents' wedding rings, one giant and the other petite. And in the second were the rubies of the "V" in the shape of a heart, set upon a golden leaf to make a brooch. When I picked it out of its box, I extended my other arm to auntie Ada, whose crooked fingers sought out mine and weaved themselves around them.

And now she was quiet by the covered window, looking at her brooch as though in all the light in the world. When the telephone rang, just four or five times, no one moved. I was waiting to see if it rang again, but it didn't.

I tore my envelope open. Then Jack did exactly the same.

Tonight you and Jack made me happy. I had reminded him of something his grief and self-loathing had made him forget... Was this his explanation? Could he really have imagined it might do as consolation? *To Jack I owe a different explanation...* I read the second paragraph quickly. He owed Mia-Mia the gift of temporarily losing his mind, and his absence wouldn't do me lasting harm... I started again from the beginning, in case I might have missed hidden clues. This time I read through to the end.

What my father had left me was an outpouring of love, for everyone else but not for himself. What small concession he had made to the facts, he had brushed off as the consequence of madness. *But the past always has a way of catching up...* Wasn't *I* a part of the past? Wasn't Jack? *Be kind to Ada...* At the jumble of my father's closing words, a swelling of hardness took possession of me. Kindness should always begin with the truth.

I stood up from the bed in a slow and deliberate way, and I read my father's words out loud.

My dear Jane,

As if I didn't already owe you too many explanations, by the time you're reading this I will owe you one more. Tonight you and Jack made me happy. This may sound strange, coming from a man who is about to end his life, but the truth is that my life came to an end at the same time as your mother's. It's difficult to love when your heart's been broken, and I know that I've cared for you badly, but even with a broken heart I've always loved you very much. Already that was more than I felt I deserved, and so by hiding my love I hoped I could deprive myself of yours. I let Ada blame me because I blamed myself, but tonight you reminded me of something my grief and self-loathing had made me forget: that your mother and I couldn't have been happier, and that a big part of that happiness was doing what we did.

To Jack, to whom I also owe with gratitude the debt of temporarily losing my mind, I owe a different explanation, but seeing you two together tonight, on the same day I lost Mia-Mia, has made me realise that you're blessed with the gift of finding people's goodness. You will never want for friends and people who love you, and when you have got over the sadness, my absence won't do you lasting harm. From tomorrow all the decisions are yours, but if you'd like Jack to stay, as long as he could still have a life of his own I'm sure it would be good for you both. I think he'd be brilliant at running the shop, if you'd like to keep it going.

Too many words might imply a pretence that words can make up for what we both know they can't. And you're better at words than I am, so the more words I write the greater you'll find the temptation to read them again and again in search of different meanings. Because you love me I would like you not to grieve me. Try instead to be as grateful as I am to Jack for bringing a corpse back to life. Without him Mia-Mia would have been someone else, and I can see now that I lost my mind to Jack as much as I did to Mia-Mia. But the past always has a way of catching up, and I would rather go now, before it has a chance to lay my happy madness to waste.

Be kind to Ada. All the love she's ever felt in her life, for Jane and for your mother and even for me, has now become a part of the love she feels for you. The impurities of sadness have never made it weaker or less real. I must leave it to you to decide what you should or shouldn't tell her you know.

Goodbye, my little magic angel. Tonight I would have kissed you goodnight without hiding.

By the time I had finished, I was reading out the words as though hurling back at life all the violence it had dared to hurl at me. A brittle coldness was beginning to take hold of me that I wouldn't have been able to endure, but already Jack was standing beside me. Leaning towards me and with one arm around me, he read out the words my father had written for him.

My dear Jack,

I've just written to Jane that to you I owe with gratitude the debt of temporarily losing my mind. I see now that Mia-Mia was the sum of many parts, and that the best part was Jack. Jack was the part I loved most, and the part that was able to make me forget. There would have been no madness without Jack, because without him I would never have escaped from the past. But the past was only biding its time. It was never far away, and slowly it was encroaching on the madness that had kept us together.

You mustn't think that any of this implies I couldn't love you enough. What I realised tonight was how impossible it had become to continue to live with that love, or without it for that matter. Instead I choose to leave with it intact.

It makes me happy that the truth has made friends of you and Jane. Your goodness and your youth will see you both through in whatever path you each choose to take. You must also have a life of your own, but Ada will not stand in your way if you and Jane decide that you'd like not to be far apart.

Writing these inadequate notes is painful enough, and I think that if I made myself reread them I would probably destroy them. I know they fall short of a clear explanation. But my mind at least is clear, and I hope that you'll all find some comfort knowing that I'm choosing this freely, without either fear or regret.

I've always loved the whole of you.

George

Jack had hurried to read out his note the moment he had made my body still, and as soon as he had finished I knew why. As the hardness subsided, I was filled with my father's outpouring of love.

'I'm so sorry, auntie Ada, that was cruel,' I said, but auntie Ada was no longer in the room. Auntie Ada was no longer in the house.

'Stay here, I'll go after her. Jane? What is it?'

In the shadow of the window I was looking at the brooch in the shape of a heart I had just found on the floor.

'I'm coming with you,' I said.

'You should stay here in case she comes back.'

I could feel my head shaking. 'The last time you asked me to stay where I was...'

'The notes,' said Jack, and when I handed him mine, he returned it with the jewellery and his to the magic secret drawer in the headboard. 'Don't worry, she can't have got far.'

'She likes to walk when she's upset, and I know the way she takes when she walks home.'

'We should've caught up with her by now.' Already we had walked along the Pentonville Road all the way to Kings Cross.

'The streets are busy, maybe we missed her,' said Jack.

'There's no way we could've missed her.'

'It's possible she took a different route, if she wanted us to leave her alone.'

'She was tired, I think she must've taken the Underground,' I said. 'We should do the same.' We were now at the bottom of York Way, by the side of Kings Cross Station, wasting time while I tried to decide what we should do.

'That's not a good idea,' said Jack, after wiping his face on his sleeve. 'She can't be thinking straight, she's upset, she hasn't had a wink of sleep or anything to eat, and if she's out in the streets in this heat...'

'It's not that hot yet, it's early.'

'It's nine o'clock, that's not really early. And if you're right and she did take the Underground, she'll be safely at home when we get there.'

'Not if she does something silly, and if she does it'll all be my fault.'

My eyes had been so busy scanning both sides of the road that I hadn't looked at Jack even once. But now he was in front of me, blocking my way.

'Jane, that's ridiculous. Stop being so melodramatic!' His face seemed shrunk with irritation, his words like a belligerent command.

'How can you say that after what happened last night?' I walked almost through him as he flew to one side.

'You're right, I'm sorry. Let's take the Underground if that's what you want.'

'Taxi!' I had stepped into the road, and was waving to the driver to stop, but he already had a fare and after beeping me out of the way he drove on.

'What the hell are you doing, you're going to get yourself run over!' Jack was barking at me now, but I stayed off the kerb with my right arm still half raised, waiting to flag down the first available taxi.

'I need to get there as soon as I can, you can go back to the house if you want,' I yelled over the noise of the traffic, taking two more steps into the road as much to get away from Jack as to make myself easier to see.

'Get back onto the pavement at least, you're being hysterical!' Instead of trying to help me he was howling at me still, but I didn't care, all I cared about right now was auntie Ada. I'd been mean and nasty and horrible to her, and if anything...

'Jane, watch out!' I heard the horn and then Jack's voice and then the screech of wheels. I went rigid in the middle of the road as a car jerked to a halt right in front of me. The man next to the driver was half out of the window and screaming ugly words that made me scared.

My legs had given way, but Jack already had his arm around my waist and I managed to follow him back to the pavement. 'Jesus, Jane,' he said. 'Now come on, we're taking the Underground. Can you walk?'

'I think so.'

'Here, hold onto me.' I put my arm through his and spread my fingers round it. 'Does Ada live far from the station?'

I shook my head to say no.

'But first we need to get you some breakfast, just something quick at the station.'

'I still have the money from last night,' I said. 'You must be hungry too.'

'Starving.' Jack was smiling at last. 'And it won't take long, I promise.'

From now on I would do as he said. My tiredness and my stubbornness had nearly got me killed, and besides, Jack was right, auntie Ada was probably at home doing practical things. That had always been her way of getting on. By now she would have called the library and told them that she wasn't going in, and there were many other arrangements to make. To get started on making them, she might already be on her way back to the house, making sure that Mr Magikoo got the memorable send-off he deserved.

Auntie Ada's was one of six flats in a two-storey building, on the top floor overlooking the street. There was only one bell, but it rang very loudly, and as long as she was in auntie Ada would hear it.

As we turned left into Cyprus Street from Brecknock Road, I tightened my grip of Jack's arm. A police car was just driving off, and one of auntie Ada's neighbours was still at the door.

'Jane, thank God you came!'

'What's wrong, has something happened to auntie Ada? Is that why the police were here?'

'Yes, I mean no. Ada's upset but she's fine. Her flat was broken into but apparently nothing's been taken.'

'Her flat was broken into?'

'And today of all days, well, not broken into exactly, no evidence of breaking in, the police said, so Ada thinks she might have left her door open, which would hardly be surprising. Jane, love, Ada told me, I'm so sorry about your father.'

'Thank you,' I said.

'Come in, come in, where are my manners. He must've come in through this door, it was an easy lock to pick, the police said, definitely we should change it, and then, bingo, Ada's door was open, although her locks are also not so difficult to pick, so who knows... And he was still in the flat, but he ran off as soon as Ada walked in on him, pushed her out of the way and disappeared like a shot down the stairs. You can imagine how frightened she was, he had this black balaclava on, and all Ada could see were his eyes.'

'A black *balaclava*?' I had heard the words but they hadn't quite sunk in, and I repeated them as if to have them contradicted. Could so much really have happened in such a short time?

'She ran downstairs trembling, and I locked my door first and then I called the police.'

'We should check on Ada,' said Jack.

'Jack, this is Miss Williams.'

'Florence, please,' said Miss Williams. 'Your aunt was very lucky, the police said, these people are usually ruthless. And when they took her back upstairs, she couldn't see that anything was missing, the silly balaclava man had run off empty-handed. We were *both* very lucky, it's a small block of flats and no one else was in, God only knows what might've happened if he'd panicked. And if I'd heard any commotion on the stairs, probably I would've opened my door, I'd have been curious, you see, the place is normally so quiet. But first thing I heard was Ada banging on my door. Big, burly man, she said, and he'd slipped down those stairs without a sound.'

'Jane?'

'I'm sorry,' said Miss Williams, 'it's my fault for rabbiting on. Jack's right, you should go on upstairs straight away, Ada said she needed a lie-down but I'm sure she'll be happy to see you, poor thing's had the shock of her life. And make sure she has a nice cup of tea, nothing like a cup of tea to calm your nerves.' She was shouting by then, we were already more than halfway up the stairs.

'Make sure she knows it's you when you knock,' said Jack. 'She's probably still feeling shaken.'

'You're so sweet,' I said, and I reached up on tiptoe and gave him a kiss on the cheek. And just before I knocked on auntie Ada's closed door, 'Auntie Ada, it's me, Jane.' I was about to knock again when I heard auntie Ada unlatching the door from inside. 'Oh my God, auntie Ada, are you okay?' I threw myself at her and squeezed my arms around her, but auntie Ada's stayed limp by her sides.

'I'm fine,' she said stiffly. 'No need to make a fuss.'

'Of course we need to make a fuss, Miss Williams just told us what happened. I mean a man with a black *balaclava*? Inside your flat?'

'Jane, dear, when you get to my age...'

'But it must've been awful for you.'

'Yes, well, Florence likes to exaggerate.'

'She's ordered us to make you a cup of tea,' said Jack.

'Then you better come in.'

The most striking thing about auntie Ada's flat was the wallpaper. Dating from the '50s, its busy abstract pattern had faded, giving it a muted watercolour feel that matched the flat's predominant theme.

'Nice place, Ada,' said Jack. 'Very traditional.'

'You mean old-fashioned,' said auntie Ada.

'But timelessly tasteful.'

'If you say so.'

'I do, I do... although... where's the famous sofa?'

Auntie Ada looked at him vacantly.

'You know, the one I've been sleeping on most frequently.'

As Jack and an unamused auntie Ada sank into opposite armchairs I went to the kitchen to make tea.

Auntie Ada was distant but otherwise remarkably composed for a woman who had just been confronted by an intruder. But after losing her brother in dramatic circumstances just the night before, and then protecting him by lying to the police only to learn from a note addressed to me that her confidences were betrayed and her secrets revealed, it was perhaps no wonder that balaclava man's moment had been a damp squib. We were none of us functioning normally. Bereavement with all its collateral feelings (hurt, anger, distress), intensified by hunger and sleep deprivation, could not but have taken its toll. After my deliberate act of unkindness had caused auntie Ada to flee, I had nearly got myself run over trying to get here. And Jack, who had yelled at me and then saved my life, was now complimenting auntie Ada on her taste, seemingly as unmoved by balaclava man as she was.

But his compliments had failed to break the ice. When I carried the tea back to the living room, while Jack cracked jokes at chatty Florence's expense, auntie Ada was staring at the floor while she twiddled her thumbs in her lap. I poured the tea and sat with my cup on the footstool next to Jack.

'Auntie Ada, I'm so sorry.'

'Mm, what was that, dear?' Auntie Ada had answered too loudly, scraping her stare off the floor and darting it at me as though she had been snapped out of a daydream.

'I'm sorry,' I said again. 'What I did was unforgivable.'

'What you did?' Auntie Ada pinched her brow so hard that her eyes had almost shut.

'I shouldn't have read out daddy's note.'

'No, dear, you shouldn't have. That's why I left the room. The note your father left you was between you and him.'

'I thought you were upset by what he wrote.'

'I haven't got the foggiest what he wrote. *My dear Jane*, that's all I heard.'

'But we were worried, auntie Ada. You could've just asked me to stop.'

'I had no right to ask you to stop. But I had every right not to want to be there.'

'And the brooch?'

'The brooch, dear?'

'I found it on the floor after you left.'

'Then I suppose I must've dropped it.'

I didn't know what else to say. Were we condemned to a permanent conspiracy of silence in which the secrets of the past, which had been unspoken but were now being denied, in effect became lies? Perhaps the truth really was overrated; I kept remembering it had already cost my father his life. Auntie Ada's past was her own, and if she found it too hard to acknowledge, who was I to say that it shouldn't stay hidden? Wasn't this what my father had meant by *the impurities of sadness*?

'I feel like I shouldn't be here,' said Jack. 'I'm nothing to you, Ada, you might want to talk to Jane alone.'

'To talk to Jane alone about what?'

'Things that don't concern me.'

'Auntie Ada, would you rather Jack left us alone?'

'Jack's family now, he's as welcome here as you are, I'm sure it's what George would've wanted.'

'Thank you, Ada.'

I had a taste of my tea. I took the jug of milk out of the tray and stirred a little more into my cup. Then auntie Ada picked up hers and took short consecutive sips.

'Breakfast, auntie Ada, have you had any?'

'I've had no time for breakfast.'

'I could make you some porridge,' I said, but auntie Ada swept away the talk of food.

'Florence said the burglar left completely empty-handed,' said Jack.

'Look around you,' said auntie Ada. 'There's nothing here a thief would want.'

'Oh my God, auntie Ada, where's the Giacometti sculpture?' A thief would want a Giacometti sculpture, at least if he knew what it was, which a random balaclava man probably wouldn't. The train of thought had made me turn to the spot on the mantelpiece, between the reproduction carriage clock and the Staffordshire vase, where the Giacometti sculpture had stood ever since I could remember. And today it wasn't there.

Just as automatically, at the mention of the Giacometti sculpture, auntie Ada's gaze had also shot directly to the very same spot, but then it was immediately averted. 'What Giacometti sculpture?'

'The one you had right there, on the mantelpiece,' I said, pointing with my finger at the missing matchstick figure on a plaster plinth.

'If you mean the copy I overpaid ten francs for, I've thrown it away. I was dusting and I dropped it on the floor and it broke.'

'But you can't have,' I said.

'It's the arthritis, I'm afraid. It's made me rather clumsy.'

I knew she was lying, but I wasn't sure exactly about what. Auntie Ada had walked in on a burglar who had thankfully fled. And now her Giacometti sculpture was missing. The pretence had gone too far.

'Daddy told us the story, auntie Ada. The sculpture was genuine, it wasn't a copy.'

'You're confusing me with all your questions, have you come here to call me a liar?'

'Daddy said in his note that *I* should decide what I should or shouldn't tell you I know. Well, I know how much you love me, and I know you know I love you just as much. But I also know the story of the sculpture.'

'Then I suppose you must know about Jane.'

'Are you sure you wouldn't like me to...' Jack started to get up, but auntie Ada's raised hand had him back in his seat.

'Yes,' I said. 'We know about Jane. But hadn't you already guessed that when you said last night that everything was true?'

'I meant about your mother's accident. George had no business telling you anything else.'

'He also told us how horrible he'd been to you as a child.'

'None of that was his fault.' Auntie Ada sat back in her armchair and brought the fingers of her two hands together.

'And he told us...' I hesitated, partly trying to remember and partly to decide what not to tell.

'George surprised me...' Auntie Ada hesitated too, as though temporarily lost in memories she had suppressed for too long. And then, looking up from the tip of the arch she had made with her hands, 'He was a good man, your father.'

'I know he was.'

'And all I ever did was bear grudges.'

'That wasn't all you did, auntie Ada.'

'But it's too late for everything now.' Again her head was bowed, and it looked like the worst of the past was about to get the better of her.

There was not enough distance. Some of the worst of the past had only just happened, but an unstoppable avalanche was keeping us all on the run, looking over our shoulders at ghosts.

'Ada, would you like a glass of water?' Jack was leaning forward in his chair, his hands already bent on its arms.

'It was supposed to go to you. And now it's gone.'

'But you told the police that nothing was missing,' I said.

'I hadn't realised that anything was, not until you mentioned the sculpture. I mean, how could he have known? None of it makes sense. For the first time in my life I leave my door open, and when a burglar comes in he takes only that. It's like that's what he came for, but it can't have been, no one knew about the sculpture except George. And it looked like nothing, just a small, insignificant thing. That man was a thug, not an art connoisseur. If I'd known it's what he had in his holdall, I'm not sure what I'd have done, not because it was a Giacometti but because it was precious to *me*, the only thing I had to remind me of Jane.'

'I thought there were also some letters,' I said.

'Letters aren't really things.'

'Are you absolutely sure that the burglar was a man?' Jack asked.

'Oh,' said auntie Ada. 'I just assumed he was, but no, I can't say that I'm absolutely sure. Strange that the police never thought to ask me that, I mean I never heard him speak and I never saw any part of him other than his eyes... blue I think they were, but they might've been green, I can't say I felt like staring into them for any length of time.'

'So you didn't see his hands,' said Jack.

'That's another thing,' said auntie Ada, 'middle of summer and he was wearing gloves.'

'Fingerprints,' said Jack.

'But he was definitely big under that coat, had his arms around that holdall, clinging on to it like his life depended on not letting go, so I couldn't even tell you if he had breasts. Yes, I'm pretty sure it was a man, for what it's worth. Unless of course it was a woman.'

'What did the police say?' I asked.

'That I was lucky I wasn't hurt, and lucky that nothing was taken.'

'And is that it, they're not even going to look for him?'

'Jane, dear, I don't *want* them to look for him. How would I explain the sculpture if they found him?'

'But don't you want it back?'

'It's never really mattered what I want...' She pursed her lips and made an effort to swallow. 'It's only a thing, why rake up the past for the sake of a thing?'

'It's an incredibly valuable thing,' said Jack.

'Oh, what difference does it make if it was valuable.'

'It could've got you killed,' I said.

'But it didn't, and now it can't, so good riddance I say,' said auntie Ada. 'It would've made a nice inheritance for you, I know...'

'That's really not important,' I said.

'But at least you'll still be getting the flat. Now please, let's not talk about the sculpture any more, it's gone and that's the end of it. Yes, Jack, I'd like that glass of water if you wouldn't mind fetching it.'

'We're all still in shock,' I said, and I was already getting up to give auntie Ada a hug.

'Are we? I wonder,' answered auntie Ada, and after I had poured myself another cup of tea, which I didn't really want, I made a silent return to my footstool.

'Has Jane been in touch at all?' Jack came back from the kitchen with two glasses of water. He handed auntie Ada hers, and then he offered the other to me. 'Recently, I mean.'

After a long, unmelodious guffaw, auntie Ada was baring her teeth. 'Has *Jane* been in touch?' she snarled. 'Why, Jack, what are you suggesting? That Jane came back to England to steal back the sculpture she gave me?'

Auntie Ada was right. Jack's suggestion, if that was really what it was, was far too outlandish. 'A coincidence is probably more likely than what you're implying,' I said.

'I'm not implying anything,' said Jack, 'except perhaps that sometimes people talk.'

'Did *you* talk, Jack? Because obviously George did.'

Jack raised both his hands above his head. 'You've got me,' he said. 'Balaclava man was Sharon from the hairdressing salon. She's fat and she's *always* wearing gloves, so she fits the description. Oh yes, and she also has blue eyes.'

'Jack didn't know about the sculpture. Daddy told us only yesterday... Auntie Ada, are you sure that it's missing? Mightn't you have moved it somewhere else?'

'I think that if I had I'd remember.'

'Then Jack might have a point.'

Auntie Ada clambered out of her armchair and disappeared into her bedroom.

'Should we tell the police?'

'It isn't up to us to tell them anything,' said Jack. 'You think your father might've told other people?'

'And they just happened to burgle auntie Ada the day after he died?' No sooner had I spoken the words than their meaning resounded in my ears: the day after he died, and already I was speaking of my father as though he had been dead for a year, almost coldly, with the detachment of time that hadn't yet elapsed. But that wasn't how I felt. While I juggled with clues about the disappearance of "a thing" that had not made any difference to anyone's life, in another compartment my grief was being held in abeyance, pleading with me to go home and lock myself up in my box room and cry.

By Jack's distracted gaze I realised auntie Ada was back in the room, but I didn't turn around.

'In case you thought I was lying again,' I heard her say while she was still behind me. 'Here, these are all from *The Times*.' Loose newspaper pages were being spread out on the table.

Socialite, author, philanthropist, Jane Knox Parker...

'Jane's dead,' I said.

'Unless you think *The Times* are in on the burglary too.'

'That's terrible.' Jack leaned forward to turn around one of the pages.

'I'm so sorry, auntie Ada.'

'That's just how I remember her,' said auntie Ada, steadying herself by resting her hand on my shoulder to look over at the page in front of Jack.

'It's a lovely photograph,' said Jack.

'Let me see.' Cupping auntie Ada's hand with mine to hold it in place, I rose from my stool to crouch beside Jack. The obituary had used a formal portrait, which was too funereal. The contrast with the photograph Jack had in front of him couldn't have been greater. Relaxed and smiling broadly, two women sat beside each other on a sofa next to... 'Oh my God, auntie Ada, isn't that Rock Hudson?'

'And that's Jane sitting next to him and looking quite magnificent,' said Jack.

'Oh my God, auntie Ada.'

'"The late Jane Knox Parker sharing an intimate moment with companion Miss Elizabeth Briggs and close friend Mr Rock Hudson."'

'Imagine how miserable I'd have been if I'd gone with her,' said auntie Ada.

'Oh,' I said, 'is that what they mean by "companion"?'

'"Jane Knox Parker, 1921 – 1969",' Jack read out in a whisper.

'Three years older than me and she looked ten years younger,' said auntie Ada. 'She died one month before your father, peacefully in her sleep after a short illness. At least that's what they wrote.'

'Let's go home, auntie Ada, daddy said in his note that you have to look after me now. And he also said he'd like Jack to stay and help us run the shop.'

13

Preparations

Did I believe auntie Ada's story that when the notes were being read out she had already left the room? If she honestly thought that she had no right to hear what my father had written, why couldn't she have asked me to stop? And if she thought that she didn't have the right to ask me to stop, why couldn't she have said she was leaving? *My dear Jane*, a heartbroken man's affectionate words to his daughter, written just before he died and read out when he was dead. Could they really have caused auntie Ada not only to flee, but to also leave behind a brooch that should have been more precious to her even than the Giacometti sculpture?

'Are you sure these were the only two notes?'

Even if her brother's pointed omission had made her feel slighted, auntie Ada had always been a very curious woman.

'I don't think she's telling us the truth, do you?' I'd been sharing my doubts with Jack, who seemed reluctant to have an opinion.

'I've no more idea than you have how much Ada heard, and there's no way of knowing unless she's forced to admit to another lie. What good would that do? She's already been through enough. If they give her some comfort, I think that she's entitled to her secrets and her grievances.'

'And to lies, too?' And when Jack shrugged his shoulders, 'I can't decide either,' I said.

'You don't have to. It's not necessary to decide everything now.'

Jack put his hand over my shoulder and pulled me to the side of the pavement. Ladies' summer hats adorned the crowd of dummies in the window; overlarge and fussy, they seemed hopelessly out of tune with the hats women wore in the streets. But the display of so many dummies and so many hats staring out at passers-by was mesmeric, and we were standing side-by-side looking in.

'I've been meaning to say that I'm happy you heard from your father himself about his good night kisses.'

So it wasn't for the hats or the display that Jack had made us stop. 'It was supposed to be our secret,' I said, not turning to look at him but taking a swing at his arm with my shoulder.

'See? We all need our secrets.'

'But how did you know? Daddy told me you were fast asleep, that he waited until you were snoring. Snoring like a man, he said.'

'Yes, well, the earlier he could kiss you good night, the earlier I could have him back in bed. The first time I saw him sneaking out of the bedroom…'

'You followed him.'

'It nearly made me cry when I saw him standing over you in the dark, watching you sleep before he bent down to kiss you. And I guessed he must've told you…'

'From his note,' I said. '*Tonight I would have kissed you goodnight without hiding.*'

It was unpleasantly hot and humid again, and we were walking home from Angel Station. Sometime in the middle of the night we had both thrown some water over our faces and given our teeth a quick brush, and Jack had replaced his bloodstained T-shirt. I was still in the clothes I had worn to look pretty for Karl. Auntie Ada had asked for a little time alone, to rest, maybe have a quick bite to eat before getting ready. Jack promised that he'd wait with me at the house, but later he'd be off, he wouldn't be staying.

'Ada needs the space to settle in, and I could do with a few days to myself, to give all of us a chance to think things over. And to get some clean clothes, now that I'm not wearing Mia-Mia's.'

Every single mention of auntie Ada brought with it another suspicion of lies. The more I turned the burglary around in my head, the less it made sense. How could auntie Ada not have noticed that the sculpture was missing? The only thing she had to remind her of Jane, that was how she had described it, and yet her first reaction when I saw that it was missing had been to shrug it off as a valueless copy that got smashed while she was dusting.

'If auntie Ada hadn't wanted the police to get involved, why would she have rushed off to Florence and asked her to call them?'

'Because she panicked,' said Jack. 'And to be fair, it can't have been much fun being crept up on by Sharon in a trench coat and a black balaclava. That'd be enough to scare anyone out of their wits.'

'Assuming the burglary actually happened, an hour ago she was accusing you of being the mastermind, and you're still making jokes and trying to find excuses for her.'

'Oh, but she wasn't really accusing me, she was defending Jane. Poor woman, she's had shock after shock after shock, it's hardly any wonder that she's being a bit unstable. And why would you even doubt that the burglary happened? The sculpture is obviously missing.'

'It's missing but she doesn't seem to care about getting it back.'

'And she's explained to us why.'

'I don't believe she hadn't noticed it was missing, and I'm not sure it's missing because it was stolen. Don't you think it's possible she smashed it herself? I mean deliberately, not while she was dusting. Jane's death must've really upset her. Then she saw those pictures in the paper, and maybe she got jealous.'

'Jealous of what, Jane canoodling with Rock Hudson?'

'Of Jane canoodling with Rock Hudson and her new companion.'

'I don't think so,' said Jack. 'But even if she did, she didn't know you knew that the sculpture was a genuine Giacometti, so why would she have gone to all that trouble of inventing balaclava man and calling the police?'

'Because unless she was still in the room when we both read them out, she didn't know what daddy might've written in the notes... And if she's lying and she was in the room and she *does* know, then maybe she smashed the Giacometti this morning because she was angry... But then why would she have called the police?'

'Listen, Jane...' We were already at the heart of the spaghetti maze that led to the house, around one more intestine and we'd be there. When Jack stopped, I stopped too.

'I know,' I said. 'It's not necessary to decide everything now.'

'I'm just worried that it's all been too crazy, you've not even had a minute...'

'To think about what happened to my dad?'

'To think about *yourself*... Ada's right in a way, this isn't the time to be worrying about "things". It doesn't really matter what happened to the sculpture.' When Jack gave me his hand I took it, and we zigzagged one last time before...

I hadn't been mistaken. A woman in dark glasses and a headscarf was hesitating at the bottom of the steps, looking up at the house as though to gauge the likelihood of it collapsing if she went any further.

'Jesus,' said Jack. 'These people are like vultures.'

'These people?'

'Hacks.'

'Is that another word for Germans?'

'It's another word for tabloid scum, not for Germans,' said Jack. 'It looks like our sergeant's been busy. Don't say a word, I'll handle this.'

'But Dr Schmidt isn't a hack, she's Karl's mother.'

'Ah, so that's the Reichian therapist. Then I'll leave all the talking to you.'

'Dr Schmidt,' I said coldly, letting go of Jack's hand as we drew near the gate.

Karl's mother jumped, but managed to compose herself quickly.

'Jane,' she said, 'I wasn't sure if you were in.'

'I wasn't,' I said.

'No,' said Dr Schmidt, and after a short awkward silence, 'I'm so sorry about your father; I came over to tell you in person as soon as I could. Inspector Cambridge came to see us this morning to have a word with Karl, and he told us what happened.'

'I see.' I was annoyed with the Inspector, who should have known to keep his mouth shut, and irritated with Frau Angela's presumption. Had she asked herself before just turning up if I would want to see her? Could she really have imagined that the answer might be yes? And yet here she was, and I was too polite to ask her to leave. 'Jack, this is Dr Schmidt. Jack's a family friend.'

'This is an intrusion, I know,' said Dr Schmidt after shaking Jack's hand, 'but after everything that's happened... Jane, could we talk somewhere more private?'

'Jack was there, Dr Schmidt. He probably knows more about what happened than you do.'

'I have a couple of phone calls to make, and a million things to do in the shop. Perhaps you could offer Dr Schmidt a cup of tea?'

'Angela, please. And thank you.' Dr Schmidt bowed her head to Jack, and as she tilted it in my direction she took her sunglasses off. 'Just ten minutes,' she said. 'I think it's important.'

I agreed with a half-hearted nod and led the way up the steps.

I showed Dr Schmidt straight to the kitchen, and after I had made and poured the tea, I joined her at the table. Jack, as promised, had already disappeared into the shop. He had asked for my permission to put up a sign to say that owing to bereavement the shop would be closed until further notice.

'How are you feeling?' It was too big a question, but Dr Schmidt had asked it in a way that seemed to take the complexity of my emotions for granted. I felt it more as an acknowledgment, rather than a question.

'I'm feeling like I've just lost my father.'

'Yes, of course,' said Dr Schmidt. 'And that goes without saying, but at the same time it's important to be said. Talking is *extremely* important.'

'It hasn't really sunk in yet.'

'That's perfectly normal.' Dr Schmidt put down her cup and sat upright, with her hands in a knot on the table. 'In my experience your feelings will crystallise slowly. Right now there's just too much to process, and it can't all be processed at once, so this isn't the time, I think it's too soon. But my door is always open if you think it might be helpful to speak with a professional. You'll feel better if you're able to let go of your anger.'

'I don't know if I feel any anger.'

'You mustn't feel bad if you do,' said Dr Schmidt.

'We finally managed to talk.'

'You made peace.'

'Yes.'

'But then your father...'

'Yes. And I miss him.'

'As I say, my door is always open.'

'Dr Schmidt, your son tried to rape me.'

'Karl is immature, and that's *my* fault...'

'I was asking him to stop, I asked him again and again and he wouldn't. He was violent, Dr Schmidt, and if I hadn't found the strength to push him off, both our lives would've probably been ruined. He's seventeen years old. He tried to rape me and it was *his* fault. Can't you see? It's Karl who needs help, not me.'

'Jane, this could destroy his career if it ever...'

'It won't,' I said, 'but I think you should go now.'

'We told Inspector Cambridge...'

'I don't care what you told Inspector Cambridge, and it's not Inspector Cambridge you should care about either, *or* Karl's career. But that's between you and your son.'

'Karl's genuinely sorry, he wants you to know that.'

'And you can tell him I'll never be able to stop feeling sorry for him.'

I was glad to have got rid of Dr Schmidt so conclusively. Had auntie Ada been around, the conversation could have hardly moved beyond commiseration; to take all the blame for the violence of her "immature" son, Karl's mother would have had to come back. It wasn't untrue; Karl really was immature. His genius and the mollycoddling by his mother had combined to make it hard for him to know where the lines were that should never be crossed.

When auntie Ada arrived with her suitcase, Jack had showered and had nothing clean to wear. I had washed his T-shirt from the night before, but the stains hadn't budged, so he had taken off the one he had changed into and I had washed that as well. It was hanging on the back of a chair in my father's bedroom, drying in the scorching patch of sun that now flooded one third of the room – Jack had pulled the heavy curtains wide open. His jeans were dirty too, but they would have taken too long to dry, and they were wearable. He insisted that he didn't need underwear or socks, and I left him stretched out on the bed while he waited for his T-shirt to at least not be soaking.

I wanted Jack to stay, but the deeper truth was that I missed Mia-Mia and my father. "The truth" again... Dr Schmidt had been right about one thing: my feelings were in constant flux, and apparently so was the truth. I missed Mia-Mia and my father only because Mia-Mia had been Jack, and through Jack I had discovered that behind his façade of indifference my father had been someone else.

'Hello, Ada.' At last Jack had emerged from the bedroom fully dressed.

'I hope you're hungry,' auntie Ada smiled at him over her shoulder.

'Starving.' He was stretching out his tallness at the kitchen door, while auntie Ada chopped up vegetables for a chicken casserole.

'Are you sure you have somewhere to go?' I asked Jack from my perch on the stained wooden worktop.

'It's bad luck to swing your legs,' auntie Ada told me.

'I've spoken with Sharon already,' said Jack.

'Who's Sharon?'

'You know Sharon, she's the blue-eyed fat girl who stole your auntie Ada's Giacometti.'

'That was never a woman,' mumbled auntie Ada.

'Is she nice?'

'Sharon's lovely. She'll be glad of the company, she said, and while I'm there I'll give her something for the rent. She's got a roomful of my clothes already, and she lives right above the salon, so it's handy for both of us really.'

'She's single then, I take it,' said auntie Ada.

'Um,' said Jack, 'that depends on the night of the week.'

Still with her back to him, auntie Ada swung the chopping knife in circles through the air. 'Swinging '60s,' she quipped, 'it'll all end in tears.'

Motherless, then fatherless, hadn't it all ended in tears already? I refused to let the thought take hold. 'Will you still be Mia-Mia at the salon?'

'No more Mia-Mia,' said Jack.

'All those clothes,' lamented auntie Ada.

'Jumble sale,' said Jack, and as he pulled out a chair he beckoned me to join him at the table.

'They're all much too modern for a jumble sale. And those shoes are monstrous.'

'Oh, stop it, auntie Ada, who cares about the bloody clothes.'

'Watch your mouth, young lady.'

'They should stay where they are for the moment,' said Jack.

'But I liked Mia-Mia, you can't just kill her off!' With my arms folded over my chest, I was staring at the table ready to burst into tears. Neither the bad luck of swinging legs nor the tears of the '60s had upset me, but to hear Jack pronounce the demise of Mia-Mia was like hearing for the first time that my father was dead.

'*She* had a mouth on her too,' said auntie Ada, 'especially after visiting her brother's bed-and-breakfast in Torquay.'

'You don't know anything,' I said, lashing out at her viciously without looking up. 'You think you're clever and we're stupid but it's actually the other way around. For years you blamed daddy for what wasn't his fault, but you throw a silly tantrum just because he hasn't left you a note. He's dead, auntie Ada, he's dead and you're *still* telling lies. You're just bitter and selfish and you can't get over messing up your life.'

'Jane, you're not being fair, that's enough,' said Jack.

'You made daddy happy and she made your life hell, but you're always defending her.'

'I'm defending her because I know she loves you. Look at me, Jane.' And when I let him lift my head up just a little, 'Can you remember what you said to your dad? Last night, when you were trying to explain how you felt about losing your mum.'

'But I couldn't,' I said. 'I couldn't explain it, it didn't make sense.'

'You told him that you didn't have to say you didn't blame him because you knew that he wasn't to blame.'

'He wasn't, auntie Ada, he wasn't.'

Jack took my hands into his. 'Can you remember what you told him after that?'

'That for everything else I forgave him, because the things that happened after we lost mum didn't count, they were all part of a madness that couldn't be helped.'

'The madness of grief, isn't that what you called it? His and yours but also Ada's, that's what you said to your dad. And it's true now more than ever.'

'But it made no difference, how can it be true if it wasn't enough?'

'If your father was here he'd say that it was more than enough, that no words in the world could've made him feel more loved or more grateful.'

'But what about *me*, what about how *I* feel?'

'Sometimes it's enough to remember, because the madness has to end and there's no other choice.'

'I'll not stay if I'm not wanted,' said auntie Ada meekly, and I sought out her gaze to give her the briefest caress. Then I fell forward and covered my face with my hands, to weep for my father again.

The next few days were quiet, dulled by the concentrated drama of those terrible twenty-four hours. While she busied herself with making arrangements, auntie Ada wore her brooch every day, but her love for my mother remained undeclared, and the notes had stayed hidden. After my outburst I decided not to mention them again unless auntie Ada herself brought them up. And everyone had known not to allow my angry words to take root. It was as if they had never been spoken.

Jack called me every day. The ladies he coiffed were apparently delighted with his male incarnation, and glad to see the back of Mia-Mia.

'They didn't like her prickly sense of humour, apparently it grated on their nerves - and they *are* all rather nervous, my ladies.' He was always making jokes, trying to cheer me up. 'Whereas Jack, as you know, is unremittingly charming, and so incredibly handsome too!'

'You mean you flirt with them,' I said.

'And my tips have trebled. Flirting's proving much more popular than gossip, my ladies are lapping it up!'

'Have you told them that Jack used to be Mia-Mia?' I was fascinated with the transformation.

'Even if I did at the beginning, they all seem to have quickly forgotten.'

'But aren't they curious about your *other* life?'

'My other life's always been private. I never discuss it, except in general terms.'

'You must've discussed it with Sharon.'

'In general terms.'

'So she knows...'

'That I'm gay? Oh, I think everyone knows *that*, it adds to the attraction. And we've talked about the riots, of course, which were much more important than landing a couple of men on the moon, but no one knows about your dad or Shepherd's Bush.'

'Gay?'

'Apparently that's how we like to call ourselves these days. Personally I've never minded "queer".'

'I prefer "gay",' I said.

'So do most of the ladies who flirt with me,' said Jack.

'But I didn't know there'd been any riots.'

'Not here, in New York, end of June, just hours after Judy Garland's funeral, and yet another brutal raid on a gay bar. Having already cried their hearts out for Judy, people felt raw, and they finally decided that enough was enough. I make jokes, but actually it was quite a big thing - and a long time coming, believe me. Now if Ada's around I'd like a quick word.' At the end of every call, Jack would always make a point of including auntie Ada, and not only for just a quick word. I would stay close by, and the three of us would discuss in a three-way conversation the arrangements auntie Ada was making.

We were all in agreement that Mr Magikoo should get a fitting send-off. When auntie Ada arranged for a notice to be placed in *The Weekly Magic News,* inviting friends and colleagues to his funeral at *Hypnos Crematorium* in Essex, for a couple of days the telephone didn't stop ringing. Neither auntie Ada nor I had appreciated just how well respected and loved Mr Magikoo had remained right up until the end of his life. The numerous condolences were invariably overfilled with accolades: one of the few true greats; tragically cut down in his prime; sorely missed after retiring from the circuit prematurely; his brilliance undimmed even after tragedy had struck; bold; inventive; without the shadow of a doubt a true original.

Monsieur Legerdemain had been particularly effusive, and had charmed us into agreeing that the secular service should be part of a grand show of magic in whose spectacular finale Mr Magikoo would be cut into two, before being dispatched to be cremated.

'Oh no, I don't think we'd like *that*,' a horrified auntie Ada had gasped. 'He wants to cut your father in half,' she whispered, covering the speaker with her hand.

'I know,' I whispered back. I could hear Monsieur Legerdemain's every word: he spoke incredibly loudly, and auntie Ada always held the receiver away from her ear.

'But, Madame, we're illusionists, n'est-ce pas? It will be a special coffin, and the corpse will not be harmed, you have my word. And the word of Monsieur Legerdemain is his bond.'

'It'll be a special coffin, he says. Your father won't be harmed, we have his word.'

'I think daddy would've *loved* the idea, tell him yes.'

'Hello, Monsieur Legerdemain, are you there?'

'At your service, Madame.'

'My niece and I both like the idea *in principle*, but we were wondering how much this special coffin would cost?'

'But now you are insulting me, Madame. Mr Magikoo was one of us, a dear friend and a comrade, you will not be charged a single penny for *any* of our illusions.'

'That's very generous, Monsieur,' giggled auntie Ada. 'Thank you, then my niece and I are happy to accept your proposal.'

'Excellent, excellent, and it is, I believe, what Mr Magikoo would've wanted. Naturally we shall all coordinate with *Hypnos Crematorium*, and I promise you a day to remember. Please convey my regards to your charming niece, and assure her, Madame, that we all share your pain most sincerely.'

When I told him the news, Jack wasn't quite as thrilled as I had hoped.

'A show of *magic*?'

'It's what daddy would've wanted.'

'At his *funeral*?'

'Yes. He wasn't a conventional man.'

'No, you're right, he wasn't.'

'And he held Monsieur Legerdemain in *very* high regard, he always said so.'

'But are you sure he'd have wanted him to cut him in half?'

'He's not *really* going to cut him in half. It'll be a special coffin, I told you.'

'With your father inside it?'

'I suppose so,' I said, but I wasn't sure.

'And the *Hypnos* people are okay with it?'

'Why wouldn't they be? We don't have all the details yet, but there's going to be a programme and everything. All the arrangements are being made...'

'By Monsieur Lemonade.'

'Please don't make fun, Jack, daddy's funeral isn't a joke.'

'You're the ones who want to cut him in half.'

'No we *don't*! Monsieur Legerdemain is an illusionist, he's not the local butcher.'

'I'm sure that's what the rabbits used to think about your dad.'

'Well, there won't be any rabbits at the funeral,' I said. 'There won't be any animals at all, auntie Ada made that clear. Just a single white dove at the end.'

'Oh God, in how many pieces?'

'You're just *mean*,' I said, and I hung up, but Jack called back straight away and I answered.

'You're right, it's just what your dad would've wanted.'

'I really think so,' I said.

True to his word, Monsieur Legerdemain had taken care of everything. The programmes were ready to be printed, *Hypnos Crematorium* had expressed some very minor reservations regarding noise and the use of pyrotechnics indoors, but they had all been ironed out, and yes, there would be a switch of coffins just before the cremation. By the time my father disappeared behind a curtain to be burnt, the coffin that transported him would be the solidly solemn Hypnos Triple Deluxe.

In a later call, Monsieur Legerdemain had insisted that the cutting of the coffin in half would be very much short of a spectacular finale unless people had seen with their own eyes that Mr Magikoo was actually inside it.

'So during the performance, the top half of your brother's special coffin will naturally have to stay open.'

This had come as a rather unexpected shock.

'Oh no, I don't think we'd like *that*,' a horrified auntie Ada had gasped again. 'He's insisting on a half-open coffin,' she whispered with her hand over the speaker. And then returning to Monsieur Legerdemain, 'My brother's been dead for almost a month, he'll hardly be looking his best.'

'But, Madame, I've just seen him, and I assure you, they've done a splendid job at *Hypnos*, our Mr Magikoo looks like an angel asleep. He has a *beautiful* colour, he's so rosy it's hard to believe that sadly he's no longer of this world.'

Again I could hear every word, but this time I snatched the receiver out of auntie Ada's crooked hands. The idea of my father's bloated head, chemically embalmed then smeared with garish make-up and presumably bereft of its toupee, staring out of a coffin while Monsieur Legerdemain was pretending to be cutting it in half, had made my eyes pop. It was literally sacrilege, and I wouldn't allow it.

'Hello, Monsieur, this is Jane Hareman... that's right, his daughter... yes, she did pass on your condolences, thank you... I wouldn't say we're looking forward to it exactly, no... Look, Monsieur Legerdemain, there's no way we'll agree to an open coffin, and if that means a less spectacular finale... your *reputation*, Monsieur? No, I don't see why people need to *see* him in the coffin... but it's his funeral, where else would he be?'

I would have rather had the funeral cancelled than agree to an open coffin, and in the end Monsieur Legerdemain had given in.

'Fine,' he said. 'But this is *not* what your father would've wanted.'

'What a hideous little man,' auntie Ada screeched as soon as the receiver had returned to its cradle. 'The truth is, I've *never* liked the French. They're rude, and they deliberately lose their wars so that other people have to fight them for them!'

'Auntie Ada, that's not true. And anyway, the hideous little man isn't actually French.'

'He's not?'

'He calls you Madame and throws in the occasional "n'est-ce pas", but to be fair to him he doesn't even try to sound French.'

'So where's he from if he's not French?'

'According to *The Weekly Magic News* he's from Wales. Monsieur Legerdemain is just a stage name.'

'He's from *Wales*?'

'Aberystwyth,' I said. 'I thought you'd be glad.'

'Glad? Why should I be glad? At least the French have class, what on earth do the Welsh have?'

'Auntie Ada, you're a snob.'

'They did have Dylan Thomas, I suppose... Oh, I'm only pulling your leg. Of course I knew Monsieur Legerdemain wasn't French. N'est-ce pas, my foot!'

Jack's reaction to the suggestion of an open coffin had less of the "I told you so" about it than I had expected.

'To be honest, Jane, I can't say I'm surprised. These people are showmen...'

'My father was a showman too.'

'And maybe he's right, this Monsieur Legerdemain. Maybe it's what George would've wanted.'

'To be displayed without his toupee as a prop, looking like a clown? I don't think so!'

'Because it isn't what *you* want, nor is it what *I* want. And it's too late to ask George, so I think that's where the flaw is, pretending that we're doing all this for him. We're doing it for ourselves, but in the end it hardly makes any difference. What we'll remember is your father and the fact that he's gone, not how good the show was at his funeral.'

'I miss you,' I said. 'You haven't been to visit me once.'

'I call you every day.'

'It's not the same. And daddy wanted you here.'

'That's not fair.'

'I don't care about being fair.'

'After the funeral I promise we'll sit down and discuss things. I just need these few days to myself.'

'And then you'll come back?'

'Only if you still want me to.' Jack's words had fallen short of reassurance. I suspected there were other factors too – auntie Ada, perhaps, or his job at the salon – that were weighing against what I wanted.

I clung to Jack's advice – to let go of but also to learn from the past - and I tried to be nice to auntie Ada, which generally meant keeping out of her way. As the day of the funeral drew closer, instead of becoming more subdued, she seemed to almost revel in the petty distractions of detail. While I gorged on every scrap of paper that helped piece together my father's career, preparing for the few words I wanted to say while my father changed coffins, she was either on the telephone or out – window-shopping for a funeral dress, checking up on the florist, running around on unspecified errands. Jack was right. When it finally happened, the funeral would last but a very short moment, followed by anti-climax and the eternity of life without my father. But for now it was keeping us busy.

With just forty-eight hours to go before the big event, while auntie Ada was out again I felt a sudden urge to take a look inside *Mr Magikoo's Magik Shoppe*. Since going on a search party for auntie Ada I had barely stepped out of the house, and as I squinted at the brightness of the sun after I had double-locked the door, wondering if I should buy myself a pair of sunglasses before the funeral, the shifting, animated blur at the end of the road gradually began to take shape. It was Sergeant Morris, engaging Auntie Ada in what appeared to be a deep conversation. When auntie Ada moved, blocking my view of the sergeant, I unlocked the door to the shop and closed it very quietly behind me. After the Inspector's warnings, I suspected that the sergeant was probably attempting to extract from auntie Ada the kind of "colourful" or "lurid" information he knew he would be able to sell. And no doubt auntie Ada was telling Sergeant Morris to sod off.

There was a pile of mail on the doormat, an untidy little mountain, unusually multi-coloured. The brown of officialdom was sparse, and as I scooped all the envelopes up, not intending to go through them until after the funeral but rather just to move them from the floor to the counter, I could see that the bulk of them had been addressed to "Mr Magikoo", some in calligraphic handwriting, others typewritten, and quite a number of them in a childish scrawl. Like The Beatles and Santa Claus and Hollywood stars, my father had fans! Some of them might not even have heard that Mr Magikoo had passed on. Their letters would make painful reading, but I was determined to reply individually to all of them.

And then I saw it: the only envelope without a stamp, addressed simply to "Jane", the four letters almost etched into the paper in Karl's characteristically tight, left-handed scribble. His separated, non-cursive handwriting had always reminded me of musical notes - I would have recognised it anywhere. And as I did, all the other envelopes fell out of my hand, cascading like a waterfall of paper back into a pile on the floor.

Leaning with my elbows on the counter, I held it right in front of my eyes, looking at the unopened envelope without really seeing it, as though it existed not in any physical form but only as a dilemma. My alertness was so acutely without focus that I felt my sudden wetness and the thumping in my chest only as the symptoms of a distant disturbance. Lost in thought, I was conscious only of not being able to think.

It was my body that was first to kick back into action. I wouldn't have known if Karl's unopened letter had filled me with anger, or excitement, or uncertainty, or some other entirely new emotion that I couldn't have described. Any sense of sequence was absent, until my hands had removed from the envelope the single sheet of paper and my focus had returned and the marks became letters that combined to form words that united into sentences that made up the letter I had just finished reading, and then had finished reading again.

Containing neither an excuse nor an explanation, it was as if Karl's real intention had not been a matter of choice, as if tomorrow at 3pm was also not a matter of choice...

At 3pm every day of the week except Saturday, with all the windows open I sit at the piano to play, and I always start with "Jane". It's a piece I've composed as a favour not to you but to myself, and for a short time it brings back to life the Jane I will always remember...

The letter asked for nothing, and by asking for nothing it succeeded inadvertently in asking for everything. I knew Karl well, and in spite of what had happened I knew that this effect could not have been the consequence of calculation. Karl was an innocent who wrote as he spoke, and in that artless, unstudied impulsiveness I might have found a reason to forgive him. The Karl who had tried to force himself on me was different from the Karl I remembered, but their difference somehow stemmed from their sameness, and this made it easier to consider his lapse as a single stray moment in "the madness of love". Or perhaps all the madness was mine.

14

"Jane"

I had hardly slept, and it made me feel selfish and ashamed that on the day before my father's funeral not only had the cause of my sleeplessness been something else, it had also given me pleasure. And now that I had staggered out of bed, glad that the night was behind me and the day had begun, I felt my selfishness and shame dissolve like a dream, leaving behind, in some distant corner, just a dull pang of remorse. The pleasure, however, continued to be overwhelming.

It had occurred to me often that all the world's suffering stemmed from disagreement between men as to what was good or bad. Well, that might be true, but in my recent experience suffering was often self-inflicted, and stemmed from a similar dispute within one's own conscience. I thought of how my father's life had ended, how auntie Ada had only half-lived hers, how Mia-Mia's had almost been perverted by her visits to her brother's bed-and-breakfast in Torquay. I was more than just assuaging my guilt. I was asserting my right to override it.

What I was feeling after reading Karl's letter didn't contradict or diminish how I felt about losing my father, or about anything else. But it had an urgency that I was powerless to resist. All my other feelings were passive; Karl's letter was pressing. It required me first to make and then to act on a decision, and the uncertainty of that process was too overcrowding, leaving little room...

'Penny for your thoughts.'

Coming to with a jolt, I was in the kitchen, looking into the refrigerator as though the answers to all the questions in the world were to be found on its shelves. I hadn't even noticed auntie Ada, who was standing with a mop in the corner of the room behind the table. I was barefoot, and when I looked at the square linoleum tiles of the floor they were wet, and I could trace the imprint of my footsteps backwards all the way to the door.

'I'm sorry, auntie Ada, I didn't see you.'

'If you're looking for the milk it's on the table.'

Milk, cornflakes, sugar, it was all on the table, along with bowls and cups and saucers.

'Breakfast,' said auntie Ada. 'We have it every morning. I'll put the kettle on, shall I?'

'Breakfast, yes,' I said. 'Have you not had yours already?'

'I thought I'd wait for you today, to make sure you're okay. Are you okay? Sit yourself down, you still look a little bit off.'

'Off?'

'And you're still acting odd.'

'Acting odd?'

'There you go again. Maybe you should get something down you and go back to bed, it's the funeral tomorrow.'

'I'm not sure what you mean, auntie Ada.'

I sat at the table, and after putting the kettle on auntie Ada joined me.

'Why, why did you have to go upsetting yourself, two days before your father's funeral?' She passed me a spoon and filled our bowls with cornflakes. 'I mean you've *never* liked the shop.'

'Things are different now,' I said. 'And I've already told you, I was checking the post. In case there was something urgent.' While auntie Ada made the tea, I sprinkled one, two, three tablespoons of sugar on my cornflakes and drowned them in milk.

'And was there?'

'I don't think so,' I shrugged. 'I just put it to one side, I didn't go through it.'

'And how's that "checking the post", may I ask? You went in there for nothing and came back in a *right* state, wouldn't talk, wouldn't eat, and so flushed that I thought you must be running a fever.'

'I'm feeling much better now.' And to prove it, I took a large mouthful of my soggy cornflakes, but they were far too sweet, even for me. I forced myself to have another mouthful, but if I had any more I'd be sick. If I were auntie Ada, I'd be worried too. After coming back from the shop, where I had stayed for many hours, everything had seemed like a monumental effort, and under some pretext I couldn't remember I had managed to escape to my room.

'Did you sleep well at least?' Auntie Ada poured the tea.

'Like a baby,' I said. 'I'm still a bit groggy, that's all.'

'Go on, get that down you, it's no good just stirring it about with your spoon. And I'll make us some toast. Are you sure you're okay?'

'I'm fine, auntie Ada, really. You're right, I shouldn't have gone to the shop, but I've been cooped up in here for so long that I felt like a change.'

'And you got yourself upset.'

'I suppose so.'

When the toast arrived, to make up for abandoning the cornflakes I asked for three slices, munching them down quickly, to prove to auntie Ada that my appetite had been restored.

'I thought I might pop out later on, to get some fresh air and try and clear my head of all the cobwebs.'

'I've a thousand calls I still need to make,' sighed auntie Ada.

'Then you'll be glad to have me out of the way.'

'I daresay, if you're sure you're okay.'

'I'm feeling fine, auntie Ada, I promise. By the way, when I was going into the shop I saw you talking to that awful sergeant...'

'What awful sergeant?'

'Sergeant Morris; the Inspector warned us he'd be fishing for dirt.'

'Oh, yes, the sergeant, he completely slipped my mind.'

Auntie Ada looked embarrassed, as flushed as her description of how flushed I had looked the previous evening.

'Was he rude to you, auntie Ada? If he was we should call the Inspector.'

'No, no, he was perfectly civil, we just happened to bump into each other on my way back from the shops, and he was asking me about the funeral, that's all.'

'I hope he's not thinking of being there.'

'He never mentioned.' Auntie Ada hesitated, as though trying to remember. 'But no, I shouldn't think so.'

I had again paid attention to what I was wearing: a stiff white blouse, a pair of blue jeans and my sandals. I was in Cross Street at 3 minutes to 3, and at 3pm exactly came the proof that I had made the right decision. Any traces of doubt that I may have harboured still were washed away by the furious first minutes of the music that gushed through the open windows. That initial violence struck me not as any tribute to myself, as Karl had claimed in his letter, but as a visceral and abject self-denunciation, until it literally broke into a drifting in the wind of a thousand elegiac lamentations. And then, just as abruptly, it shuddered as it struck out far, far ahead of itself, as though in a cajoling exhortation to the future: in the language of despair, it spoke to me only of hope.

I had always thought of music simply as the stirring of emotions with sound. I had never understood it in any other way, and could judge it only by the strength of the emotions it had stirred. I saw no difference between Beethoven and Bowie, and whenever Karl had asked me I had never been able to put into words why I might have found Rachmaninoff's *Etude Tableaux* more stirring than Liszt's *Feux Follets*. 'What does that even mean, you found it more "stirring"?' Karl would ask. 'Can't you give me something more concrete?' And I would always answer that I couldn't, because wasn't that precisely the thing about music, that it wasn't something concrete?

"Jane" was different. It had stirred my emotions, but it had stirred them very specifically, in a way that had communicated meaning to me. 'There's nothing in the world that's more concrete than music,' Karl had told me, but only now had I understood what he meant. And when "Jane" came to an end I remained where I stood, alone in a street that was rarely so deserted; it was as if it had reserved itself exclusively for me. Then Karl came to the window, as he must have every other day since delivering his letter by hand, and when his gaze fell on mine I held on to it tensely; when he lifted the open palm of his hand I did the same; when his face dared to break into a smile so did mine, at exactly the same moment. And when he disappeared from the window, I knew that very shortly he would be at the door, and already I had stepped into the road and was crossing the street.

With the door still ajar just behind us, we put our arms around each other, and when I rested the side of my head on his shoulder I could feel the warmth of his breath in my hair. Then I broke away a little, to lean back and look at him directly in the eyes. But as my lids became heavy, I felt the distance between us dissolve, and our mouths came together in a kiss that had the softness but also the passion that all our other kisses had lacked.

'I'm sorry,' said Karl, and when I told him to shush while our noses and our foreheads still touched, he shook his head lightly and he said it again. 'I'm sorry.'

'I know,' I said.

'What I did...'

Tilting backwards again, I put the flat of my hand against his mouth. 'Let's just forget it.'

'I don't want to forget it. I want it always there, to remind me what I don't want to be.'

'But you're not. And if I thought that you needed reminding I wouldn't be here.'

'It wasn't me who called the police.'

'I guessed that,' I said.

'I left the note in the shop in case it was too soon to get in touch. I'm really sorry about your dad.'

'At least we managed to talk.'

'You made peace, Frau Angela told me.'

'Yes, she came to see me.'

'I'm sorry about that too.'

'She's your mother, what choice did she have?'

'The choice to let me pay for my mistakes,' said Karl. 'But everybody wanted to protect me, even you.'

'You got a broken nose for your mistakes, let me see?' I held his face in place to examine it closely, and could see the fading bruises under his eyes, but the nose seemed as straight as it had always been. 'Just a bloody nose and a pair of black eyes,' I corrected myself.

'When he came to see us the second time, I think the Inspector knew, but he wouldn't let me tell him. He said I should write you a letter instead, if there was any explanation to be made it was you it should be made to. But there wasn't, so I wrote you a letter without one.'

Only then did I notice as though in the haze of a daydream that Karl and I were practically dressed in identical clothes. His white shirt had bigger collars and was better ironed, and his jeans were a slightly lighter shade... I was too close to him to see what he was wearing on his feet, but I imagined him wearing his flip-flops. It was a stupid detail, but it did make my feeling more intense: without Karl I would never feel complete. It was a feeling that brought with it a new anxiety - what if I was wrong?

'I'm glad you did,' I said, refusing to even countenance a thought that perhaps only a lifetime together could settle. 'And I'm even more glad that I found it when I did.'

'I would've waited,' said Karl.

'But I'm not ready for sex yet.'

'I'm obviously not either,' Karl answered without looking at me, and after I had used all my fingers to ruffle his hair, 'Can I play "Jane" one more time for you? Or don't you want to come in?'

'Only if you have ice cream,' I said, and when Karl nodded I pushed the door shut.

'It's been too hot,' he said, as we made our way through to the kitchen.

'Let's not talk about the weather, it reminds me too much of auntie Ada.' I leaned against the bright Formica worktop and watched Karl scoop some ice cream into bowls. It was mixed vanilla and chocolate with pieces of crushed meringue.

'How is she, your aunt?'

I couldn't help rolling my eyes. 'I wouldn't have a clue where to begin.' And when Karl's curiosity had united his eyebrows, 'Come to the funeral,' I said, 'it'll be fun.'

'Fun?'

'We thought we'd celebrate his life with a magic show. It's what we think dad would've wanted.' Karl gave a tentative nod. 'Mm, the ice cream's divine,' I said. 'Oh, and he's being cut into two for the finale, I nearly forgot.'

'Your *father*?' Now Karl's incredulity had made his eyebrows part and twist upwards into spirals.

'You pull such faces,' I laughed. 'Don't worry; he's not *really* being cut into two. And someone's going to be there I'd like you to meet.'

'Can I ask you a personal question?' Karl was nervously stirring the last of his ice cream. And when I answered with my eyes that he could, 'Why would your father want to kill himself? Especially after you talked. And what about this girl he was seeing, you said they were happy.'

'Come to the funeral,' I said. 'It'll make it easier to explain.' I thought about that word, "explain", and immediately I wanted to change it. 'Not explain, exactly. I mean it was a shock, the last thing I expected, but then so many unexpected things have happened... I think I lost my dad when we all lost mum. I'm trying to accept it without feeling angry or loving him less. In fact I've never loved him more. Does any of that make sense?'

'My dad ran off to Australia with a leaning tower of Pisa from Sweden, do I actually want things to make sense?' Karl's smile moved closer to mine.

'Someone's stolen auntie Ada's Giacometti,' I managed in a heavy breath, just before my cold lips met Karl's.

Watching Karl play it made "Jane" even more categorical. I stood in my usual place by the piano, taking in Karl - the abrupt and brittle movements of his head, the tension on his face and neck, the deftness of his long slender fingers - while being stirred in my entirety by the first piece of music that was speaking to me personally.

When he stopped and placed his spread-out fingers on his legs, his eyes briefly shut, exhaling as though to let out any remnant of the music before getting up, already I was moving behind him, to reach over his shoulders and tighten his chest with my overlapping forearms, the side of my head lightly nestled in the nape of his neck.

'Thank you,' I said.

While he was locked in that contorted position, his hands found mine and briefly brushed against them. 'It's me who should be thanking you. "Jane" would never have happened without you.'

'It did happen without me,' I said, standing back as Karl swivelled round to face me.

And as I offered him my hands, which this time he held onto, 'There hasn't been a moment without you,' he said.

'But it wouldn't have happened if we hadn't fallen out, is that what you meant?'

'If the slightest thing had been different.'

Perhaps it should have made me uncomfortable, this theory of his that everything had happened for a reason: if anything, the last few days had been governed by unreason, and I had clung to that unreason to make sense of them, or rather to be able to endure them. But now the unreason of being here with Karl, by transporting me over impassable borders had made life *unendurably* delicious. And Karl wasn't trying to defend himself. He was simply conceding that the intensity of everything was interrelated, that perhaps he had needed the burden of so much regret...

'What's a "Giacometti"?' I heard him ask.

'Similar to an Otto Dix, but not really; he's a famous modern artist, but a sculptor, not a painter.'

'He died you know.'

'Who did?'

'Otto Dix.' Karl got up from his stool, and led me by the hand to the sofa.

'When?' I asked, when we had snuggled up together in a corner.

'July 25, just a few days after... But no, that's not a nice way to remember.'

'Just a few days after Nixon's propaganda?'

'Don't take any notice of Frau Angela's nonsense,' said Karl, almost indignantly waving it out of the way with the back of his hand. 'I doubt she believes it herself. She's just angry that Germany's caught in the middle, but whose fault is that? Caught in the middle and cut into two like your father tomorrow, except that it's not an illusion, I hope *unlike* your father tomorrow.'

'I hope so too,' I said, 'not that it would make any difference.'

'And Giacometti?'

'As dead as Otto Dix, I think.'

'But what do the police say?'

'The police?'

'About the stolen sculpture.'

'Oh, nothing, they don't actually know it was stolen, auntie Ada hasn't told them.' I slipped out of my sandals and gathered my legs on the sofa. 'My feet are clean,' I said, and as I twisted my body to face Karl from nearer the edge, he put his arm around me as though to protect me from falling.

'Is it valuable?' he asked.

'Probably very, even though it's little.'

And holding me still on my perch, he was asking me why with his eyebrows – if a valuable sculpture had been stolen, why hadn't the police been told?

'She always said it was a copy,' I said, and the pinching on Karl's forehead brought his eyebrows together again.

'I've just thought of something,' he said.

'About the Giacometti?'

'About your father's funeral.'

'If you don't feel like coming...'

'When a magician cuts someone in half with a saw, you can see at least part of the person being cut sticking out of the box – I think it's usually the head and the feet – otherwise what's the illusion, if you can't be sure the box isn't actually empty? But I don't suppose they're doing that with your dad – even if they wanted to, I'm sure you wouldn't let them.' Now his eyebrows had collapsed and made his eyes narrow.

'Of course not,' I said. 'Monsieur Legerdemain did try to insist on a half-open coffin, but we told him that we hadn't agreed to a freak show.'

'Then he might as well use an empty coffin. Or better still he should leave your father's coffin alone. I bet you he's not even French.'

'He's from Aberystwyth in Wales. And you're right, we shouldn't be allowing even the pretence of cutting my father in half, and *not* because it wouldn't be a convincing illusion. Grand finale or not, as soon as I get home I'm going to call him and tell him it's off.'

'Don't be too surprised if he's upset.'

'He'll make some grumbling noises, I'm sure. But actually I think he'll be relieved.' Already he had been unhappy at our refusal to consent to an open coffin, and even if he didn't care about inflicting an indignity on his friend, the hideous little man from Aberystwyth cared about Monsieur Legerdemain's reputation, which would hardly be enhanced by his sawing of a coffin into two in the absence of the scantiest illusion of a body. 'Thank you,' I said to Karl. 'One more reason why I'm glad I came to see you.' And with one sharp movement I leapt to my feet, unknotting myself like an acrobat. 'But it's late, auntie Ada might need me.'

'So was it an original or was it a copy?'

'The coffin?'

'Your auntie Ada's Giacometti.'

'Oh, it was definitely an original. You know, from her Paris days.' And to Karl's inquisitive squint I replied by fluttering my lashes. 'Her lover gave it to her as a gift.'

'Your auntie Ada had a *lover*? In *Paris*?'

'Her name was Jane,' I said. 'And then she fell in love with my mother.'

'Jane did?'

'Not Jane, auntie Ada.'

'I suppose she might be hiding it,' said Karl.

'That she'd fallen in love with my mother?'

'The Giacometti sculpture. It wouldn't be too hard if it's little.'

15

Betrayal

As I made my way back home from Cross Street, I found the streets unbearably busy. I wanted to be alone with my thoughts, but it was rush hour, and from I didn't know where a throng of clockwork people had emerged to walk in the direction of the Underground or to line up in bus stops as they all fought to make their way home. It struck me how sullen they seemed, and how solitary too, even while they formed part of a crowd. What kind of lives did they lead, all these smartly dressed people, what kind of homes were they returning to at the end of that part of their daily routine that required them to travel?

'A rat race, that's what it is, and if that's how I'd been forced to live my life – if I'd gone to University and joined the civil service – maybe I'd have had a bigger house and a car, but I bet you I'd be dead by the time I was forty.'

'And maybe Val would still be alive.'

'Aye, Ada love, maybe she'd still be alive, but I'd never have known her, and you think that's what Val would've wanted? At least for the little time we had, we knew what it meant to be happy, and that's more than a lot of folk will get in a lifetime. What good would it have been, being alive, if I'd never met Val?'

Even without a bigger house and a car, my father was dead before he was forty. And although it seemed absurd, the living second-guessing what the dead would've wanted, I knew that my father couldn't have been wrong, that the last thing my mother would have wanted was a different life without him.

At last I had stepped out of the main road and the crowds, and instead of what had passed and belonged to the past, which would always be a part of who I was, I tried to turn my mind towards the future. Jack, auntie Ada and Karl, and to some degree Frau Angela too - the details may not have yet been settled, but life would go on and be good.

Karl had promised he was definitely coming to the funeral tomorrow. He would be at the house before 11, to travel with us to the *Hypnos Crematorium*. Auntie Ada had insisted on the largest limousine, and I was glad that there would now at least be four of us to only half fill it.

'Miss? Excuse me, miss?'

'Jane, is it? Can we have a word, love? It's important, me and Barry were friends of your dad's.'

Although I hadn't stopped, they were almost touching me, a fat middle-aged man in a worn out fedora, shabby, sweaty and short of breath, talking to me with a half-smoked cigarette sticking out of his mouth, and on the other side his much younger sidekick, a mafia-looking type with joined up eyebrows and combed back thick black hair held together with brilliantine, and if I wasn't mistaken a camera over his shoulder – he had briefly overtaken me, and I had caught just a glimpse of it.

'There's really no need to be frightened, we're respectable professionals,' panted the fat middle-aged one.

'That's right, love, and we need to check some facts with you, that's all,' his brilliantined sidekick explained.

My pace had quickened automatically as soon as they had spoken, and I pushed my elbows out to keep their intrusion at bay, but the mafia type was constantly half turning as he took one step in front of me before falling back, and with the fat one on my heels my movements were encumbered by my fear of tripping over either one or the other, or possibly even both of them at once.

'It's in your own self-interest to talk to us,' the fat middle-aged one snapped at me bad-temperedly.

'If I've learned one thing in this job, it's that there's more than one side to every story, and me and Barry are giving you the chance to tell us yours.'

'Go away!' I barked at them, violently swinging my elbows and catching just the fat one in the ribs.

He gave a whining shriek and swore with words I didn't understand, and when he pushed into my back with his shoulder, I had to slow down to recover my step, but then I sprinted a short distance, and as I turned around to face them I stopped. They collided with each other to avoid me, and came to a sudden halt when the sidekick pulled the fat one two steps back.

'If you don't leave me alone I'm going to scream!' I had spread out my arms and was yelling already.

'This hostility, love, I'd say that it's uncalled for.' While the fat one huffed and puffed, the sidekick did the talking, and I could see the camera clearly. 'Come on now, calm yourself down, all we're trying to do is have a word. A word to your advantage, I might add.'

'I know what you are, you're *hacks*.'

Now the fat one sniggered, but he cut himself short to spit on the ground before lighting up another cigarette.

'Respectable professionals, love, that's what we are, just like Barry said. Here, let me give you my card. See, Mr Colin Webb, full-time employee of *The Daily Fox*, it says so right there.' And when I swiped the card out of his hand, 'But, Barry, we're so rude, we've not even had the decency to offer young Miss Hareman our condolences, it's no wonder she's taken offence.'

'Go away!' I said again, turning on my heels to stomp off in the direction of the house.

'Will the elusive Miss Mia-Mia be attending the funeral tomorrow, we hear she was particularly close to the dear departed Mr Magikoo, rather sordidly so we've been told, given Miss Mia-Mia's little secret. Well, I say little, but we wouldn't really know, would we, Barry?'

At the obscene sound of their chuckling, I turned around with the intention of swearing, but before I had time to I was stunned by the blast of the camera's flashbulb.

'Gotcha! And may I say how pretty you are too.'

I was rubbing my eyes, on the verge of bursting into tears. So now I knew exactly what "hacks" were.

'One last chance, love, would you care to add a comment to our version of your daddy's goings-on, yes or no?' And when I made no answer, 'I guess that's a no, then. So we'll bid you goodbye and we'll *definitely* see you tomorrow. We're looking forward to it already, aren't we, Barry?'

Barry gave an affirmative wheeze full of self-satisfaction.

Magnified by shock, my fury had initially been all-consuming, but as it began not so much to subside as to become assimilated by my nervous system, gradually one after the other all the mental and physical constituents of my consciousness were being restored, not in any orderly or logical sequence, but rather in a random and disorganised mêlée. When at last I had uprooted myself from that spot in the middle of the road where I had stood stock-still as though frozen, when I had opened the front door to the house and then slammed it shut behind me, and when slowly the hysterical woman in the hallway had taken the form of auntie Ada, only then did my mind begin to formulate thoughts that were asking impossible questions: Who? How? Why?

'Jane? Oh, my dear, dear child, it's those bastards, they've been hounding you too, I did everything I could to put them off, I even threatened them with the police if they tried to harass you, "she's a child," I said, "and she's just lost her father, I beg you to show some compassion," but they're obviously *ruthless*, like a pair of savage hounds scenting blood. And now look what they've done to my poor little angel, how, how can human beings be so callous? But what am I thinking, just wittering on instead of getting you a chair to sit down on, you're pale as a ghost and trembling like a leaf, some water, a cold glass of water, I'm sure that's what you need, if you hold onto my arm...'

When auntie Ada went to touch me I recoiled, making fists of my hands and bringing them together to press against my breast. 'Jack,' I said, and it was as if by the effort of speaking my lungs had been filled with fresh air.

Auntie Ada brought her fingers to her mouth as she took a step back. 'Jack, dear?' she winced.

'Has he called?'

'Has he called?'

I tried to control my confusion, and to rein in my assumptions.

'I'm sorry, auntie Ada, are you okay?'

'No, I should think I'm not, those men said *horrible* things about George. And it'll all be on the front page of their filthy little rag tomorrow morning. The day of his funeral and they're making him a laughing stock, and worse, much worse!'

'So you talked to them.'

'Talked to them? But I've already told you... Let's at least sit down... please, I need to sit down, first those men, then you arrive in this terrible state, snapping at me like you think it's all my fault...'

'I'm not snapping at you, auntie Ada.'

'Oh, you are, dear, you are, but it's all right, I know you're in shock...'

'Come on, let's get you off your feet and I'll fetch us both some water.' I had taken auntie Ada by the arm and was leading the way.

'Oh, please, dear, not your father's chair... there's more air in the kitchen, I'm sure.'

In the cold light of the kitchen auntie Ada looked a mess. She had collapsed onto a chair, fidgeting until she dug into the table with her elbows, anchoring herself into a more fixed position by holding her head with her hands. When I had filled two glasses from the water jug in the refrigerator, I sat beside her. After pushing one in front of auntie Ada, I drank mine in one gulp.

'You were right,' I said, 'I was thirsty.' I even attempted a smile, but auntie Ada had her stare somewhere else.

'I've already told you,' she resumed in a drone, when I tried to make her look at me by touching her arm. 'I begged them to leave us in peace, I told them you were only a child and if they came anywhere near you I'd call the police...'

'But did you talk to them?' I asked again.

'All I did was try to protect you, but they were brazen, they just laughed in my face, what they wanted was to run through all those dreadful accusations and have me confirm them.' She paused, and her head became tilted as she shot her eyes upwards through mine. 'They've branded your father a deviant and a pervert – not *just* a homosexual, as if that wasn't enough, but one who preyed on vulnerable boys and liked them wearing dresses. And yes, Jack's been calling, there's a number there for you to call him back on. Although really...'

'Really what, auntie Ada?'

'Well we know, don't we, what he's likely to say.'

'Does he know about those dreadful men?'

'Oh, Jane, how could he *not* know about those dreadful men? He's the "vulnerable boy" they're saying your father preyed on. Where else could they have got that if not from Jack himself?'

'So you're accusing him.' Sitting opposite auntie Ada, I had again spread out my arms and was pinching the sides of the table.

'Go on, call him if you like.'

'Has he told you that he knows about those men?'

'He was pretending to be upset about something, but I wouldn't ask him what, and I'm not sure he'd have said if I had. He knows I'm not as gullible as you are.'

'You've always mistrusted him, first when he was Mia-Mia and then when he was Jack.'

'Mia-Mia was the reason...'

'But she wasn't, auntie Ada.'

'It's a coincidence, then. She decides that she's a boy and that same night your father is dead.'

'Jack's not a boy, he's a man; he was always a man. I told you what happened. It was daddy who pretended, not Jack. And Jack tried to please him by doing things he hated, like visiting his brother's bed-and-breakfast in Torquay, which was really some hell in Shepherd's Bush, where they tried to...'

'Please, stop it, I don't want to know!' Auntie Ada had lifted her head even higher and was shaking it in tandem with her hands. 'I don't, I don't. I've heard enough disgusting stories from those men.'

'But the truth wasn't disgusting, isn't that what matters, auntie Ada? And daddy's gone, no one can hurt him.'

'There were other calls too.' Auntie Ada's snarl was ugly, almost unhinged. Her mouth was twisted, and her narrowed eyes shimmered like liquid incisions seeping poison. 'There won't be any magic show tomorrow, everyone's pulled out.' She was tugging at clumps of her hair as though to impress on me the tragedy of what she was saying. And leaning forward on her elbows, *'Everyone's* pulled out,' she repeated. 'It'll probably be just you and me.'

'Who's "everyone"?'

'Let's see now,' answered auntie Ada, with the same distorted glee. *'The Weekly Magic News* won't be coming. Somehow they got wind of *The Daily Fox* story and the Editor called to express his regret, but at least he was polite. Two minutes later there was a call from Monsieur Legerdemain, who I must say was exceptionally *French* in his rudeness. "Your brother, Madame... the man I had believed to be my *friend*... to think that only yesterday I was rehearsing with his coffin... that I almost cut a sodomite in half! Your brother was quite simply disgusting, Madame." A view that he assured me was unanimously shared by his colleagues.'

'I don't suppose you tried to defend him.'

'Defend him, dear? From what, exactly?'

'From all the lies,' I said.

'And which part of the story do we think is untrue?'

Momentarily I felt at a loss. But in the next breath I understood the violence of auntie Ada's abrupt transformation all too clearly. Under shock, I had pushed my suspicions to the back of my mind, but already they were percolating through, throbbing at my temples with a vehemence to match auntie Ada's. There were only two possibilities: either Jack had betrayed my father's secrets and his own in exchange for financial reward, which I found too hard to believe, or an overwhelming residue of bitterness had reduced auntie Ada to a smallness which I wanted to refuse to believe.

But the evidence was there, and all of it was stacked against auntie Ada: the notes had made her jealous; she had lied about the Giacometti, perhaps inventing balaclava man as a means of attracting attention. She had never stopped blaming my father: for what had happened to my mother; for permanently taking her for granted; for daring to become involved with Mia-Mia; for making her responsible for me, and then expecting her to share me with Jack; for revealing her secrets, and perhaps most of all for being dead – who knows how the madness of grief might have made her behave? I had seen her with my own eyes talking to the sergeant.

'Karl's coming too,' I remembered, as though numbers made the slightest bit of difference.

'Karl? Are you sure? But I thought...'

'That was all just a big misunderstanding,' I said, 'so he's coming here tomorrow at 11, and I'm sure Jack will be here as well.'

'You haven't called him yet,' said auntie Ada. 'And you should warn Karl what to expect if he's coming.'

'We're not lepers, auntie Ada.'

'And no one's going to want to set foot in the shop, so the sooner we close it the better.'

'Daddy wanted Jack to run the shop.' I felt a shiver of shame as I began to put my thoughts into words, taking auntie Ada's hand into mine as I spoke them. 'Would you, auntie Ada? Would you really have gone to such lengths just to sabotage daddy's last wish? Was that what you were doing when I saw you with the sergeant?'

'Now listen to me, Jane...'

'But why, why should I believe a word you say when already I know that you're a liar?'

'My secrets are my own,' said auntie Ada possessively, her wet crooked fingers wriggling out of my grip one by one.

'And my father's secrets, whose were they?'

'You really think those horrible things came from me?'

'They can't have come from Jack, and who else could they have come from if they didn't come from you? Unless... Oh my God, auntie Ada. The Inspector, it must've been him. Don't you see? He wasn't trying to help us at all... It was all just an act, to make us trust him... And we fell for it, all of us. We told him everything he wanted to know. Then he twisted it and sold it to those horrible men.'

'I don't think so, dear. And really I think it's time you spoke with Jack. If I were you I'd call him now. I'll be upstairs in my room if you want me.'

'Yes?' A woman's voice answered.

'Hello, could I speak to Jack, please?'

'Who is this?'

'It's Jane,' I said.

'Jane, thank God, I thought it might've been those people from the papers again. They've been ringing on and off all afternoon, honestly, Jane, I've lost count how many people I've told to fuck off. Of course by then it was already too late. I mean, how was I supposed to know that the first call was a trap? Jack says it wasn't my fault, he never warned me what to say if someone rang and asked to speak to Mia-Mia, so when they did, like an idiot I gave Jack a shout and put him on, and half an hour later those creeps from the paper were here. Jack went outside to talk to them, I could see him arguing with them through the window, and then they took some pictures and they went.

Oh, Jane, Jack said not to mention any of this if you rang, he didn't want you worrying yourself, and I wouldn't have, I'm not even sure what exactly this frightful palaver's about, something personal, Jack said, and he doesn't like to talk about personal things, but I gather the story's got something to do with your dad, so it's best if you're prepared, don't you think? I mean, it's the '60's, for God's sake, not the middle ages - if no one's getting hurt, who *cares* what anyone gets up to in their bedroom? I'll tell you who – all the hundreds of thousands who buy *The Daily Fox* for titillation. We're a nation of hypocrites pretending to be prudes, that's what we are.'

'Am I speaking to Sharon?' I finally managed to ask.

'Listen to me prattling on, and I've not even remembered to introduce myself. Dear oh dear, Sharon, what's the matter with you? The poor girl asked for Jack and got a ruddy diatribe instead... Jack's popped out, love, he had some arrangements to make, but he'll be back later on to pick up all his stuff, and if you called he said to let you know that he'll phone you just as soon as he's back. He shouldn't be too long now, he's already been gone quite a while...'

'But why's he picking up all his stuff, is he moving?'

'Taking time off to try and think things through, I think that's what he said, but Jack being Jack I wouldn't have a clue what these things are that he needs to think through...'

'Did he say if he was coming to the funeral tomorrow?'

'The *funeral tomorrow*?'

'My dad's.' My head was swimming, and the whispered words had sounded like an echo.

'Your *dad's*? You mean he's *dead*?'

'Please remember to ask Jack to phone me,' I said. 'And thank you.'

'Yes, yes of course, just as soon as he comes back.' Sharon sounded flustered, genuinely taken aback. 'Jane, I'm so sorry about your dad, Jack never said. Obviously if I'd known...'

I tried not to draw any conclusions from my long, one-sided conversation with Sharon until after I had spoken with Karl. Auntie Ada had a point, I did have a duty to warn him that tomorrow would not be going ahead as planned, that the papers had got hold of a story about my father, and the journey to and from *Hypnos Crematorium* was likely to be fraught. Now more than ever I needed him to be there, but naturally I would offer him the choice to stay away, which of course he would turn down without a blink.

And he did, after listening in silence to my long preamble – about my father and my mother and about auntie Ada; about my father and Mia-Mia and Jack; about the notes and auntie Ada; about the Inspector and the sergeant and my run-in with the two men from *The Daily Fox*; about my conversation with Sharon; about Jack's possible absence tomorrow.

'You don't have to come if you don't want to.'

'*Of course* I'm coming. I'll be there before 11 like we said. And that's the second time I should've walked you home and I didn't.'

I had only told Karl the bare facts, careful to omit all the clues, or even any hint of my half-formed contradictory suspicions. I didn't want Karl coming to a conclusion before I did.

If the story hadn't come from the Inspector, then it might have come from Frank and Norma of *Captain Cook's Fish and Chips*. They knew Mia-Mia, they knew she was Jack, and they had sent their regards to Mr George. The scoundrels from *The Daily Fox* might have squeezed the story out of them somehow, although how would they have known about Sharon? Well, quite possibly Mia-Mia had told them, her job as a hairdresser in Chelsea was hardly a secret.

'Hello, Jack?'

Ten minutes after my long conversation with Karl, the telephone had barely started ringing when I picked it up with a start. I had moved the pouffe to the hallway and had sat on it cross-legged, so intensely waiting for Jack's call that in my rush to answer I had yanked at the handset too hard, and the telephone had nearly tumbled to the floor. And now it was making crackling noises in my ear...

'Hello, Jack, can you hear me?'

But no amount of crackling could have caused me to mistake the voice that answered for Jack's.

'It's me,' said Karl.

From his cheerless intonation I knew why he was calling. I listened to his muddled, convoluted explanation of why Mami had "forbidden" him to join me for the funeral tomorrow. His attendance could only do both of us harm, and for my sake as much as his own it was better if Karl kept his distance. What good would it do if we were both embroiled in scandal? As long as I had nothing more to do with the young man at its centre, who was obviously disturbed, the scandal would eventually die out. In just a couple of months, it would be like it had never happened, and "things" could then go back to normal.

'Is that what you think, that I'm "embroiled in scandal"?'

Karl stayed silent.

'And that Jack must be "disturbed"?'

'I don't know him.'

'Neither does your mother. In fact I don't think she even knows you. Certainly she doesn't know me. But she thinks she knows what's best for me.'

'For both of us.' His voice was of defeat and unconditional surrender.

'You've used your mother's words, don't you have any of your own?' I found myself struggling for feeling. 'Does it mean *anything* to you that I needed you to be there? Oh, but Mami's forbidden it, I'm sorry, I forgot. And you think that after this, "things" can just go back to normal? I mean, really?'

'But isn't this nothing, compared to...'

I hung up; I returned the handset to its cradle with as much emotion as I'd been able to draw out of Karl. How could he have dared to compare? It was the comparison that had caused my revulsion. How spineless was he, how beholden to "Mami", that he could have allowed himself to be "forbidden" after I'd forgiven him for *that*? And how hollow was his music after all... I felt deceived, but also relieved that this second betrayal – I had yet to decide who had been the perpetrator of the first - had freed me from an error of judgment that no doubt I would have paid a heavier price for later on.

"Mami" was a curse and she wasn't going away. She would stifle Karl and stunt him as a man and a musician; he seemed to be completely under her sway. The hideous thought returned that in all likelihood it had been Mami who decided it was time for her son to have sex, and that perhaps he ought to have it with me. It would have never crossed her mind I might say no, and crushed by a refusal that Mami must have left him unprepared for, Karl had gone berserk. I didn't doubt the honesty of his feelings, which Mami in all her wisdom had completely either missed or misread. And the saddest thing of all was that even after *that*, Karl had still not broken free. But I refused to feel sad; truly there were more deserving claims on my sadness.

I had sunk into the pouffe with my hands intertwined in my lap, staring at one thumb as it revolved around the other. Again I jumped when the telephone rang, but my movements now were slower. First I brought my feet together on the floor, then I dug into the pouffe with the palms of my hands and gave myself a gentle upwards thrust, just enough to lift me up onto my feet, and finally I picked up the receiver.

'Hello?'

'How are you?' Jack's voice trickled through the wires. 'I suppose it would be too much to hope for that they wouldn't have bothered a child.'

'Too much, yes.'

'The bastards promised, you know – I made them. But they were hardly men of honour, so I can't honestly say I'm surprised.'

'And you, what did you promise?' I asked the question only as a matter of fairness. After accusing auntie Ada and doing away with Karl, I wanted to at least hold on to Jack, but not at the cost of more lies.

'I sold out. I told them what they wanted to hear.'

In the short silence that followed, I was unable to interpret what Jack had just said. No, he was not being ironic, but perhaps he was not being altogether literal either.

'You mean you told them the truth,' I almost demanded.

'Oh no, they weren't interested in the truth, so I helped them make it up.'

'You mean you went along with their story.'

'They didn't have a story until I sold them one.' Jack was closing up every loophole, as though to stop me from inventing mitigation and excuses.

'But Sharon said it was a trap, that they rang and asked for Mia-Mia, and she passed them on to you. I thought Inspector Cambridge, or maybe Norma and Frank...'

'I know what Sharon said, I was there when you called.'

'But why?' I had asked a thousand different questions in one.

'Money,' said Jack. 'Quite a lot of money, too.'

'But why, I still don't understand.'

'Enough to get away and make a new start,' Jack went on, as though blurting out the truth to a script. 'So I thought, why be mean and pin the blame on poor Ada, it really wouldn't have been fair. I can't say I'm particularly fond of the woman, but she's all you've got, and as I'm very fond of you, it would hardly be decent if I turned you against her.'

'So you had Sharon lie, and then you changed your mind.'

'That's about the size of it, yes. At least now you can stop blaming Frank and Norma or the Inspector.'

But Frank and Norma and the Inspector had long since been dispensed with as excuses. 'And it was you who told those men that my father preyed on vulnerable boys?'

'Is that really what they're saying? No, I never told them that.'

'So you didn't tell them lies.'

'I *almost* told them Ada's story, it was rather too delicious to resist, but I managed to restrain myself.' Jack's laughter was forced, and it fizzled out quickly. 'I've been a disappointment, I know.'

'But you didn't tell them lies,' I said again.

'If I hadn't told them *anything*, then there wouldn't be a story and there wouldn't be any lies.'

I steadied myself by leaning with one side of my body against the wall. 'You're being too cruel,' I said.

'Oh yes, didn't you know? We queers are traitorous people. That's why half of us are working for the Russians – half the clever ones at least.'

'Stop it, please! You're being deliberately horrible and mean, I don't understand!'

'It's all for the best,' Jack answered dully. 'And you're young, you'll soon forget...' As though he had thought better of what he had intended to say, he stopped. 'You'll soon forget,' he said again, but more finally now.

'You're trying to make me hate you.'

'And you must. I would rather you hated me today than tomorrow. Then tomorrow you can hate me just a little bit more.'

'Are you really not coming?'

'Don't let them cut your father in half, or even pretend to. It really isn't what George would've wanted.'

'That's all been cancelled,' I said. 'No one's coming, not even Karl.'

'Karl?'

'He promised he'd come, but Mami won't let him.'

'You've seen him?'

'And I wanted him to meet you, but now neither of you is coming.'

'Why would you even want me to come?'

'Because I don't believe you, I don't, I don't! I don't think Sharon was lying, I think *you* are. And if all you've told those men is the truth, then why should I have to hate you, I don't *want* to. Please come tomorrow, I don't want to be alone with auntie Ada!' At my own mention of auntie Ada, I was struck by an unanswered question. 'But how did auntie Ada know?'

'Know what?'

'She said you spoke but that you didn't really talk.'

'That's right, we didn't. I gave her this number and asked her to ask you to call me.'

'So how did she know that if I talked to you you'd take all the blame?'

'She can't have known.'

'But she did. "I don't think so, dear," she said, when I blamed the Inspector. And then she told me I should call you. So she *did* know, don't say she didn't.'

'She can't have,' Jack insisted. 'When I spoke with her I didn't know myself.' But after a pause he came up with a different explanation: 'She must've guessed that I wouldn't have wanted to harm you more than I already have. And that's what I'd be doing if I told you more lies.'

'Yesterday I saw her talking to the sergeant, and today I was chased by those men.' I was flailing about, uncertain what exactly I was doing or why I was doing it. Perhaps Jack was telling the truth, and instead of trying to exonerate him I should offer to forgive him. I had forgiven Karl for more, and he hadn't deserved it. I knew Jack well enough to know that he was *not* who he was trying to come across as, and even if he was telling the truth, when it came to it he had not wrongly accused auntie Ada. He, too, had every reason to be angry with my father – for the hell in Shepherd's Bush, for not loving him enough to be able to live with the truth, but again most of all for being dead. I felt too bereft to let go. I had lost too many people already.

'The sergeant?' I heard Jack asking, perhaps for the second or third time.

'It doesn't matter,' I said. 'Can't we just say that bad things have happened, but that we're not going to let them make *everything* bad? I don't want to lose you. I can't. And I'm never going to hate you.'

'Sweet Jane...' Jack faltered, his voice at last surrendering its hardness, like a bug breaking out of its shell and revealing the softness within. I waited for more – a sign at least, something to hold onto. But I waited in vain.

'You're not changing your mind,' I said.

'Or my feelings,' said Jack.

'Then the distance between us will only be miles, and you'll always be close to my heart.'

Jack's laughter was tender. 'If any grown-up had said that... but then grown-ups are jaded.'

'At least they can decide things for themselves. I needed you and Karl both to be there tomorrow, but you and Mami have decided something else.'

'And I think we've both done you a favour.'

'Mami *definitely* has, but you definitely haven't.'

'Or maybe it's the other way around. You're too young to be sure about anything,' said Jack.

The very next morning I had to decide if Jack had been right. If I changed my mind after thinking I had made it up *definitively*, perhaps it was because, like Jack had said, I was too young to be sure about anything, rather than because I was too weak. In the end I decided that I ought to do what felt right *today*, not what had seemed unshakeable yesterday. It was a matter of reflection but also of instinct, and surely it was as much a sign of maturity not to be stubborn as it was not to be rash.

Already last night, at the end of my long conversation with Jack, I had become unsure about everything else, while at the same time being certain seemed to matter much less. I had gone upstairs and knocked on auntie Ada's door, and the little that was said while we pressed against each other had signified a mutual letting go of our claims and counter-claims on the truth.

And now, in the simple clothes I had decided to wear for the short ceremony by which we would be bidding my father a modest farewell, half an hour before the excessive limousine from *Hypnos Crematorium* was due I was holding the front door ajar while Karl, magnificently sombre in a black suit and tie, his hair cut short and neatly parted, was being photographed by one of the several men he would have had to walk past before knocking on the door, to ask me when I answered if perhaps I might be able to forgive him.

Should I hold it against him that, rather than being clouded by the well-deserved dread that the door might be shut in his face, his whole countenance glowed with that same familiar confidence that had once so endeared him to me? If I thought that it stemmed from the arrogance of taking me for granted, then I probably would. But that wasn't what I thought. The impression he gave me was one of an immense relief that he had made the right decision, regardless of how I might react. And I reacted badly.

'Does Mami know you're here?' As soon as I had asked it, my question made me feel like a grudge-bearing child pretending to be a sensible adult, and I was glad when Karl shrugged it off.

'I suppose I deserved that,' he said with a self-deprecating smile, 'but please can I come in?' I had already made my mind up *not* to shut the door in his face, and I was about to step back so that I could open it more widely. Karl's smile broadened as he gave me a wink. 'I'd rather we did this in private,' he said, casting a cursory glance over his shoulder. And as soon as he was in and the door was shut, 'So where's your friend Jack? Has he decided what he's wearing for the funeral? I know you said that he's a boy now, but why not make a point by dressing one last time as a girl, or do you think I'm being disrespectful?'

'Jack's not coming,' I said, half expecting one more knock on the door.

'Oh,' said Karl, 'his Mami won't let him?'

'It's complicated.'

'Ah, but that's just grown-ups for you, they think *everything's* complicated. They just need to be snapped out of it sometimes.'

'Is that what you did, snap Frau Angela out of thinking this was complicated?'

'That's exactly what I did. "I'm going with Jane to her father's funeral," I told her. "But first I'd like you to listen to this." And then I played "Jane" for her. "I wrote that for Jane," I said when I finished. "After what I did to her the *real* scandal would be if I let her down again, and I'm not going to allow you to make me do something I'd never forgive either one of us for." She didn't dare to speak a single word, not even when I asked her to iron my shirt.'

'And here you are.' I tightened his tie, but then I loosened it again. 'We don't want you choking,' I said.

'Come here,' said Karl, and as I yielded to what I felt like doing *today*, already one absolute certainty had sweepingly overridden another.

II

1984

16

The Signing

In a small patisserie in Soho, somewhere off Old Compton Street, I was washing down my second giant slice of Black Forest Gateau. As a matter of fact I had not even wanted the first, but the ritual, a reminder of both happy and unhappy times with loved ones long lost, served as a bittersweet antidote to nerves, so effective that it made even the inevitable onset of heartburn worthwhile. Well, "worthwhile" was perhaps overstating it. It suggested something rarefied, which clearly heartburn was not. Really it was the memories that calmed my nerves, not the number of slices of Black Forest Gateau, but it was in the nature of rituals, once they had become entrenched, that they were indivisible – magic recipes sacrosanct in their irrational entirety. One tampered with them at one's peril.

But the restless voice inside my head was making a simple thing sound unnecessarily pompous, and I gobbled down another mouthful of Black Forest Gateau in a last-ditch attempt to shut it up, grinning at its silliness widely. My teeth felt thick and sticky with chocolate, but here, where I was just another stranger eating cake, brown teeth were almost de rigueur. I would have plenty of time to brush them, restoring their immaculate whiteness in time for the event. I always carried toothbrush and toothpaste in my handbag.

'More tea, Madame?' asked the new waiter, bending over the small round table as though to take in panoramically the view of my greed.

I looked up at his smile – refreshingly friendly, I thought – and just shook my head, my hand over my mouth self-consciously.

'I am Pierre,' said the new waiter.

'Pleased to meet you, Pierre, I'm Jane.' The hand had not moved.

'Ah oui, the patron 'as told me. Jane 'areman, the writer.' While every "H" was silenced, the "J" in Jane was pronounced in that mouth-wateringly French way that I loved, and at the sound of it a little laugh of pleasure escaped me, and I let my hand drop.

'You must excuse my chocolate teeth,' I said.

'Ah but why, I don't see any chocolate teeth. You must excuse my terrible English, I think. But not so terrible that I cannot read your books.'

'Really, you've read them both?'

'But of course, and I adore them.'

'Thank you, Pierre, that's very kind.'

'Ah oui, trés gentil, you think I am polite. But I am not polite when I say I adore them, I am honest. *The Giacometti Riddle* especially, it is more personal, non?'

'Pierre!' The patron, a corpulent debonair Frenchman who had never let on that he knew who I was, looked incensed that his waiter was being so presumptuous.

'And the sculpture on the cover, it is exquisite!'

I looked at my watch.

'But I take up your time, my patron is right, please excuse me.' And with a deep bow of the head, Pierre was about to walk away.

'No, Pierre, wait! I have a signing round the corner at Buchner & White – you know it? It's a bookshop on the Charing Cross Road. You turn right at Cambridge Circus, and then it's just on the other side of the road, you can't really miss it. It's on the corner with Litchfield Street, I think. Between six and eight, can you make it?'

'But my book, it is at 'ome. I mean *your* book, *my* book it is still in my 'ead. And I think you will be 'appy it is in French.'

'I'm sure we can spare you another copy, and if you're able to come you'll be doing me a favour. I'm not a big fan of these events, they make me very nervous.'

'So you come 'ere first for something very sweet,' Pierre ventured with a flourish, but when I didn't laugh, 'Don't worry,' he whispered, 'I am flirt but I am gay, very single since I come to this city. Perhaps why I like so much *The Giacometti Riddle*? Very melancholy, I think. Little bit like Kafka, non? And the character of Jack it is so real!'

'Excuse me, could we order?' someone called from a distant table.

'Buchner & White, I will be there,' Pierre went on in his conspiratorial whisper. And then, already on his way to the distant table, 'Monsieur, Madame, what would you like?'

It was only 5.20 when I waved to Pierre that I was leaving. A few minutes' extra walk might help to clear my indigestion, which had now become a bloating in my tummy that I hadn't factored in when choosing what to wear for the signing – a plain scarlet dress, a black and purple Spanish mantilla draped around my shoulders, and black shoes I could kick off under the table while I signed *The Giacometti Riddle* for the few people I expected to turn up.

It was a clear spring day, gorgeously colourful and bright, but a spring day nonetheless. Spring was far from being my favourite season. I found its dusks particularly gloomy for some reason, and it brought on all the allergies I had inherited from my father. I even disliked the names of its months: March I found cacophonous and bossy, May made me think of indecision, and as for April... It was April now, and I was already looking forward to July - a rich month for memories, of "life being lived in the present", but of tragedy too. As "infinitely more exciting than stories" was how I had experienced those heady days around the landing on the moon back in 1969. I had told myself on one of them that "stories" was how auntie Ada and I had dealt with the past, and that "life" already belonged to the future. But then "life" had somehow again become the past.

As I made my way slowly towards Buchner & White, I took in the seediness of Soho, so *authentic* compared to what life had become like under Thatcher. I had not cared for politics much in my life, but I found the prevalent climate depressing: everything, including one's happiness, was suddenly being measured in numbers — one's unhappiness too, if one happened to number among those unequipped to "get on". The race for the fulfilment of greed had made our lives more cutthroat.

Success was naturally also being measured in numbers, and at least by the yardstick of numbers Jane Hareman, author, was very successful indeed. But this "success", what did it really add up to? Could I honestly say it was making me happy? Was it perhaps not self-indulgent even to be asking the question, when so many people's lack of happiness stemmed from far more fundamental deprivations than some vague, egotistical feeling of inadequate self-fulfilment?

Pierre had not been part of anything that could be counted, and yet our short conversation had brought to my day more joy than all the astronomical numbers my agent had been quoting at me since *The Giacometti Riddle* went on sale. That meaningless comparison made me wonder if perhaps I might have made a mistake by not changing Jack's name in the book. It had been a deliberate act, borne out of frustration. All my attempts to trace him had failed, and it was fifteen years already since that telephone call on the day before my father's funeral. Too much time had passed, and what use was my "success" if it had failed to make it easier for Jack to get in touch? If he had read my first book, he would have known I still wanted him to, and the second was an undisguised plea.

It would have been so easy to find me. I had not moved from the house in Angel, where now I lived alone, still sleeping in the windowless box I had steadfastly refused to dismantle. I could not bear to part from the dreams I had dreamt in my bed, and every time I walked into the bathroom without knocking first, I would remember with a flutter my all too brief encounter with Mia-Mia's penis. The house was still *full* of Mia-Mia, and so contrastingly empty of everyone else. What little memory I had of my mother consisted mostly of remembered sensations – fleeting moments not attached to any one place. My father I remembered all too well, but had intentionally disconnected from the house. He would forever be the one and only, the inimitable Mr Magikoo, not the man who had withdrawn into himself after losing his wife and then lived his last years in a fantasy world. The recollection of his body lying lifeless in a bath full of blood had retained only the essence of Jack's magnanimity. Like all the rabbits my father had pulled out of two different hats, the macabre reality of that scene would have otherwise been haunting me still.

To be able to live in it, I had cleared the house of all its ghosts. And conversely I had filled *Mr Magikoo's Magik*

Shoppe with all of my leftover love. Contrary to another of auntie Ada's predictions, the shop had continued to thrive, helped by people's fondness for Mr Magikoo and also by their liking for scandal. To this day, through the maze of streets around it, they wormed their way along to its doors in their droves - in spite of all the changes it had lost none of its magic.

Auntie Ada and I had been rooted together by a mutual affection that the years had made a part of who we were, too resilient to be broken by the keeping of secrets or even by the telling of lies.

'My secrets are my own,' auntie Ada had declared, and perhaps because the bulk of her secrets had already been revealed (even if they had remained unspoken), she had wilfully clung on to the few that had not, until almost the end. These details were like knots in the untangling of the truth from that complex web of lies auntie Ada had spun overnight and had then locked away - in a place that had for years seemed inaccessible even to her, until she had been favoured with foreknowledge of her death.

The years we had shared in the house, although they had been marked by the effort of saving *Mr Magikoo's Magik Shoppe* while at the same time preparing for Oxford, had for me belonged mostly to Karl, perhaps partly as a means of tolerating auntie Ada. It had taken me some time to accept auntie Ada on her terms, in other words without more discussion. Whereas everyone else had in one way or another asked for my forgiveness – my father with his note, Karl with "Jane" and his last-minute defiance, and finally Jack with the enormity of his false confession – as far as auntie Ada was concerned the present was too pressing and the future too uncertain, and therefore practicality dictated that the past must be held very firmly at bay. And I could see now that she hadn't been wrong. If the pretence that she had carefully constructed had collapsed too early, certainly the shop would not have been saved, and who knows what other ugly, long-lasting repercussions the baring of the truth might have wreaked. With Karl no longer in the picture, perhaps I might not have left Oxford at the end of my first year, already confident enough in my writing to insist on taking over the house, and on running the shop with the help of a part-time assistant. Auntie Ada had not tried to dissuade me, and had even seemed impatient to return to Tufnell Park. Her mark on the house had been fleeting.

When it came, the end of Karl was a relief, and it came without regret or explanations or even surprise. Acknowledged by both of us at once in the sharing of no more than one short final glimpse, it was the end of a chapter with too many changes of heart, rewriting itself time after time in a stubborn refusal to end. The stubbornness of course had been ours.

We had both suffered loss. Karl had compensated with a sense of his place in the world that had made him feel entitled, and I had drummed into myself the instinct to cling on, almost at all costs. But really we were children growing up, and our moment together had passed, long before the final betrayal: we had sex on my eighteenth birthday, and the next time I saw him, less than one week later, his hands were all over April Fowler.

Looking back, I didn't need a Reichian therapist's help to pinpoint what had crystallised my doubts about Karl, and it wasn't Frau Angela's hold on her son, or the self-centredness I had mistaken for confidence, or even his violence. It was simply the starkness of the contrast between him and Jack, encapsulated in my memory of a group of children with a ball.

At the corner with Greek Street I stopped. I could see the trees of Soho Square, my refuge on that icy sunny Sunday in the winter before I went to Oxford.

In defiance of the cold I had walked all the way into town, and this small oasis had appeared out of nowhere to offer me a quiet place to sit. In my trips to the West End with auntie Ada, the winding streets of Soho had been out of bounds, but I had just turned eighteen, and at last I could wander wherever I pleased.

'Jane? Jane Hareman?'

I looked up from the bench I had all to myself, but the noon sun was low, and even with one hand over my eyes, I struggled for some time before I could decipher the tall hatted shadow hesitating in the footpath barely a metre away.

'Inspector Cambridge?'

'I've startled you, I'm sorry.'

All at once my mood had lifted. 'You haven't,' I said, 'but I hope you're not here because there's been another complaint of assault.'

'Why, is one likely?' And when I shrugged my adult shoulders, 'Is the same young man still causing you trouble?'

I patted the bench for the Inspector to join me. 'Not since one hour ago,' I said.

'I see. And isn't that good news?'

I shrugged my adult shoulders again before changing the subject. 'I almost rang you *many* times,' I said.

The Inspector took his hat off and put it upside down in the space of bench between us.

'I'm sorry about what happened,' he said.

'Yes, it was horrible. But the kindness of the people at the funeral made up for it. We weren't expecting anyone, and all his so-called friends stayed away, but we arrived in that enormous limousine to find literally dozens of his fans, kids, grown-ups, all queuing to shake my hand and say how much they'd loved daddy's magic.'

The Inspector nodded as though he already knew. 'I'm glad to say the sergeant isn't with us any more.'

'Jack took all the blame, but I don't think he was telling the truth. I even said to auntie Ada that it might've been you. But she seemed to know it wasn't.'

'She was right.'

'But how would she have known it?'

'Is that why you almost rang me?'

'I thought...'

'You wanted certainty, I expect.'

'Certainty? I'm not even sure what that means.'

'I've often wondered too, but I don't think I'm any the wiser, which is perhaps why I didn't call you. And other people's families and friendships, they're minefields to be getting involved in, hard to know if one was doing good or harm. I'm speaking hypothetically, of course.'

'Would one be able to say if one knew something I didn't?'

Inspector Cambridge laughed. 'One wouldn't,' he said, 'but in any case one doesn't.' And then more seriously, 'Whatever certainty you've settled on, cling onto it if you can.'

I took a deep breath, and sighed its vapour out into the cold. 'And now Jack's disappeared...'

The Inspector shook his head. 'Perhaps one day he'll just turn up,' he said, and as he took his cigarettes out and looked through all his pockets for a match, he asked me about my plans for the future.

It was time. I turned my back to Soho Square, where thirteen years before I had put Karl behind me, and I walked across Old Compton Street towards Cambridge Circus.

I had never stopped hoping that Jack would get in touch, but the certainty I had settled on would waver. One moment I would *know* that he had taken the blame on behalf of Mia-Mia, whom auntie Ada had wrongly accused of blighting our lives. But then missing him would make me suspect him. Too many strange things had happened all at once, and as I turned the details I remembered around in my head, goaded by my sadness I would sometimes rearrange them into elaborate scenarios in which Jack and auntie Ada would take turns at being cast as the villain. I would then become convinced that there had to have been a degree of collusion - an exchange of some sort. And the idea of an exchange between Jack and auntie Ada would always have at its heart the missing Giacometti.

Either Jack had been bribed with it, or auntie Ada must have threatened to accuse him of its theft. Hadn't he, on that fateful night before the burglary, when he was still half expecting my father to show him the door, wheedled out of me auntie Ada's address? "Cross" sounded *nothing* like "Cyprus". Hadn't I then left him by a telephone box, with plenty of time to call balaclava man? Had the burglary not happened just hours after Jack had found out that auntie Ada kept a genuine Giacometti on her mantelpiece? And hadn't the telephone rung at the house in some sort of signal, just a short time before auntie Ada had fled unexpectedly? Hadn't Jack been acting peculiarly while he and I were trying to catch up with her?

But no, it was all too far-fetched. We had *all* acted peculiarly, in those hours after my father's death. And there had not been a moment, after our discovery of his body in the bath, when Jack had been out of my sight. He had not been near the telephone once, so how would balaclava man have known when auntie Ada would be away from her flat? Nor did the "signal" hypothesis make any sense, unless Jack could have predicted precisely the course of unpredictable events, at the time of making the phone call in Cross Street. As for any bribery suspicion...

I no longer sought all the answers. The truth was on the cover of *The Giacometti Riddle*, so beautifully complex that it had become a work of fiction.

'I have something for you,' auntie Ada said. 'There, on the trolley, no, not the box of chocolates, the shoebox.'

I wondered how a shoebox had found its way to auntie Ada's room at the hospice. As far as I knew, her only other visitor was Edith, who had brought the box of chocolates the day before.

'Edith brought it in this morning,' auntie Ada explained. Her voice came in waves of whispering gasps, with all her crooked fingers in the air as though to punch her words through. 'She's known it was yours since I gave it to her, but really you deserve an explanation, so you should have it now, not after I've croaked it.'

'Auntie Ada...'

'Oh, passed away then, if you'd rather. Now go on, open it.'

It was wrapped in plain brown paper and had a dusty ribbon around it, tied up on the top into a multiple knot. And no sooner had I picked it up than I knew what was inside it. I untied the knot patiently, and then I lifted the lid. I removed one by one the crumpled sheets of white tissue paper. And there it was. I took it out and stood it on the trolley, a mere nine or ten inches tall, including its plinth. I turned it around very slowly, so that both auntie Ada and I could see it from every angle.

'You'll find the receipt in the box, in case you want to change it.'

'Very funny,' I said. I reached out and squeezed auntie Ada's hand. 'It's even more beautiful than I remember it, thank you.'

'Jane's letters,' said auntie Ada, taking back her hand as though without its movements she might not be understood. 'They're all in there too.'

I lifted the rest of the tissue paper, to uncover a bundle of letters bound together with another piece of ribbon.

'Can I read them?'

'I'd like you to. And I wasn't joking. In one of them you'll find the receipt. In case you need to sell it one day.'

'I'm never going to part with it, *ever*!'

'She was a wonderful woman. Nearly as wonderful as you and your mum.'

'But not nearly as wonderful as you.'

'That's nonsense and you know it.' Auntie Ada's laughter was weak, and it tapered into a cough. 'I tried to convince myself that I was doing what was best for you, but of course even that was a lie.'

'Shush, auntie Ada, none of that matters now.'

'You've forgiven me, I know, but I think you need to know what you've forgiven me for.'

'But I don't.'

'For Jack's sake.'

'Okay then, for Jack's sake.' I took a handkerchief out of my pocket and wiped my eyes dry.

'That's your father's handkerchief,' said auntie Ada.

I nodded. 'To wipe away his allergies,' I said.

'He was an odd sort, our George, but he knew how to make your mum happy. And if anyone deserved to be happy...' Her fingers danced about her and finished the sentence.

'They made each other happy.'

'They did. And Jack would've been good for him too. Much better than that silly Mia-Mia.' This time her laughter was barely a wheeze. 'But he'd never got over your mum, none of us had.' Auntie Ada brought her hands down to rest on her chest. 'I told Jack that he had to stay away or you'd end up in care. You were right, I'd spoken with the sergeant and then with those men, and unless Jack took the blame you'd have hated me, and who'd have looked after you then? The boy who dressed up as a girl and caused your dad to take his own life? So Jack went along with it and took all the blame. And that's when I knew I'd been unfair.'

A longer silence might imply recrimination, and when auntie Ada's hands began to slowly rise up, I took hold of them lightly.

'Was big money dangled?'

'Dangled, yes,' said auntie Ada. 'But neither Jack nor I took a penny. What I did was unforgivable, and I've carried it with me all these years, but I didn't do it for money. Jack did it for you and I did it for myself, so I wouldn't have to share you.'

'And the burglary?' I asked without demanding.

'It happened,' said auntie Ada.

'But the sculpture wasn't taken.'

'That man was an incompetent, nothing was taken.'

'It wasn't in its place on the mantelpiece.'

'That's because I put it away.'

'That same morning?'

'When I heard you at the door.'

'So already...'

'Yes, dear, already.' She took away her hands and used them to cover her mouth, but a movement of her head shook them off.

'Later on, did you offer it to Jack? And did Jack refuse it, or did he take it and then give it back?'

Auntie Ada's mouth stayed pursed, both her hands taking flight before landing again by her sides. But then, as though to stop me from asking again, 'Edith's had the sculpture for years,' she said. 'And really that's as much as I remember... Oh, don't look so surprised... Now please, let's talk about something else.'

First it was a copy, then it was broken, then it was stolen, and now here it was. Was I really surprised? Did I believe this final version of "the truth"? I had plenty of time to decide by myself, and only little time to spend with auntie Ada.

'I did have some news,' I said.

'Good news?'

'My book's going to be published, so yes.'

'It's going to be published and I've not read a page of it yet.'

'I can read it to you if you like.'

'Yes, let's start tomorrow morning. *Violence Likes the Dark*, it's a wonderful title.'

That night's dark had brought with it peace, and auntie Ada had been spared "tomorrow morning".

Three years had passed since auntie Ada's death – three years that had not seemed to me to pass quickly. But they had given me time to decide.

The distant green of Soho Square had not left me feeling sentimental. Rather it had left me with a fresh sense of wonder at how a mistake that had been so longstanding could have been so easily erased: barely had I blinked and Karl was gone, almost as though he had never existed.

Greta Buchner was at the open double door, looking splendid in a flowing black dress and her customary single string of pearls. Already quite a number of people were waiting in line.

Buchner & White was a large shop with old leather armchairs and heavy mahogany tables, creaking wooden floors and not enough light. Complemented in some strange way by the whiff of Greta's perfume, the air was of dust and old paper, but also of something else, a familiar intangible essence.

Greta made a little speech, and the line, which had now spilled outside, throbbed with a short burst of applause. I took my seat behind the designated table. Pen in hand, I looked up with a smile.

The next time I looked at my watch it was almost eight o'clock. I raised my head again, as I had after opening every other copy of *The Giacometti Riddle* on the page with the short dedication:

For Jack

My smile had become brittle, exhausted. Impatiently I waited for a name, already counting the few people left behind the silent woman holding everyone up. Pierre was not among them.

'For George and Mia-Mia,' said the woman when she finally spoke.

My focus fell on her sharply.

'Oh my God, Mia-Mia, *oh my God!*'

'Just for you, just for today,' Jack's voice answered.

By the same author

The Dead of August

"A sophisticated, comic novel that brilliantly captures the triumph and folly of art, media, and publishing."
Kirkus Reviews (starred review)

Bowl of Fruit (1907)

"BOWL OF FRUIT (1907) is an incredible read, with well-crafted characters and a plot that is refreshingly original."
IndieReader (5 star review)

POLK, HARPER & WHO

"As with other Cacoyannis novels, the language, the cleverness, the juxtaposition of heartbreak and humor and the presence of truly hilariously drawn characters is at least half the pleasure of reading the book. The author has a way of describing mundane scenes in ascending lines of subtle humor that, for me, often results in an outbreak of irrepressible laughter by the end of the scene. The attention to detail and the complexity of his descriptions of both character and setting are captivating."
Casey Dorman - Lost Coast Review

"In this literary novel, family secrets, friendship, and the resilience of love play out in a dinner party between two couples... A thoughtful, observant, and often humorous tale about real connections."
Kirkus Reviews

26173260R00143

Printed in Poland
by Amazon Fulfillment
Poland Sp. z o.o., Wrocław